SEA STORM

"The fast-paced plot is filled to the brim with fascinating characters, and the locale is exceptional—both above and below the waterline. One doesn't have to be a nautical adventure fan to enjoy this nail-biter."

—*Publishers Weekly* (starred review)

"Strong pacing, lean prose, and maritime knowledge converge in this crackerjack thriller."

—*Kirkus Reviews*

BLACK CORAL

"A relentless nail-biter whether below or above the waterline. Even the setbacks are suspenseful."

—*Kirkus Reviews* (starred review)

"Mayne's portrayal of the Everglades ecosystem and its inhabitants serves as a fascinating backdrop for the detective work. Readers will hope the spunky Sloan returns soon."

—*Publishers Weekly*

"Andrew Mayne has more than a few tricks up his sleeve—he's an accomplished magician, deep sea diver, and consultant, not to mention skilled in computer coding, developing educational tools, and of course, writing award-nominated bestselling fiction. They are impressive skills on their own, but when they combine? Abracadabra! It's magic . . . Such is the case in Mayne's latest series featuring Sloan McPherson, a Florida police diver with the Underwater Investigation Unit."

—*The Big Thrill*

"Former illusionist and now bestselling author Andrew Mayne used to have a cable series entitled *Don't Trust Andrew Mayne*. If you take that same recommendation and apply it to his writing you will have some idea of the games you are in for with his latest novel titled *Black Coral*. Just when you think you might have things figured out, Andrew Mayne pulls the rug out from under you and leaves you reeling in fits of delight."

—Criminal Element

"The pages are packed with colorful characters . . . its shenanigans, dark humor, and low view of human foibles should appeal to fans of Carl Hiaasen and John D. MacDonald."

—*StarNews*

THE GIRL BENEATH THE SEA

"Distinctive characters and a genuinely thrilling finale . . . Readers will look forward to Sloan's further adventures."

—*Publishers Weekly*

"Mayne writes with a clipped narrative style that gives the story rapid-fire propulsion, and he populates the narrative with a rogue's gallery of engaging characters . . . [A] winning new series with a complicated female protagonist that combines police procedural with adventure story and mixes the styles of Lee Child and Clive Cussler."

—*Library Journal*

"Sloan McPherson is a great, gutsy, and resourceful character."

—Authorlink

"Sloan McPherson is one heck of a woman . . . *The Girl Beneath the Sea* is an action-packed mystery that takes you all over Florida in search of answers."

—*Long and Short Reviews*

"The female lead is a resourceful, powerful woman and we're already looking forward to hearing more about her in the future Underwater Investigation Unit novels."

—Yahoo!

"*The Girl Beneath the Sea* continuously dives deeper and deeper until you no longer know whom Sloan can trust. This is a terrific entry in a new and unique series."

—Criminal Element

THE NATURALIST

"[A] smoothly written suspense novel from Thriller Award finalist Mayne . . . The action builds to [an] . . . exciting confrontation between Cray and his foe, and scientific detail lends verisimilitude."

—*Publishers Weekly*

"With a strong sense of place and palpable suspense that builds to a violent confrontation and resolution, Mayne's (*Angel Killer*) series debut will satisfy devotees of outdoors mysteries and intriguing characters."

—*Library Journal*

"*The Naturalist* is a suspenseful, tense, and wholly entertaining story . . . Compliments to Andrew Mayne for the brilliant first entry in a fascinating new series."

—*New York Journal of Books*

SEA
CASTLE

OTHER TITLES BY ANDREW MAYNE

UNDERWATER INVESTIGATION UNIT SERIES

The Girl Beneath the Sea
Black Coral
Sea Storm

THEO CRAY AND JESSICA BLACKWOOD SERIES

Mastermind
The Final Equinox

THEO CRAY SERIES

The Naturalist
Looking Glass
Murder Theory
Dark Pattern

JESSICA BLACKWOOD SERIES

Angel Killer
Fire in the Sky
Name of the Devil
Black Fall

THE CHRONOLOGICAL MAN SERIES

The Monster in the Mist
The Martian Emperor

OTHER FICTION TITLES

The Grendel's Shadow
Knight School
Hollywood Pharaohs
Public Enemy Zero
Station Breaker
Orbital

NONFICTION

The Cure for Writer's Block
How to Write a Novella in 24 Hours

SEA CASTLE

A THRILLER

ANDREW MAYNE

 THOMAS & MERCER

Published by Thomas & Mercer, Seattle

www.apub.com

Amazon, the Amazon logo, and Thomas & Mercer are trademarks of Amazon.com, Inc., or its affiliates.

ISBN-13: 9781662506413 (paperback)
ISBN-13: 9781662506420 (digital)

Cover design by Shasti O'Leary Soudant
Cover image: © Nestor Rodan / Arcangel

Printed in the United States of America

SEA
CASTLE

CHAPTER ONE
NIGHTTIDE

A crescent moon casting glimmers of light onto the rolling waves of the ocean would normally be a relaxing sight to me. But not tonight. As I walk down the beach, I can already see the pale-white legs of a corpse through the gaps in a protective screen.

The Fort Lauderdale Police Department and two detectives from the Broward County Sheriff's Office arrived before me. We're at the north end of Fort Lauderdale on the border of their respective jurisdictions. I had to get myself out of bed barely thirty minutes ago when they notified me.

It was more of a courtesy than anything else. Suarez, the detective who called me, knew I was with the Underwater Investigation Unit—currently in bureaucratic limbo while politicians fight over whether to dismantle it. Our last case brought down a South Florida financier who had enough money stashed around to continue to make our lives difficult and politically connected friends who didn't want to see our investigation go much further. Presently I'm working for the Florida Department of Law Enforcement as a seat-filler while all of that gets sorted out.

"Hey, McPherson!" shouts Suarez as he spots me walking toward the enclosure.

"Good morning," I reply.

I avoid using his nickname, "Crash." He's somehow managed to total three unmarked police cars. There was even a joke going around that he was getting kickbacks from the auto body shop.

"It's not morning until I have breakfast. It's only four a.m.," Suarez responds with a grin that wouldn't seem awkward if it weren't for the fact that I can see the body behind him.

I recognize the other detectives and nod at them. "What's the situation?"

"Dead girl. Beach," replies Waterman, a Fort Lauderdale PD detective known for using words sparingly—as if she had to pay for each vowel. Most cops love to talk. Waterman, not so much. The fact that she's volunteered this without me asking her directly should feel flattering.

I walk around the edge of the screen and get a better look at the body as a forensic technician named Mandy Fonseca takes photos and collects samples that otherwise might get lost or contaminated when the body is moved to a pouch.

She nods. "Solar says hey," she tells me, a reference to my former boss, before returning her attention to the corpse.

Corpse. It's a weird word. One moment you're a person, the next you're a corpse. I've given CPR to two people and brought them back to life. Did they become corpses and then not?

This is the kind of question my daughter, Jackie, likes to ask in the typical way precocious young teenagers challenge reality.

From the looks of the body in front of me, there's not much chance of her coming back.

She's nude, lying facedown with her head turned to the side and mouth visible. Her skin is pale and her lips deathly blue.

Definitely a corpse.

The standout feature is the long rope: one end is twisted around her neck, the other runs all the way into the waves.

"Anchor rope?" I ask.

"It appears so," replies Fonseca.

I turn to Suarez. "Anybody call in a missing swimmer?"

"Nope. I thought you might find this curious."

"I don't exactly come to these things for thrills, Suarez. I'm a day person, not one of you night ghouls who waits by the radio for the latest creepy misadventure."

He laughs. "Yeah, but this is when all the good stories happen."

"I could go a decade without another good story and be perfectly happy. I want boring ones about burnt brownies and my daughter telling me the latest school gossip," I reply.

"Have you ever even made brownies?" he asks.

"Once."

"And?"

"I burned them. What's your point?"

"You should stick to what you're good at." Suarez sees that Fonseca has pulled the rope in from the waves. "Can we take a look?"

She holds up the rope's end under her headlamp's beam. The rope was cut clean, with only a few frayed fibers.

"Clean," says the laconic Detective Waterman.

"It definitely didn't snap," adds Fonseca.

"It wasn't cut with a typical fish knife. That would fray the edges more," I observe.

"That's the kind of nautical knowledge we bring you in for," says Fonseca, not unkindly.

I want to point out that almost every entry-level criminal-investigation textbook contains the diagram. I'd bet that even ancient Egyptian cops had stone tablets showing the same thing: all the different ways rope can be snapped or cut or severed so they could tell whether the rope used to tie up Bill the golden idol–maker during a robbery was the same type of rope used to bind Joe the silversmith when he was robbed.

Law enforcement is mostly about boring things like rope and treads on shoes and tires. It's not what you see in movies, where cops sit around drinking coffee while trying to unscramble the clues in some coded letter from a serial killer.

"Look," says Waterman, pointing to a small object gleaming in the waves.

"Shouldn't we have a boat out here?" I ask the group.

"Engine trouble. That's why we asked you," says Suarez.

"Fine," I sigh, stripping off my FDLE jacket and sweat suit down to my swimsuit.

As a police diver, I never know when I'll have to go into the water and whether I'll have the luxury of a place to change in privacy. It's become a habit to wear a swimsuit whenever I'm on call. Scott Hughes—my partner at UIU, currently away at training—on the other hand, has a preternatural instinct for wearing shorts whenever we're going to end up in the water. Me, not so much.

I'm ten yards away from shore, breaststroking my way toward the shiny object Waterman spotted, when I hear Suarez shouting: "I meant we called you because we wanted you to bring your boat!"

Oh. Well, that's information I could have used half an hour ago.

I keep swimming hard until I get close to the object, then slow down. I don't want to reach my hand out and grab a fistful of a Portuguese man-of-war. I've made that mistake before. Unlike my dad and grandfather—who built up an immunity to jellyfish stings, like loggerhead turtles do—I'm not so lucky.

The Nobel Prize was given to a researcher in 1913 for pioneering research on severe allergic reactions after observing the effect of injecting jellyfish venom into animals.

The animals all died.

Even trying small doses to inoculate them first only made them sick and didn't improve their chances of survival. Further evidence that the men in my family are just plain weird. Although I'm kind of curious if my daughter, Jackie, who takes after her great-grandfather and namesake, inherited some of that immunity. Not that I'd ever ask her to touch a jellyfish . . .

I don't see a dorsal sail, and unless this is an Australian box jellyfish that got very, very lost, I decide it's a garbage bag and reach out for it.

Nothing stings, so I grip it tight and start sidestroking back to shore.

Fonseca is waiting with a tarp on the ground for me to set the bag on to avoid contamination from the sand. I'm getting strange looks from the other officers, who are unsure how to react when a colleague strips down to a two-piece and dives into the waves at a murder scene.

I put on my clothes and carry on like nothing happened.

"We're going to feel real stupid if it's just someone's garbage," says a Broward Sheriff's Office detective named Nathan Offerton.

By "we" he means "me." And no, I won't feel stupid. I'd have retrieved it even if this weren't a police investigation. It's one less trash bag floating in the ocean.

These people occasionally visit the sea. I live here.

Fonseca carefully unties the bag and aims her light inside.

Clothes . . . probably whatever this woman was wearing before she died. Possibly an important clue.

"Damn. Nobody tell Wylder or she'll cancel her retirement," says Offerton.

"Who's Wylder?" I ask.

"Inside joke," he says dismissively.

Fonseca hands the bag to Detective Waterman, who dips into it, then looks up at me. "That was a good save, McPherson."

Six words. Damn.

CHAPTER TWO
ROPE BURN

Josh Kaperman, a Broward County medical examiner, is standing next to a widescreen television in a room with a window that looks into the medical exam laboratory where the corpse is laid out on a table.

A robot arm with a high-powered microscope is going over every square inch of the body while another instrument using submillimeter radar is probing deeper, in three dimensions. This kind of thing was science fiction a year ago; then someone donated the device to the ME's office.

I'd heard rumors of controversy over the donation of the robot and some other high-tech equipment. Some speculated that the money might have actually come from a hacked crypto wallet that belonged to a criminal.

Their loss, our gain.

From the look on Kaperman's face as he uses his iPhone to guide his toy around the body, he gained the most.

He explains it almost like he's making a sales pitch. "Berta can inspect every single section of the body in microscopic detail and then build up a high-resolution map that we can zoom in on. With the radar module, we can see things like tissue damage and burst blood vessels."

"I think he's in love," whispers Suarez, sitting across from me.

"I heard that. And yes, I probably am. As I was saying . . . the really interesting thing is the software. We can use artificial intelligence to look for certain patterns and call out anything unusual." Kaperman points to a stack of folders sitting on a counter in the exam room. "Hopefully with this, we'll have fewer unsolved cases like those."

He zooms in on the bruising around the neck. "If we take a closer look, we can see that these blood vessels were burst in large sections and not in small ridges."

"Ridges?" asks Suarez.

"If there were ridges and the troughs between them were the same diameter as the rope, that would tell us fairly conclusively that the rope was used to strangle her," explains Kaperman.

"Meaning her death was no accident," Offerton injects.

Kaperman sits back and points to his screen. "Well, in that scenario, she could have been strangled by someone using the rope or it could have been accidental. The ridges wouldn't tell us that."

"Then what use is your little toy?"

Kaperman is taken aback by Offerton's response and doesn't immediately react.

"There are zero ridges, Offerton," I tell the BSO detective. "Try to keep up. If there aren't ridges, then it wasn't the rope that strangled her."

"So she drowned," Offerton fires back. "Why didn't you just say it?"

"Because she didn't drown," explains Kaperman. "Not exactly. It's too early to tell, but it looks like she was strangled by hand."

I turn to Offerton. "He says she was probably murdered. But not by the rope."

He glares at me. "I heard him, McPherson. What I haven't heard is why you're here. Is this an FDLE case now?"

"I asked her to be here," says Suarez. "We can use her expertise."

"If we need anyone to dive for shiny objects in the bottom of a canal, we know where to reach you," says Offerton.

"What the fuck, Nathan?" Suarez's use of Offerton's first name changes the tone of the discussion.

Offerton fumes silently for a moment, then holds up his hands, palms out, in a peace gesture. "I just don't like jurisdictional overreach. We do the work, you take the credit. That kind of thing."

If the body of someone who was recently a living person with dreams and ambitions weren't lying on the table in the other room, I'd get up and tell Offerton where he could shove Kaperman's robot. But I'm here to find out what happened to this woman and see that justice is served.

I've been in other situations where nobody gave a damn. It sickens me. In fact, that stack of unsolved murders sitting on Kaperman's counter burns in my consciousness. How many of those investigations were only one lucky discovery from being solved? How many of them got derailed because of bickering over hours and who was right and who was wrong?

"Do we know her name?" I ask, trying to focus the detectives on what's important.

"We have a few potential matches from social media searches," says Suarez. "Nobody who's been reported missing, though."

"How long had she been dead?" I ask Kaperman.

"No more than twenty-four hours. I put the window between eighteen and twenty-four."

"So nobody might even know she's gone yet," says Offerton, thankfully back on track.

I give him a nod. "Any sign of struggle?" I ask Kaperman.

"We checked under the fingernails for skin or blood and found nothing. The ocean has a habit of scrubbing things like that away, though."

Tell me about it. I once had to perform an amateur autopsy underwater because of strange and extenuating circumstances. I literally watched clues float away before my eyes.

"Could it be suicide?" asks Offerton.

"The pattern of burst blood vessels makes me want to say no, but I can't rule it out," answers Kaperman.

Offerton pushes further: "What if her clothing was between the rope and her neck? Could that make it look like she was strangled?"

"Maybe?" Kaperman answers hesitantly.

"Her clothes were in a bag," says Waterman, who has been characteristically silent until now.

"Some of her clothes. She owned more clothing than what we found in there. And it's not the first time we've found a suicide with their clothes all bound up," Offerton replies.

"With a rope around their neck?" I ask.

"Yes. Ever heard of an anchor? We pulled someone out of the water who committed suicide that way. I think it's happened multiple times," he insists.

News to me. But I don't read every police report.

"Okay, next question. Did she come from the sea or did she go in via the beach?" asks Suarez, looking at me as if I have the tide tables and currents memorized for South Florida.

Okay . . . I kind of do. "It could have been either. We had a strong wind earlier last night. She could have died at sea and drifted to shore. Or died right offshore and drifted around until she floated to the beach. In that case . . ." I pause to do the math. "She could have been south of Miami when she was put into the water. That would have given her enough time to drift to where we found her."

"So she couldn't have been killed offshore of Broward County?" asks Suarez.

"If she was in the ocean for twenty hours, that seems unlikely. Unless . . ." Something strikes me.

"Unless?" asks Suarez.

"I'm assuming she was free-floating. The other end of the rope could have been tied to an anchor and she was in one spot for most of the time until the rope came free."

Suarez makes a face. "So then it could still be our problem."

"I'm FDLE, emphasis on the *F*. So it's my problem no matter where she died. If it was an anchor, then that really reinforces that she was murdered," I add.

"How so?" asks Kaperman.

"I checked for reports of boats washing ashore. Whatever she was in would have likely beached itself in the wind," I explain. "Assuming she was alone in the boat, or left there alone."

"Unless she swam out there," says Offerton. "That would imply suicide."

"How do you swim with an anchor?" I ask.

"A strong-enough swimmer could," he fires back defensively.

Waterman says nothing but has an expression of pity on her face.

I keep my mouth shut. It's not impossible. It would have to have been one really light anchor or the dead woman a much more powerful swimmer than she appears to have been.

"Next steps," says Suarez. "McPherson, would you guys mind checking the marinas? See if anyone saw a woman matching this description get on a boat?"

By "guys," I presume he means me. I don't actually have the full weight of the FDLE behind me, and Hughes and Solar, the two other members of the UIU, are off doing other things.

"Sure. I have an email list with most of the managers. I can get on that right away. Time is ticking. Our best chance is within the next day or so, before memories get foggy and details lost."

Suarez nailed it. I'm not buying Offerton's conjectures about suicide. This woman was murdered.

CHAPTER THREE
MARINA

Tomas King, first mate of the *Chandelier*, an average-size yacht that docks at the Miami Beach Yacht Club, is hosing down the aft deck of the boat when I approach. He waves at me and shuts off the water. It's not yet noon, and I decided to come here first on a lark after sending an email to all the marina owners.

While owners can be a good source of information, sometimes the best intel comes from people like Tomas who work the boats and talk to other people in similar positions. They see everything. They gossip with each other.

People like them don't often gossip with the police, but my family has history in South Florida, and my father fixed the engines of the *Chandelier* when the owner was in a financial bind with the IRS.

Stuart Grumman, the owner and Tomas's employer, is a controversial figure, to say the least. He owns several strip clubs and adult bookstores in South Florida and for almost a decade has found himself the center of some investigation every time a mayor or prosecutor needed to do a quick U-turn into the politics of morality by going after the local porn kingpin.

I can't say that I can vouch for the legitimacy of all Grumman's business dealings, or the ethics of them. I have a problem with them, to be honest, because the kind of people I want to protect are the commodities he uses to make money.

The *Chandelier* is just one more sleazy venture. Besides Grumman's clubs and bookstores, he hosts private parties in international waters. While advertised as merely "R-rated" fun, stories abound that more goes on than that.

Nobody has ever looked deeply into this, as far as I know, and I'm not about to make waves. Mainly because it's not my call but also because, sleazebag or not, Grumman has always been good at paying back favors and has helped my dad and uncle out of a few binds.

"Heya, Sloan," says Tomas in his Kingston accent, using my first name because he also knows my dad and grandfather.

"Hello, Tomas. Permission to come aboard?"

"Of course," he replies warmly.

Technically, as law enforcement, I have to ask permission unless I have probable cause or a warrant. Tomas doesn't even bother asking me what this is about.

"I need to ask you about a girl," I explain.

"Right place, wrong time," he says.

"Story of my life. You wouldn't happen to be missing any girls?" I ask.

"Not the last time I checked."

I take out my phone and show him a computer-generated photo of the dead woman that makes her look . . . well, alive. "Have you seen her? Do you know if she works for Grumman or someone else?"

Tomas takes my phone and studies the woman. "No, I have not." He hands it back to me.

"Did all the young women come back the last time the boat went out?"

Tomas suppresses a grin. "I think I would notice that. I keep a head count."

I have no doubt about that.

"Is this the girl that was found last night on the beach?" he asks.

Word travels fast. "It's related to that. We don't have a name yet. We're hoping someone may have seen her."

"A pretty girl like that, I'm sure lots of people saw her." He taps the radio on his waist. "Five minutes ago, Hank over in the fuel depot called me up and said there's a pretty one walking this way. And here you are. People notice."

"Thanks for the compliment, as stalker-y as it sounds. That's why I'm talking to you. Do me a favor: if anybody else mentions maybe having seen this missing woman, don't hesitate to call me. Okay?"

"Anything for a McPherson—that's what Mr. Grumman says," he replies.

"In this case I'm asking as a cop."

"I think that would be okay too."

I say goodbye and walk back down the pier lined with million-dollar yachts. Although it's a quiet day and nobody is looking at me, I'm now aware that there are probably lots of eyes watching.

Tomas was correct that an attractive woman would get noticed. I doubt it will take more than a day to identify her.

That'll be the easy part. The real question is what happened to her.

It's not just a matter of achieving some kind of resolution; it's about making her life matter by not ignoring the fact that she's now dead.

I feel a twinge of pain in my gut at the thought of Amelia Joltz—a young woman I shared a college algebra class with. I spoke to her once or twice and didn't really notice her beyond that.

Nor did I notice when she wasn't there for our class on Monday or Wednesday. Nobody did.

Nobody noticed she was missing for a week. That semester she hadn't had any roommates and lived alone.

Amelia had a fatal seizure in the shower. The water kept running until her hair fell out and clogged the drain, causing a leak into the dorm room below.

That's when maintenance showed up and someone finally noticed Amelia.

If you look back at her Facebook and Instagram posts, everything stops the day she died.

To her friends it looked like she was taking a break from social media. The lack of posts was the only sign she had gone missing from the world.

Amelia and that stack of folders in the medical examiner's office haunt me even as I stand here in broad daylight. The more time goes by, the greater the chance this new victim's life will simply fade away.

An old man in a long-billed cap is moving gear from the dock to a sportfishing boat. From the large rods and the water hose going into the bait well in the back of the boat, it looks like he might be taking a charter out for a run. The morning report said that schools of hammerhead had been spotted near shore.

One hammerhead is a sight to see. I've dived in the middle of hundreds of them, and it was surreal: sharks everywhere, fading into the distance. It feels like you're on another planet surrounded by aliens. Except in reality, you're the alien invader.

To the novice shark diver, it can be nerve-racking, but you soon realize they couldn't care less about you. That's not to say you don't get the occasional curious shark coming in close and testing how defensive you are. They're always on the lookout for food. Preferably the kind that won't put up too much of a fight.

Unlike when a large mammal comes at you, playing dead is the worst strategy with sharks. Like toddlers, sharks like to bite things to figure out whether they're edible.

Still, sharks get a bad rap. While they're not quite gentle giants with bad PR, they play by rules that can be fairly well understood. One of those rules is they'll nibble on things when they get the chance.

Which reminds me . . . it's surprising that our body didn't have any signs of bites, given how long she was in the water. I guess she just got lucky.

I get into my truck and check for any messages.

None of the marina managers have reached back to me, but there's an email from Suarez:

> To: S. McPherson
>
> Subject: We identified the body

CHAPTER FOUR
NEXT OF KIN

I take a seat in the back of a small auditorium in the Broward Sheriff's Office where Suarez is about to give us an update. Jennifer Mazin, my temporary supervisor at the FDLE, is talking to Suarez's boss in the corner—probably negotiating how the case will be handled.

One of our jobs in the Florida Department of Law Enforcement is to assist other agencies in the state. If a case involves multiple jurisdictions, we can make it easier (in theory) to coordinate how the case is investigated and prosecuted.

It's not like in TV shows, where people argue about someone taking over a case—at least not with the minor ones. It's usually friction-free. Most of what we do in a situation like this is help communicate with other law enforcement groups and assist with routine police work.

If the victim has an ex-boyfriend in Melbourne, Florida, that Broward wants interviewed, we can assign FDLE agents to handle that and save a BSO detective the trip.

That's not to say there isn't tension. As the state's enforcement agency, it's also our job to investigate other law enforcement agencies and investigate public corruption. We're not always greeted with smiles from other cops when we walk through the door.

"Let's get started," says Suarez as he takes the podium. "We have a few updates. First and foremost, we've identified the victim as Nicole Donnelly. She's a twenty-six-year-old white female from Atlanta. Her family in Houston have been notified, and this will be going out later today as a bulletin along with a request for anyone to step forward who may have information leading up to her death.

"The deceased was last seen in Atlanta eight days ago. We're building up a timeline of how she got from there to our beach.

"The exact time and location of death is still being determined, so for the present, our office will continue to conduct the investigation with the assistance of FDLE, Fort Lauderdale PD, and the coast guard."

Suarez presses a clicker, and a map of Florida appears showing the surrounding ocean and currents. A red loop covers an area from where she was found, down to the Keys, and thirty miles into the ocean.

"The challenge is determining where she went into the water. We know she was in for a while, so that means the possible search area is very large—assuming that she hadn't been weighed down by an anchor closer to where she washed ashore. Twenty hours is a long time in the water, and a body can travel quite a distance in the currents."

No joke. Entire empires were formed because of favorable currents. You could be lost at sea and find the right current and be home for dinner—or catch the wrong one and never be seen again.

Ocean routes and currents have also been state secrets. Some undersea currents still are when it comes to the best path for getting your nuclear submarine quickly from point A to point B.

"At this point we don't have a determination as to whether the deceased died by accident, suicide, or homicide," says Suarez.

I raise my hand and speak before being called upon. "Suicide's still on the table?"

"Yes, McPherson. Forensics still thinks that's an option. We don't have any evidence of struggle," he explains.

"Other than the choke marks on her neck," I respond.

"We don't have clarification on that. The medical examiner thinks they could have been caused by the rope if it was twisted the right way—that plus the buffeting from the currents could cause similar bruising."

From the looks of the other investigators in the room, I see that I'm not the only one having trouble buying this explanation.

Suarez can tell too. "Listen, we don't know anything yet. We're going to continue to proceed as if this was a potential homicide case and talk to any leads that come up. There's another factor: if you look at this map, you'll notice that she could have been dropped in the water from a small vessel out of port from Key West, the Bahamas, or even Havana. The coast guard will help us figure this out. The other possibility is that it was an accident or a botched rescue attempt and nobody has come forward."

"Why not?" asks a BSO detective named Martine.

"Bad guys have boats too. If she was a passenger on a drug boat and fell out, it's not like they're going to call the coast guard."

Damn it. They are going to put an asterisk on Nicole's case. They'll ask some questions. Check for obvious suspects, like a boyfriend with a criminal record or a shaky alibi. But beyond that, unless someone comes forward and says they saw Nicole get on a boat with someone, this case will collect dust until something else turns up.

It'll fade away.

"What about her clothes?" I ask.

"What about them?" replies Suarez.

"They were in a bag a hundred yards from where she washed up. How could they both drift together for so long?"

"We thought about that. They could have been tied to the rope and come loose when she washed ashore," says Suarez.

"That's convenient," I reply, using my outdoor voice instead of my inner monologue.

"What's your theory?" he responds.

I throw my hands up. "I don't know. Nothing makes sense."

"You're the one with the reputation for connecting unrelated dots into something useful. I'm more than open to suggestions from the person who caught the Swamp Killer."

Suarez is being diplomatic because of my reputation. I found a van in the bottom of a lake that led to the arrest of one of South Florida's most prolific serial killers.

It was mainly luck on my part, but also a lot of persistence and help from teammates. Teammates who are currently scattered to the wind because we may have been a little too good at catching highly placed crooks.

"In all seriousness, McPherson, if you have a suggestion, let's hear it," Suarez says sincerely.

Well, damn. Now I'm on the spot. The obvious suggestions—talk to her friends, retrace her steps, and seek witnesses—are already being put into place. Maybe not with the gusto and emotion I think this poor woman deserves, but with the amount you could expect in a case with this little evidence so early on.

Behind me, Offerton whispers to another detective. "She's going to turn into another one."

I turn around and whisper back, "Another what? And if the next words out of your mouth are 'It's an inside joke,' I'm going to . . . say something cruel."

"No disrespect," says Offerton. "You're a good investigator. A great one. But you're going to burn out at this rate and start chasing things that aren't there."

"So you think this was an elaborate suicide? Really?"

"No. I think someone killed her. But look at that search area. If we don't stumble into someone who knows where she was, we've got a three-country search for a suspect. Do you know what the close rate is for those kinds of cases?"

"If I can continue . . . ," says Suarez, trying to regain control of the meeting.

I catch Mazin giving me a disapproving glare. Nobody knew where to assign me at FDLE, so they stuck me with her, and she was none too thrilled. A bureaucrat who avoids actual cases as much as possible, Mazin must find managing me like receiving a wild bull as a pet.

"Okay, then. Offerton is right. We'll either know in the next forty-eight hours who our main suspect is, or it could take a long time for something else to break. So let's make this time count."

Fair enough. Most cases are cracked with boring, pedantic footwork. I'm more of an outlier in my methods. But what can I do with this case?

The map showing all the potential places our victim could have been dumped is stomach-churning. The only way to make any progress is by tracking down her contacts. But if she was abducted by a stranger, that may not help much.

No . . . to crack this case, you'd have to approach it unconventionally. You'd want to narrow the scope immediately, so you knew where to focus.

You'd have to get a little eccentric . . .

CHAPTER FIVE

BAIT

George Solar is standing at the edge of the dock looking down into the forty-foot cabin cruiser I borrowed from my boyfriend. Specifically, he's looking at the blue tarp covering the suspicious mound lying on the afterdeck.

The tip of his cigar glows orange in the night as he takes a deep puff. "Is that a body?" he asks matter-of-factly.

"You could say so," I reply.

"I'd be lying if I said I thought this day would never come. How'd you get it into the boat?"

"Run helped me," I explain.

"Well, that answers my second question. Where is he?"

"Watching Jackie," I reply.

"And that would be the third question: You still get along with Hughes?" he asks, referring to the third member of our dismantled Underwater Investigation Unit.

"Yep."

"Okay, then," he says, then hops into the boat. "That's all I need to know. I thought you were kidding when you said you needed help with a body. Then I remembered who I was talking to. Does it have a name?"

I pull back the tarp. "I was thinking Aquapig."

Solar examines the large pig carcass and nods. "Is that a reference to one of those Avengers?"

"Something like that."

I climb onto the bow and undo the line while Solar unhooks the stern.

"My mind is racing right now, McPherson, but I kind of just want to see where this is going."

I start the engine and take us away from the dock. Solar takes a seat in the chair next to me. He looks older than when I first met him—that is, met him when I was an adult. But he doesn't look *old*. He's got that quality that Clint Eastwood and Harrison Ford have, which causes aging men to become more of themselves.

My boyfriend, Run, is like that too. The laugh lines on his face only make him more Run-like.

I panic at a gray hair and understand why some of my friends dye theirs crazy colors when they reach their forties and have a midlife crisis. It sucks to be judged on your appearance in a binary way: young or old.

Men have it different. It's not fair, but at least I get to look at Run all day and enjoy him resembling the man I love more and more.

"This about the Nicole Donnelly case?" asks Solar.

"I thought you wanted to watch things unfold," I joke.

"This is part of that. I assume you're not too happy with them putting an asterisk on the case."

I'd ask him how he already knows about this, but that's who George Solar is. He's on the phone nonstop and is a nexus for Florida law enforcement information.

When Mandy Fonseca told me hi from Solar on the beach, chances are that she'd just gotten off the phone with him. Likely because she wanted to know if he had an expert she could talk to about conditions on the beach affecting the corpse.

Of course, Solar would know somebody who knew somebody.

"Right now, the search area is between here and Havana," I explain.

"I told Cynthia I'd only be gone a few hours. If we're planning an invasion, I'll need to let her know I'll be late," Solar deadpans.

I take us into the Intracoastal and gun the engine when we're out of the no-wake zone. I have to speak over the boat engine, but I'm used to that.

"There are some things that don't make sense. We found her clothes in a plastic bag still floating in the water," I explain.

"I heard some maniac stripped down to a bikini and pulled it from the waves," he comments.

I ignore that. "Anyway, that seemed odd. Maybe it was tied to the rope. Maybe not."

"You want to see how far a body could drift using our friend back there?" asks Solar.

"Not quite. I checked the tide and satellite data: the search window is as big as we feared. I want to check out another hypothesis. Maybe she was killed close to where we found her."

"That would certainly put the focus back on South Florida. But didn't the medical examiner say she'd been in the water for twenty hours?"

"Yeah. I don't have all the details right now. That's why I wanted your help with this little experiment."

I take us through the inlet and out into the ocean, heading north a few hundred yards from the beach. The towers of hotels and condos sparkle on shore, making the whole shoreline glow, except those parts declared no-light zones so the sea turtles can hatch.

I bring us to a stop a few miles south of where Nicole was found and drop anchor.

"I want to drop our friend into the water on a line and wait an hour or so. That okay with you?"

Solar's version of a grin forms at the corner of his mouth. "I think I see where this is going."

Solar helps me tie a rope around Aquapig's legs and neck and connect it to an anchor. We then push him over the transom and tie the other end of the rope to a cleat so he doesn't drift out of reach from us.

I grab ahold of the rope so I can feel where the body drifts.

"I'm guessing your theory is she couldn't have been in the water that long without something taking a bite," says Solar.

I nod. "We've had more sharks coming inshore than usual lately. From what I saw on the beach, she didn't look like she'd been snacked on." I shrug. "I know, I know. I don't have all the pieces. Maybe she was wrapped up in a tarp and tied down."

Solar thinks that over. "That could mean she went in a lot closer to shore and washed up near where she was dumped."

"Yep."

I point toward the section of beach where she was found. "Notice anything?"

South of us lies one of those dark areas kept pitch-black to serve as a sea turtle sanctuary.

"That would make this a good dumping zone," says Solar.

"It would indeed. But they have infrared cameras to watch the hatches. If she was dumped in the ocean there, we might find clues."

"We'll make an investigator out of you yet," says Solar.

"How long since we put our friend in the water?" I ask, still holding the rope tethering the pig to our boat.

"Eight minutes, why?"

"Because I already feel something nibbling on him."

CHAPTER SIX

LUAU

Detectives Suarez and Offerton, Jennifer Mazin, and ME Josh Kaperman all have masks on as we stand around the examiner's table. Lying under a sheet is Aquapig—what's left of him. I called them in for my dramatic reveal.

I may be overplaying my hand, but I want to force them to try to shut me down face-to-face instead of over email or a conference call.

"Before you start, can I ask how you got this in here?" asks Kaperman.

"Fonseca. She said this table was clear. Did I need to request a reservation?"

"No. Just curious."

"If that's another body that washed ashore, you're going to have to explain to me the sequence of events that skipped the whole crime-scene-investigation thing," says Suarez.

"Not to worry. This isn't that. But something kept bothering me about the length of time the victim was theoretically in the water. So I did a little experiment."

"This is gonna be good," says Offerton, not in a way that I feel is entirely supportive.

"Twenty hours is a long time in the ocean for a body. Especially with schools of hammerhead sharks and the bulls that have been spotted recently near our beaches. So I put this guy in the water near where we found Nicole Donnelly to see what would happen."

It's time for my dramatic reveal: I pull back the sheet.

Everyone stares in stunned silence for a moment. They've all seen dead bodies before, so that isn't what provokes their reactions. What they haven't seen in person is the aftereffects of a shark attack.

"Good lord," says Suarez. "Are those teeth marks?"

"I believe those were caused by a bull shark," I reply.

"Did it have its hind legs when you put it in the ocean?" asks Kaperman.

"Yes. Fully intact. I'm happy to show you the before-and-after photos."

"I know what a pig that *wasn't* the victim of a shark attack looks like," he replies.

"For the record, the animal was dead before he went in," I add hastily.

"Well, that's a relief," says Mazin.

"How long was he in for?" asks Kaperman.

"Two hours." I gesture toward the refrigerated section where Nicole's body is being held. "There's no way she was out there for twenty hours and didn't end up looking like this."

"Shark repellent?" asks Offerton.

I shake my head. "Do you know what shark repellent is? It's an extract taken from dead sharks. You know what it smells like? Rotten sharks. Nicole smelled like seawater."

"What if she was covered up?" asks Suarez.

"With a tarp? Maybe. But that should have washed ashore. Also, I got my first bite in under ten minutes. If she was anchored in place or covered in a tarp, she was more than likely placed in the water near where we found her. She couldn't have drifted for that long without getting munched on."

"Can I use Berta to examine the pig in closer detail? We don't have a lot of good high-resolution imagery of shark bites," Kaperman explains.

"Sure thing. Consider him yours," I reply.

"Jesus Christ," whispers Offerton.

Mazin is glaring at me. "Can I speak to you for a moment alone?"

"You can use my office," offers Kaperman as he leans in to inspect his new specimen.

I follow Mazin through the door in the back of the exam room. In its window, I catch a reflection of Offerton shaking his head.

Mazin holds the door for me, then closes it after I enter.

"What the hell is this about?" she demands.

"What is what about?"

"Are you trying to make our lives more complicated?" Mazin asks. Her arms are folded, fists clenched.

"I'm just trying to help this case."

"They have it," she responds.

"Do they? Last I checked, the entire Bermuda Triangle was their search area and they were ready to put in sixteen hours of actual work, then close the case," I fire back.

"Nobody is going to close it. Do you know how many unsolved cases I have sitting in my office?"

"More than you should," I respond and immediately regret it.

"If you were anybody else, I'd write you up for that. I knew your attitude was going to be a problem, but I took you on anyway." She watches my face for a reaction, which I try hard not to give her. "That's right," she continues. "When Solar's pet project got disbanded, nobody wanted to inherit you. I stood up and said I'd work with you."

Ouch. "Why? You know my history."

"Because I thought you wanted a break from the action. How many times have you been shot at? That gunfight in Catalina? I'd think you'd be ready to retire after that. I was wrong. You can't stop looking for trouble."

A break does sound nice. But so does not being haunted by the thought of the people I could be helping.

Mazin gets to the point. "This isn't our case, McPherson. I don't *want* this case."

What I want is to call her lazy, but she has a decade on me. God knows how I'll feel about my job in ten years. Instead, I try to calmly explain the situation to her. "If Nicole Donnelly was dumped near where she was found, that will be Fort Lauderdale's problem if BSO wants to pass the buck. Hell, if the perp set foot in the turtle sanctuary, we could make it a federal case."

"Is it ever that simple? Have you *ever* had a case that goes down that simply?" She points to the room where Offerton and Suarez are waiting. "You know what they're thinking right now? Let's push it to Fort Lauderdale and have them point out it took place in the water, which would then put it back on our plate because we inherited Solar's UIU responsibilities."

"Let me talk to someone else at the FDLE about the case," I tell her.

"No way. I'm not letting you make me out to be the bad supervisor trying to push everything downhill."

I'm about to point out that's exactly what she's doing, but I change tack instead. "What if someone else takes me on?" I wait a beat. "Nobody would fault you if I got switched to another unit."

"Nobody would have you," she says simply.

I'm sure I could get Solar to twist a few arms, but I can't pull him into every battle. I need to solve this one on my own.

"All right, how about this? I play it low-key. If I can get someone at FDLE to take me and the case on, then you transfer me. If I can't, I drop it," I offer.

She sighs heavily. "I'm not here to bargain with you."

"That's the funny thing about bargaining. You have no choice when someone else has something you want."

"And what is that?"

"I can either be the paper pusher you want to me be . . . or be myself," I explain.

Mazin thinks this over for a moment. "Okay. After tomorrow I don't want to hear about this anymore. If it ends up on my desk, I'll make your life hell. Everyone else in our unit has their hands full with cases homicide hasn't been able to handle. We don't need more."

"Fine. I won't make any waves that affect you," I reply. "And I'll try not to make you look bad. Now can we go back out there? It's getting awkward."

Mazin goes through the door first. "We were talking and decided this might be Fort Lauderdale's call," she announces to the room.

"That makes sense," says Offerton, putting up zero fight.

"I'll talk to Waterman," adds Suarez.

"That will be a short conversation," Offerton quips. "Care to guess what one-letter response she'll give you?"

"Do I still get to keep the pig?" asks Kaperman, who hasn't stopped marveling over the shark bites.

"Yes," I reply. "Waterman can get her own."

"You good with this?" Suarez asks me.

Technically, my opinion is irrelevant. It's Mazin's call.

"I'm just here to help." That's when something occurs to me. "Offerton, in one of our many delightful exchanges, you mentioned someone named Wylder. Then, a little while ago, you said something about me becoming 'another one.' What's all that mean?"

I could have belched at the top of my lungs and it would not have received a more unwelcome reaction.

"Gwen Wylder." Offerton shrugs. "Cautionary tale."

"Okay. But when you first saw Nicole Donnelly's body, you implied that Wylder would be excited about it. That she might cancel her retirement, or something like that. What did you mean?"

Offerton waits for someone else to jump in, but nobody does. "She was a detective in Miami. She got a bit obsessive over cases and went a little nuts and they let her go."

"No, they didn't," replies Mazin. "She sued to get her job back. Now she sits in a basement office where nobody bothers her."

"Really?" replies Offerton. "Damn. Some people have all the luck."

"When you say obsessive over cases—any kind of case?" I ask him.

"She had a type, you might say," he says without offering any detail.

"And that type would be?" I probe.

"Things that looked weird at first glance. Anyhow, let's go brief Waterman and get this rolling."

This Gwen Wylder clearly made everyone uncomfortable. Maybe she's a living version of my poor classmate Amelia Joltz—someone who fades away before anyone realizes it.

In this case, into borderline insanity.

People have called me insane too.

Maybe I should talk to Gwen and see what she has to say.

CHAPTER SEVEN

COBWEBS

"Fuck off," Gwen Wylder tells me to my face when she opens the door to her office and sees me standing there.

She's in her late fifties and immediately reminds me of an intense version of Sigourney Weaver.

If the message on her answering service wasn't clear enough that she didn't want to talk to anyone, the look on her face made it abundantly evident before she even spoke.

I put a foot in the door before she can close it. Behind her I see rows of filing cabinets and stacks of folders piled up between what look like more library books than one person should be able to check out.

A small window looks out over the parking lot. It's not the basement, but close.

"I'm—"

She cuts me off before I can get my name out. "I know who you are. You're the annoying pest that left five messages on my voice mail."

"That would be me. I'm also—"

"You don't think I read the newspapers or heard about the podcasts about you? My damn checkout clerk asked me if I knew you. Now I get all my groceries online."

"I just—"

"Get your foot out of my door or I'll shoot it off. Look around: there's nobody on this floor. I can get away with it," she snarls.

I pull my foot back and she slams the door.

I can't tell if this was all an act or if the woman is genuinely nuts. She might not know anymore herself.

"It was nice meeting you," I say to the door.

I hear a muffled "Fuck off."

Okay. Time for plan B.

I take a photo of Nicole Donnelly's crime scene from the folder under my arm and slide it under the door.

A few moments later, I hear Wylder pick it up.

Seconds after that, she opens the door and stares at me with her gray eyes like an owl readying to devour a mouse.

"This the girl on the beach?"

"Yes . . . ," I answer hesitantly.

She eyes the folder under my arm. "That the file?"

"Yes . . ."

"Leave it here and go get me a coffee from Lao's Donut Shop," she demands.

I hold the folder back. "Are you going to play nice?"

"Are you going to get me my fucking coffee from Lao's?"

"Fine." I hand her the folder.

"No coffee. No deal," she says before slamming the door.

I think our entire exchange took thirty seconds. I'm beginning to see why she has a bad reputation—she makes George Solar look like Mr. Rogers by comparison.

I've learned that you never win a battle of wills with a crazy person because they don't even know there's a battle. The best course of action, whether it's a bull shark that's decided to follow you or someone like Gwen, is to keep moving and not give them a reason to snap.

She wants coffee from Lao's Donut Shop, then coffee she shall have.

I stare up at the faded letters above the empty storefront in the half-abandoned strip mall and sigh. According to Google, Lao's Donut Shop closed three years ago.

Does she not know this? Or is she messing with me?

I check Yelp just in case there's another Lao's.

Nope.

This is the one. It had fairly good reviews, and people really seemed to like Johnny Lao, the owner of the shop. There are even a few sad emojis in posts where people point out that it's closed.

A sun-bleached note on the door says "Closed until farther notice." The misspelling makes it even sadder. I even see boxes of unused supplies behind the counter.

Gwen is messing with me, I decide. She's too smart not to. And the angry-lady thing? It seems like a shtick the more I think about it.

Okay, she wants to play? We play.

Sometimes, even with a bull shark, you have to surprise it by doing the unexpected.

A little over an hour later, Gwen opens her office door and makes a sad face at me. "No luck? The great Sloan McPherson strike out? Losing sucks, doesn't it?"

I bring the coffee cup into view from just outside the doorframe.

Gwen's eyes light up when she sees the Lao's logo.

Not believing it, she pops the lid off and takes a whiff of the coffee scent. "Holy shit! How the hell . . . ?"

She takes a drink, and her face approximates something close to ecstasy.

I had a cup myself. It was good, but not that good.

Andrew Mayne

"Is the shop open again?" she asks excitedly.

I shake my head.

"Do you have a goddamn time machine?"

I assume she's joking. "Are we going to talk about this case?" I ask sweetly.

"I want to know how you got me this cup of coffee," she says, walking back to her desk.

"There's more where that came from . . . if we talk."

She shakes her head. "Damn it. Fine. Sit down."

Gwen takes her chair and inhales the aroma of the coffee. "When I went off to the funny farm, Lao's closed down. Thinking about that coffee was the one thing that kept me going. And what do you know, it was gone when I got out. A fucking metaphor for my life. And then who should walk through my door with a cup of the impossible? Sloan McPherson. Karma or kismet?" She shakes her head. "One of 'em."

"I'm not sure I understand," I reply.

"Never mind. Ignore me. It gets easy after a while. Let's talk about this case."

CHAPTER EIGHT
ALONE

"Tell me about it," says Gwen as she rocks back in her desk chair and studies me with her gray eyes.

"The body was found shortly after two a.m. There was a length of rope around the victim's neck, and her garments were found floating in a garbage bag near the shore. Based on the currents and a test I did—"

"Stop," she says, cutting me off. "You sound like one of those robot assistants rattling off facts." She taps the folder. "I can read all that." Gwen takes the photo I slid under her door and pushes it in front of me. "Why did you show me that?"

"I wanted to make you curious . . . ?" I reply hesitantly.

"You wanted me to feel something. Crime is emotion. It's about what we can't have. Love, money, respect. It all comes down to that." She taps a filed fingernail on the image of Nicole's dead body. The victim's eyes are open and her cool blue lips parted as if she's trying to say something. "What does this make you feel?" asks Gwen. "Tell me about that. What did you feel when you found her?"

"I was late to the scene. Everyone else was already around her," I reply.

"I know what a crime scene looks like. Tell me what you felt."

My emotions at the time come back to me. "Alone. She looked so alone. We were right there, but the beach could have been empty. I felt like we were . . . ghosts."

"We'll get back to that in a moment. What about her and the condition you first saw her in?" Gwen asks.

"Staged. Not in the sense that she was laid out like that by whoever killed her, but the rope. The bag of clothes. It just felt . . . forced."

Gwen probes deeper. "Why would somebody do that?"

"Misdirection. To confuse us."

"Okay. But were you confused? The ME found reasonable evidence she was strangled."

"There's some doubt . . ."

"Doubt," she repeats. "It looks haphazard. Maybe it was a suicide. Maybe the person who did it didn't have the time or knowledge to cover it up. What do the other detectives think?"

"I can tell they know it's a murder. The scope of the potential dumping area and the lack of forensic evidence has them frustrated. They're assuming . . . maybe 'hoping' is a better word, that it's a one-off and somewhere down the line they'll make a connection to someone they know or a suspect who coughs up information."

"All they have is her body and her contact book," says Gwen. "Look at her . . . look at *Nicole*. Look again. Tell me what else you see."

"She's pretty."

"Pretty girls usually get killed by jealous boys. Either by ones that love them or can't have them. If Nicole had been less attractive, I don't think she would have ended up on that beach," she asserts.

"The ME found no sign of sexual assault." I shrug.

"I could sexually assault you and there would be no sign," she fires back rather aggressively. "Hell, the marks on her neck could be a sign of sexual assault."

Gwen's response and the claustrophobic office are making me uneasy. I try to focus on the case and hope she's not going to try to strangle me to make a point.

"Whoever killed her was infatuated with her?" I reply.

"Maybe. We don't want to get too into the head games. It's easy to get caught up in that and create an image of someone who's completely different from who our killer actually is. That's how we've missed on some of the bigger cases," explains Gwen. "Now tell me more about the beach. What did it feel like?"

"It's at the north end of Fort Lauderdale. Near a sea turtle sanctuary and a state park."

"Is it dark there?"

"There's dark beach for the turtles just south of there."

"Where they dumped the body," adds Gwen.

"We don't know that. She could have been drifting for hours." I'm about to explain the Aquapig experiment, but she interrupts me.

"Nope." Gwen lifts the photo. "This one wasn't drifting for very long. That turtle beach is too convenient a place for someone to dump a body."

"I can think of a lot better places," I reply.

"You're assuming they had the time and ability to do it. This looks like a haphazard cover-up, but that doesn't mean they were stupid. There could have been other factors." She stares at the image, almost admiringly. "This feels like an improvisation."

"Forensics says she was in the ocean for twenty hours."

"Bullshit," says Gwen.

"They've got a pretty accurate methodology." I lift my finger. "You can tell by the fat near the surface of the skin and how much brine builds up in . . ."

Gwen's glaring at me. "Are you seriously lecturing me about this?"

"I was just saying the ME says she was in the ocean for twenty hours. Although—"

"Yes, your little pig stunt. That proves it. But I don't need a science-fair experiment to tell me the ME's wrong."

I'd challenge her on that, but I get the sense it would be a waste of breath.

"What do you think?" I ask instead.

"About this? Your friends are going to do the very minimum and then file it away and hope for a miracle. Like you said. Unless we get lucky enough that another dead girl washes ashore, we won't be hearing about this case for a while, if ever."

"You have a strange definition of luck," I reply.

"Do I? Or do you just pretend that these"—Gwen taps the folder—"cases are something more? Do you convince yourself you care? Do you go through the little drama of pretending, *What if this were someone I knew?* Give me a break." She opens her arms wide. "This place? It's just another factory. Paper comes in. We put ink on it. Maybe a person gets moved from one spot to another that we call prison, but that's yet another factory. I don't think we care any more about these victims than someone processing insurance claims or making Nintendos. If we did care, we wouldn't go home at five and spend our weekends reading IKEA catalogs and catching up on our DVR."

I touch my side where I was once stabbed. "Some of us care and have the scars to prove it. When I go home tonight and have dinner with my daughter, I'm not going to see her face. I'm going to see Nicole's. And the only thing that disturbs me more than that is the fact that I can't quit—even if it means sometimes getting in the way of the people I care more about than anything else in the world."

"Nice speech," says Gwen.

"I'm not finished." I nod at her. "Don't tell me we don't care. Some of us care to the point of burning out and then claw our way back to finish what we started."

"Don't confuse ego for determination," replies Gwen. "I'm still here because I'm not going to let them win."

"You're still here because you're not going to let them think you don't care," I reply.

Gwen shakes her head. "Goddamn, you're stubborn."

"There's a lot of that going around. So, can you help me with this?"

"How?"

"What do you think? What do you know? Have you ever seen anything like this?"

"I've seen a lot of things. I'd have to dig through my files. That could take a while," she says.

"I can help."

"Only I understand how they're organized. Tell you what . . . you could help me with something." Gwen spins around and takes a folder down from between two textbooks on biology.

"I've been trying to close a few things out. This is a couple years old. Maybe you want to take a look?"

I take the folder from her and open it to a photo of a teenage boy with a shy smile. "Is this connected?"

"It could be," says Gwen. "An attractive young person left in a deserted place."

I read the victim's name out loud, "Michael Lougher? I never heard of this."

"He was a foster kid. Went missing. Presumed to have run away. His body was found two months later with a bashed-in skull. It made news for a hot minute, then faded away," she explains.

"And this could be connected to Nicole?"

"It's something. I need to do a search to see if any later cases might have been connected, then talk to his foster parents before shuffling it off to the basement. You do that for me while I dig through my files on any other cases that might connect to Donnelly."

I grip the folder with both hands. "I don't want to get distracted from Nicole's case."

39

Gwen holds up the photo of Nicole. "You think whoever did this is out there planning their next kill? Not a chance. They're watching the news waiting to see what we do. Right now, that's talking to Nicole's acquaintances. We have some time." She points to the folder in my hand. "Michael Lougher doesn't. That case is about to be consigned to oblivion. His last chance is you finding something relevant—and recent."

CHAPTER NINE

WARD

I'm standing in front of Michael Lougher's house—or rather the last place he lived before he went missing. It's a modest home in Sunrise, Florida, with a Chrysler minivan parked in the driveway. The paint is faded, and you can see the spots where the sprinklers have deposited a layer of calcium from the hard water.

The lawn is mowed, but the house looks like it could also use a new coat of paint. It's what an old person's house looks like when they give up maintaining it.

Lou and Claudia Terrada, Michael's foster parents, still live here, but I'm not paying them a visit today. I just wanted to see where Michael lived before he vanished.

Michael, like many foster children, had a rough time in the system. He bounced from home to home, including several times during the year he turned fourteen, when he likely went from childish mischief to adolescent criminality.

According to his file, he wasn't a bad kid in a violent way but one who learned that the easiest way to fit into a new school was by falling in with the wrong kids.

He'd run away three times before he went missing. The first time he was found in Orlando. The second time shoplifting in Miami.

From the interview transcripts with the Terradas, it's clear that they were losing their patience with their foster son. They were a devoutly religious family that had helped raise two other foster children without much difficulty. Then came Michael.

While they thought his running away "sad," that wasn't how their feelings come across in the police report. In fact, they waited two days to report him missing.

And that's why the case is complicated. His foster parents said that Michael vanished when they stopped at a highway gas station on their way to visit a relative.

The police report suggests that there might have been an argument while they were on the highway and Lou Terrada might've told Michael to get out of the vehicle in a desolate area.

The main reason for this suspicion is the family's delay in contacting the police. A gas station security camera clearly caught the van pulling into the station with Michael, then departing six minutes later with no sign of him having left the premises, unless it was in the van.

The only image showing Michael was taken when the van pulled in. It's only a few seconds long. Michael is sitting in back and Lou Terrada can be seen yelling back at him.

Why the discrepancy between what the Terradas say happened and what the police report concluded?

If they kicked him out on the highway, they could be charged with child abandonment. Whereas if he ran away while the car was parked at a gas station, the fault wouldn't be theirs.

I have no idea what miracle Gwen expects me to pull out of thin air, or if this is a good use of my time while Nicole sits in the morgue, but I don't have a lot of other options at the moment.

I take one more look at the house, then climb back into my truck. I check the map that shows the route the Terradas drove and take the same streets they likely did on their way out of town.

Having had my own share of family arguments, I can imagine it starting over something trivial and then escalating. The report said Michael was angry that he had to go visit Claudia's sister, who lived in Naples. He wanted to stay home and hang out with his friends.

The Terradas knew better than to leave Michael alone—although had they, he might still be alive.

I take the route south to Highway 41, which cuts across to the west coast of Florida.

At this point, either Michael and his foster parents were exchanging loud words or he was staring out the window with teenage anger burning his cheeks.

In the Terradas' version of events, he was already making up his mind to ditch them the first chance he got.

In the police report's version, the argument wouldn't reach a boiling point until after they left the station.

The difference is critical, because where he got out might lead to who he ran into next.

Implied in the report: after exiting the Terradas' van, he entered someone else's vehicle, never to be seen alive again.

The police theorize that Michael was killed that same night. His body was found weeks later, several miles west of the gas station in a culvert under the highway. The autopsy indicated that the back of his skull was crushed with a blunt object while he was bent over. The speculation was that he might have been forced into that position, possibly to perform a sex act on his killer.

That's where the report gets even darker in its speculation. The first time Michael ran away, he made it to Orlando by hitchhiking.

The second time, the Miami officers who busted him for shoplifting suspected that he'd been working as a male prostitute.

So, the theory goes that after Lou Terrada kicked him out of the van, Michael thumbed a ride with someone who then killed him shortly after. The police looked into vehicles that had made stops at the same gas station during that time period. A large section of Wylder's folder contains fuel receipts, images of video freeze-frames, and copies of tickets that were issued that night on the highway.

The police talked to everyone they could get a name for. Unsurprisingly, more than a few people with criminal records drove trucks along that route. The police even came up with the names of two men who had previously been charged with sexual assault. Interviews were inconclusive. Both men had solid alibis.

I pull off Highway 41 into the Lucky Stop gas station and park in the gravel lot adjacent to the pumps. It's a typical independently operated South Florida gas station with a convenience store that sells beer and lottery tickets.

The cameras that caught the Terradas' vehicle are clearly visible. Their sole purpose seems to be capturing license plates. Perhaps a deterrent to criminals who would otherwise see the remote gas station as a vulnerable target.

The bathroom is on the left side of the building. A chain-link fence runs behind it to the edge of the property line, then goes back to a canal.

Looking back confirms what I suspected: the security cameras only capture vehicles. What happens at the pumps and the bathroom isn't their focus.

I take a few steps toward the bathroom, then stop when the scent of stale urine and the sound of buzzing flies warn me off.

I walk around the gas station and take a few photos, then decide it's time to visit the location where Michael's body was found.

As I drive away, part of me feels like I left something behind. Not a physical thing, but a sense of having passed by something too hastily and not realizing what it meant.

🦋

I'm standing by the only marker indicating where Michael's body was found: a sun-bleached plastic ribbon tied to a guardrail over the culvert he was shoved into.

Thousands of people pass this spot every day without ever knowing that a young man was brutally murdered and abandoned only yards away from their speeding cars.

Being a student of archaeology (and destined to become the world's oldest PhD candidate, at this rate), I'm acutely aware of how much history lies right below our feet. In a single car trip to the store, we probably pass over several ancient burial grounds, thousands of prehistoric creatures, and the remnants of countless dinosaurs.

The faster we travel, the more history we whiz past without a thought.

Michael, a foster child—in other words, a ward of the state—was feeling judged and rejected by the people who were supposed to care for him the most. I don't know if the Terradas failed him, but as a society we sure did.

A tractor trailer flies past me, and the wind flicks my hair. The scent of the muck where Michael was found reaches my nose, along with the rancid odor of decay.

What a horrible place to be left.

I step over the guardrail to inspect the area more closely.

One of the unexplained details in the police report was the rust stains on Michael's jeans. They could have been the sign of an active teenager with poor laundry hygiene—but they also added one more clue that didn't quite fit into the puzzle.

I walk back to my truck and thumb through Wylder's folder. Police took twenty-eight statements from people they tracked down who'd traveled this highway.

Based on my experience, someone saw something and didn't realize it. Or the person we're looking for is on this list.

A yellow note is stuck to a report about one interviewee in particular: Redmond Conliff.

The note reads: "Wrong place. Solid alibi. Too bad."

The reason it says "too bad" is that Conliff, a box-truck driver for Bington Produce, had a prior conviction for sexual assault on a minor when he was nineteen. He served eighteen months of probation.

I may be cynical like a lot of cops, but when we see a pattern, we take notice. A non-cop might take a look at Conliff's record and say that it's proof that the system worked. The guy got caught, was punished, and never broke the law again.

I have friends into justice reform who throw these data points at me all the time. They tell me that, sure, murder rates and aggravated assaults may be up, but theft and other crimes are down overall.

That's when I explain that there's a difference between crime being down and people not reporting a crime the same way as before, or at all. Convenience stores frequently don't bother filing a report when someone shoplifts. It takes too long for the police to arrive. And god forbid you try to hold the person in the store: you'll find yourself facing legal action from the shoplifter's attorney for some imaginary injury you inflicted. Or be injured yourself.

There's crime and then there's reported crime. I know of some police departments that have declined to file less severe cases simply to show that their numbers are down.

I have friends who see these stats and tell me everything is fine.

When I read about Conliff, the optimist in me wants to believe he reformed himself. The cynic suspects he got smarter.

A reasonably intelligent person doesn't try to pass a counterfeit bill in the same place where they were first caught. A violent sexual predator tries to avoid making the same mistake twice.

I don't know if Conliff is reformed or merely smarter than before. One way to find out is by talking to the man.

CHAPTER TEN
Resting Place

Redmond Conliff is eating a hamburger from a plastic container when I approach him at the break tables near the loading dock. Three box trucks sit behind him with crates of oranges and other produce being unloaded by a man in a forklift.

According to their website, Bington Produce primarily serves local restaurants with fresh farm-to-table fruits and vegetables sourced from different growers around the state. I called ahead and asked if I could speak to Conliff about a hit-and-run he might've witnessed while on his routes.

This of course was a complete fabrication and is why Conliff doesn't seem too nervous when he sees me.

"Redmond Conliff?" I ask, not wanting to let on that I was staring at his mug shot only five minutes before.

"That's me," he replies after wiping his chin.

"I'm Special Agent McPherson with the Florida Department of Law Enforcement. I think your dispatcher told you I was coming?"

"Yeah. An accident, right?"

I take out my notebook. "May I sit down?"

"Sure," he says, gesturing to the concrete bench opposite him.

I flip through to a page where I made some bogus notes. "Hold on. What was your route yesterday?" I ask.

"I was off," he replies.

"Sorry, I meant when you last drove. These are someone else's notes. This isn't my case. I'm just helping out," I explain, hoping to cover my screwup.

"Day before. I was carrying oranges from up north. Ma'am, I didn't see any accident. I'm not sure why you're talking to me."

"Me either. It's just a formality. Someone probably saw your truck right before or right after and got confused. I just need to put a couple things into the report," I tell him apologetically.

"No problem," he says with a shrug.

"I do this all day," I sigh. "Trying to pick up the pieces of someone else's mistake." I flip to another page. "Huh, looks like this isn't the first time you've talked to the police."

"Unfortunately, no," he replies.

I pretend to be confused. "Seems you were a potential eyewitness three years ago for another incident."

Conliff doesn't respond to that.

I act like I'm moving on. "Well, I'm just going to put down you didn't see the blue Prius speeding . . . Oh, I forgot to ask you that," I suddenly add, playing up my ditziness. "*Did* you see a blue Prius speeding?"

He smirks. "No, ma'am. I did not."

"Okay, good. I think we're about done." I flip back to my notes. "What was the other thing the police asked you about . . . before?"

"Some hitchhiker or something," he replies.

I notice he didn't say "kid" or anything else descriptive about Michael.

"Was he a fugitive?" I lob at Conliff.

"I don't know. I don't really remember that much about it."

I look down at my notes while asking, "And you didn't pick up the hitchhiker?"

"I was driving in the opposite direction he was going. I had a gas receipt," he adds, a little too hastily.

"Uh-huh." I flip to another page. "Oh, my mistake. It seems he wasn't a fugitive. He was a kid. They found his body a few weeks later."

I can tell he's growing suspicious. So I push it a little.

"Well, I hope you didn't murder him," I say with a forced laugh.

Conliff stares at me. It's not necessarily the look of a guilty man—but definitely the look of someone with a guilty conscience.

"You didn't murder him, did you, Redmond?" I ask seriously.

The smart move would be for him to not say anything. But Conliff has been arrested before for sexual assault and he'll have a persecution complex for the rest of his life, even for things he didn't do.

The tell is in how they deny it:

The guilty tend to respond with an alibi.

The innocent issue a flat denial.

A sociopath responds with anything that comes to mind.

"I was going in the opposite direction" is his response.

"Can you prove that?" I ask.

"I already told you: I have a receipt. The gas station person saw me. I was nowhere near that kid."

The report Gwen Wylder gave me has a credit card receipt from the 88 Fuel Depot and an affidavit from the manager who said they saw and spoke with Conliff twenty miles east of the gas station where Michael was last seen.

Investigators ruled him out because he was going the opposite direction from where they assumed Michael would have hitched for a ride after being kicked out of the van.

Of course, that's an assumption on their part—based on the belief that Michael was still in the van when it left the gas station. If he wasn't, it's a different matter.

But the camera evidence supports their theory and Conliff's alibi— or rather, it doesn't contradict either of them.

I refer to my scribbles in the notepad. "It says here that you were convicted of sexual assault on a minor. What was that about?"

Conliff assesses me. "I'd rather not talk about it. I need to get back to work." He gets up and throws his half-eaten hamburger into the trash.

"Things can catch up to you, Redmond," I tell his retreating back.

He ignores me and climbs the steps to the loading dock and vanishes through a back door.

This is what Gwen wanted me to see. Conliff is the perfect fit— other than the fact that he doesn't fit.

I'm wary this is another Lao's Donuts coffee run. Except I won't be able to improvise my way through it like I did with Lao's. That one was easy. I did a search for Lao, got a phone number, called his wife, and found out that he worked at his son-in-law's diner two blocks away as a manager. I asked the landlord to let me look around the empty shop and swiped a stack of coffee cups, then told Lao I wanted to surprise a friend. He was happy to brew the coffee for me at the diner, adding a spoonful of thick cream like he did when he ran his shop.

Things lined up my way then.

They're lining up in the opposite direction right now.

Conliff *feels* guilty, but I can't prove how his and Michael's paths could have crossed.

That same challenge confounded the original investigators so much that they turned their attention back to Lou Terrada and impounded the van to look for further evidence, their new theory being that he might have killed Michael.

With no blood spatter or other forensic evidence and his wife sticking by the story, the cops didn't have nearly enough to go on, so the case got back-burnered until somehow landing on Gwen's shelf.

Did she ask for it? Or was it a cruel trick slipped under her door like the photograph of Nicole Donnelly I forced upon her?

I get back into my truck with every intention of going to her office and telling her what she can do with the case, but instead I find myself heading back to the gas station where Michael was last seen.

CHAPTER ELEVEN
AIR FRESHENER

"How's it going, babe?" Run asks me over the speakerphone.

"The usual. Parked in the middle of nowhere, chasing phantoms," I reply.

I'm back at the gas station. This time parked where I can see the whole establishment.

I'm trying to create a mental picture of what could have happened that would have put Michael on a collision course with Conliff.

The problem is that the cameras cover the area outside the pumps, not leaving much of a route for Michael to wander off from. The barbed-wire fence enclosing the back of the station and the canal make the property resemble a mini penitentiary.

The lot behind is overgrown with brambles and the overpass beyond it too steep to casually climb. Not that I would underestimate the will-power of an angry teenager. But that's a lot of obstacles.

"You going to be late?" Run asks.

It's already dusk. "I hope not. You good to watch the kiddo?"

"Always. But is the kiddo good with that?"

I'm about to reply that she loves spending time hanging out with him as much or more than me, then realize he's sending me a subtle message: I haven't been spending enough time with Jackie.

"Point taken. Let me wrap things up here and head home," I reply.

"No point intended," Run insists.

He knows Jackie is the center of my world. He also knows I sometimes need a gentle reminder that I have to come back down to their world.

"Let me call her," I suggest.

"K. See you later," he says before hanging up.

I dial Jackie's number.

"Jackie McPherson, private eye. How may I help you?" she says as she picks up the phone. She's a teenager now, but still as playful as when she was little. I hope that never changes.

"I'm calling about a missing mom," I reply.

"Have you checked the nearest swamp? I hear they like to swim around them. The more disgusting the better."

"Actually, a crappy old gas station," I answer.

"Eww. Gross. Remember that one on the way to Key West with the bathroom that smelled like a raccoon died and then rats ate him and then they died and then a cat came along and—"

"Yes. I get the picture. It was bad. This one is pretty awful too. I can see the flies from here."

"*Yuck!*" she shouts. "Hold your breath until you get home. You could get Ebola or something."

"I don't think that's quite true. Hepatitis, maybe."

I study the bathroom again. It's actually a box of cinder blocks added to the side of the station. Probably built to keep customers from using the one inside.

The chain-link fence starts at the edge of the back wall and runs all the way to the overgrown lot. The cameras don't cover the bathroom, only the entrance and exit to the station. Michael could have gone in while Lou Terrada was pumping gas. Maybe he hid there?

If Conliff's truck had pulled in, I'm sure the police would have seen it on the surveillance footage. But what if someone else pulled in?

It's not uncommon for men who are into risky hookups to meet in places like this.

Michael, sadly too streetwise for his years, probably knew this too.

"You still there?" asks Jackie.

"Yes, hon. I have to go look at this bathroom," I tell her.

"Don't do it!" she warns over the phone.

"This is work," I reply.

"Then quit."

"I'll see you when I get home."

"I'm not letting you in if you smell like the one in Key West," Jackie vows. "I'll make Dad pressure-wash you in the driveway."

"Love you too, bye," I say as I hang up.

I grab my flashlight and walk toward the bathroom. The horrible scent and the sound of buzzing are more than enough to tell a blind person which way to go, making my light completely unnecessary for this purpose. But it also makes for a handy weapon.

I'm not worried about any particular thing jumping out at me—other than maybe Skunk Ape, Florida's answer to Bigfoot. I like to be prepared.

The metal door has been kicked, defaced with graffiti, and shows the signs of years of abuse. A cardboard sign that's either meant in earnest or sarcastically says ALL GENDER BATHROOM.

Under the words, a helpful person drew in ballpoint pen their idea of what different genitalia look like. *Sheesh.* A psychology student could write a master's thesis on how this person views sex. I guess this is what some people did before Twitter.

I grab the handle and pull it open. And immediately regret that I didn't put on a mask and gloves or bother knocking first.

Although the smell is overwhelming, I'm thankful I'm greeted by only an empty toilet that looks lonely in the dark.

I turn on the light and see a swarm of flies collect around the fixture.

It would have been a lot easier to bring Gwen back another cup of Lao's.

The trash can is overflowing, and graffiti covers the wall in so many layers it's hard to make out any individual message.

A cracked sink is mounted next to the toilet with a broken mirror above it.

What's above the toilet is more interesting to me.

It's a window. A good old-fashioned slide-out window like the one convicts use to escape through in movies.

Did Michael see this?

What would his first thought have been?

Escape.

I take my life into my hands and step onto the toilet seat to peer out.

The window opens into a back area filled with junk.

I'm busy aiming my light at the bald tires and box frames and don't hear the person approach behind me.

"Can I help you, lady?" asks an old voice.

I look behind me and see the gas station attendant.

"Police matter. I'm fine, thanks," I reply as I crawl through the window.

CHAPTER TWELVE
Escape Route

I lower myself down and land next to a rusted oil drum filled with sharp metal objects that look like props from a *Saw* movie.

The entire back area is filled with old tires, metal junk, and jagged, unrecognizable objects. It looks like a *Texas Chainsaw Massacre* amusement park.

Okay, I say to myself. Let's assume I'm Michael—rebellious, pissed off at the Terradas, and wanting to make a run for it.

Now what? Hide here?

No. Keep moving.

I make my way toward the back of the yard, using my light to keep from impaling myself.

Somewhere behind me I hear the man call out. "You sure you're okay?"

"I'm fine. Thank you."

"Would you like me to turn on the lights?" he asks helpfully.

Lights? "That would be great."

A moment later, bright floods click on and illuminate the junkyard.

I realize that I was about to step onto a rusted box spring and possible snare myself like a fox in a trap. I also notice that to my left there's a gap in the fence. Beyond it, a narrow path leads between the fence and the brush to the canal.

Well, that's interesting.

I work my way around Satan's bed and slip through the opening in the fence.

A footpath takes me all the way to the edge of the canal, where a narrow concrete embankment runs along the water and under the overpass.

In the satellite image of the area, the path's hidden by the brush. From here it looks like a vagrant highway.

I walk along the embankment and under the overpass. The distance between the edge of the canal and the wall is less than a foot, and I have to move carefully to avoid taking a swim.

"Be careful!" calls the man, startling me.

I keep moving, increasingly regretting that I didn't just drive around the overpass. But hey, that's not how I do things.

I finally reach the other side of the overpass, and I'm able to place my foot on the dirt and not have to balance myself like I'm in the circus. There's not as much brush here. It's a dirt lot with patches of grass. I walk toward the road, searching the ground with the beam from my light.

I think I've now established that Michael could have escaped from the gas station and not been spotted by the cameras.

But then what?

My light catches a faded cigarette butt and a crushed can.

As I move it around, I see more trash and evidence that people have spent time here.

Doing what?

My light catches a tread mark from a large tire. I kneel to get a closer look.

"Sometime the truckers stop here to nap," says the man behind me, nearly startling me out of my skin.

I turn toward him. He's shorter and much older than I am and has a helpful look on his face.

"Who's watching the station?" I ask.

"I locked it," he replies.

"Do trucks park here a lot?"

"I guess so. I can't really see from the station. I sometimes see them parked here when I drive into work."

"Did you work here when the teenager got abducted and was found up the road?"

"Yeah. But I don't remember anything about that particular night. We gave the police the footage from the cameras."

"Did the police come back here?"

He shakes his head. "Not that I can think of. They said the boy got kicked out of the car some miles ahead."

They were *really* locked into that hypothesis.

I try to phrase my next question tastefully. "Do any of the truckers ever pick up people at the gas station?"

"You mean for sex?" he says bluntly. "We call the sheriff if anyone comes around like that." He points to the lot around us. "But here, we can't really see it from the station. I guess that kind of thing might happen."

I aim my light back at the ground and follow the tire tracks until I come to deeper grooves in the dirt carved by years of trucks pulling into the same spot. I stand where the grooves end—where the cab of a parked semi would be—and look back, imagining what could have happened.

Michael comes through the little path under the overpass, escaping the Terradas, and finds himself here.

What happens if he sees a truck?

He's not a stranger to hitchhiking. He's probably fearless enough to approach the driver and ask for a ride.

What happens if he asks Redmond Conliff?

Conliff has a history of at least one sexual assault on a young man. He probably offers him a ride. Would he ask for some kind of sexual favor? Right here?

The prior assault suggests Conliff is either ashamed of his sexuality or gets some kind of thrill from violence. Either way, soon after or before Michael had his skull bashed in, Conliff stopped at a gas station east of here, putting him in the opposite direction of where Michael was found.

This would put him out of the picture—unless he killed Michael here, drove to the other gas station, made a point of being seen heading eastbound, then did a U-turn.

Conliff had been caught before and would have been more cautious this time. He knew that driving logs would identify him being on this route, so he had to throw off investigators.

He needed three things: an alibi, a place to dispose of the body, and somewhere to ditch the murder weapon.

We know what his alibi is and where Michael's body ended up. But we don't have the murder weapon.

I turn around and aim my light into the dark. The reflection of the beam bounces off the surface of the canal.

Well played, Gwen. You must have seen this coming a thousand miles away. You didn't hand me this case because it connected to Nicole Donnelly. You pulled it out of the cobwebs because you thought it might connect to me.

I take out my phone and call Run.

"What's up, babe?"

"I . . . um. I'm going to be a little late. Go ahead and start dinner without me."

"That kind of night? I'll set a plate aside for you."

I hang up and look to the gas station attendant. "What's the safest path back? I have to get some things out of my truck."

CHAPTER THIRTEEN
DRONE

In the back of my SUV is a large case containing a device that Scott Hughes managed to have lent to our UIU team to test out. It's the latest in the lineage of tools used to explore underwater.

For as long as people have been living and working near water, they've had ideas about what could be done if they could spend more time beneath the surface. Whether it's finding things that were lost, like fishhooks and treasure-laden ships, or doing things we do on land, like building structures or searching for things to eat, we've constantly tried to think up new ways to make this easier and safer.

Some of the first underwater explorers to use mechanical devices to stay underwater and go deeper were the ancient Greeks. Aristotle described how a large cauldron could be turned upside down and lowered to the ocean floor via a rope so men could breathe inside it and recover wreckage or build foundations for bridges.

There are even accounts of Alexander the Great taking a trip to the ocean floor inside a diving bell. His alleged remarks upon resurfacing were, "The world is damned and lost. The large and powerful fish devour the small fry . . . Upon the conduct of each depends the fate of all."

The student of history in me suspects that quote was the invention of a medieval writer who had never set foot in a bathtub deeper than six inches, let alone spent any time observing life underwater.

Describing the ocean is like trying to explain "land" to someone from another dimension. You could spend days trying to describe all the different types of terrain before getting to things like rocks or mountains, let alone clouds and birds.

"Damned and lost" aren't words that I'd use to describe the ocean. But as I look out at the large moonlit canal that runs along the highway near the gas station and think about what could be lurking under the water—from used tires to beer cans and rusted fishhooks—Alexander's alleged description seems fit.

Less than two years ago, I would have strapped on a scuba tank and leaped in with a flashlight to see what was down there. A few close calls with death have made me slightly more cautious.

The contents of this equipment case is Scott Hughes's latest effort to get me to think before I dive. He's had a front row seat to a few of my close calls and has put a lot of thought into keeping them to a minimum. Given Scott's own background as a navy diver, I don't take his suggestions lightly.

One way to minimize danger is using underwater remotely operated vehicles. ROVs have been around for decades, and I keep a simple one in my vehicle to scout dive locations for hazards like jagged metal and things with sharp teeth.

ROV or not, I ultimately still go into the water because I can search much more quickly by swimming and using my own eyes.

When I strip away the bubble cushioning wrap and realize I have no idea how to work this contraption, I make a video call to Hughes.

"What's up?" he says from the hotel room where he's been staying while going to the cybercrimes school in Virginia.

"How's the family?" I ask.

"They're watching a Disney cartoon in the other room. The words 'Dada boring' may have been thrown around. But I won't say by who," he jokes.

"I can guess. So, I'm looking at your infernal new machine and want to make sure I don't dump it in the water and accidentally create something else that has to be salvaged," I explain.

"Okay. It's a lot easier than it looks."

"It looks like a Roomba and a stealth jet had a cyborg child," I reply. "I don't know if I should put it in the water or throw it in the air."

Half a meter wide, the device resembles a small, artificial manta ray.

"I also can't find the controller," I add.

"There's an app for your phone if you need one," says Hughes.

"If I need one?" I ask. "How the heck do I control it?"

"You don't. See the VR goggles in the case? There's a microphone. You just tell the URV what you want it to do," he says.

"URV?"

"Underwater Robotic Vehicle."

"So, I say, 'Go left'? That sounds tedious."

"More like, 'Search for a gun within five meters of where you are.' You talk to it like a diver."

"Huh," I say skeptically. "So simple words and grunts."

"I said talk to it like it's a diver. Don't talk to it *like* a diver."

"Hardy har. So I just drop it in the water?"

"I'd turn it on first."

I set the unit on the bumper so its camera can see me and push a rubberized switch on the back of the device.

A voice emits from the goggles attached to a long, thin tether coiled up in the case. "System starting. GPT calibrated. Please place me in the water so I can orient myself."

"That voice sounds oddly familiar," I say. It's Hughes's voice.

"A buddy of mine worked on this. I helped with some of the systems. They asked to sample my voice," Hughes explains with a hint of embarrassment.

"Cool. So I just drop Tiny Hughes into the water?"

"It's called the URV1," he replies.

"That's what *you* call it."

I install the app for the device. I then put the goggles on and my AirPods in my ears so I can still hear Hughes and unfurl the cable and walk the URV to the edge of the canal.

"Dropping it into the water," I call out.

"Please be gentle. Make sure I'm not placed on any rocks or in a strong current," says Hughes's voice from the URV.

"That's just creepy," I say. "Is there a way to keep it from always listening to me?"

At the same time both Hughes and the URV say, "There's a 'mute all' button on the side of the headset."

"For crying out loud," I groan.

I gently place the URV into the canal like a little baby Moses. The device's impellers start to spin, and it glides away from my hands.

The URV moves a few yards, then makes a sharp turn. It then moves a few more yards and makes another turn. I assume this is the calibration part.

A moment later it flips over and dives into the water, pulling the cable behind it.

"Okay. It just dived or else we're out a few thousand dollars," I reply.

"Watching it now," says Hughes. "We're good."

I turn back and look at my phone, which I left on the bumper of my SUV. How can Scott see that far?

"Wait, you're watching this through the gadget?" I ask.

"Yes. It's using your phone to send video. It's low-res. You have a better image in the goggles," he explains. "I thought you'd be more impressed."

"The goggles?" I reach up and realize they're still sitting on my forehead. "I haven't actually tried them yet. It seems pretty dark for video."

"Just try them," Hughes says with the same kind of voice he uses with his kids to get them to eat broccoli.

"One second."

I pull them down over my eyes. It takes a moment for them to adjust.

"Holy cow."

CHAPTER FOURTEEN
VISUALIZER

I was expecting to see a grainy black-and-white image of murky water. Instead, I'm greeted with a 3D full-color view of the bottom of the canal.

By turning my head in any direction, I can see all around the device. I've played with Jackie's VR headset before, but this is different. It feels like I'm really in the water—only with heightened senses.

Muck-covered rocks and grass are clearly visible. A turtle swims by, and a virtual box appears around its body with the label "Florida Softshell Turtle. 18.3 cm. Specimen 2."

"What's going on? How come I can see color underwater at night?" I ask.

I must be muted to the URV, so the real Hughes answers: "The image is processed by an AI algorithm using data from the ultrasonic sensors and a feed forward transformer."

"Uh. So it's making it up?"

"In the same way your brain is adding in the details around what you think you're seeing. The system is constantly making predictions and updating them. Like it guessed that was a turtle and used that to update how it was representing color," he explains.

"What about the 'specimen' part?" I ask.

"It logs everything and keeps track of all the wildlife and other items. You can then search it later in a spreadsheet. It tries not to count the same thing twice by tracking its position," says Hughes.

"Cool. How do I use it to find what I'm looking for?" I ask.

"What *are* you looking for?"

I realize I never even told Hughes why I was out here.

"I'm helping Gwen Wylder, a Miami homicide detective, with a cold case," I explain.

"That's mighty nice of you."

"She's a tyrant. Nobody else can deal with her. But she's also wicked smart. I think she's going to help me with the Nicole Donnelly case," I explain.

"I heard about that. It's not an FDLE case yet, is it?"

"We're assisting. But I can't sit still. So I'm out here chasing down a potential murder weapon in the hopes that this Wylder might cough up something helpful relating to Donnelly. I miss our team," I sigh.

"What do you miss more? Being trapped on a sinking ship or almost getting asphyxiated by a serial killer?" asks Hughes.

"Not being alone while it happened," I blurt out.

"Yeah, I hear you. To be totally honest, I'm up here doing this course so I don't get partnered up with some NPC unit," says Hughes.

"NPC?"

"Nonplayer character. It's a videogame term for the computer-generated characters that just sit there and let things happen. It's also a bit of an insult these days. I've been using it for years. I should change that up," he muses.

"I wish Solar would get the UIU back together. I don't see why that's not happening."

"He's trying to keep us protected. Not all our enemies are in jail yet. Some sit in the statehouse. Others preside in courtrooms. I know he's been twisting the governor's arm. But there's only so much he can do at a time."

"I know. I know."

"Underwater mapping complete," says the URV. "What would you like me to do now?"

"So how specific should I be?" I ask.

"Tell it what you're looking for."

I unmute the VR goggles' microphone. "I'm looking for a man-made metal object between ten and thirty centimeters in length."

The image zooms as the URV zips through the water and shows me a metal drainage pipe that looks like it broke away from something.

"You can be more general," says Hughes. "Like, 'a potential murder weapon.'"

"Okay. I'm looking for a blunt metal object that could be used to strike someone in the back of the skull. Possibly a hand tool. It might be concealed in a sack or something similar," I prompt Tiny Hughes.

"Searching now," says the URV.

"Too specific?" I ask Hughes.

"We'll see."

The URV starts to move around the floor of the canal, inspecting rocks and debris with a spotlight and then moving closer, almost touching them.

An outline appears around an object using various colors, depending on whether it's a rock, grass, or something else.

"What do the colors mean?" I ask.

"What do you want them to mean?"

Thanks, partner.

"Make anything that's metal red," I tell the URV.

The image changes as it's overlaid with a grid that goes far beyond what I can see visually. Red outlines appear in random locations. Some are clearly cans or car parts.

"How is it getting this?" I ask.

"Magnetometer and sonar," says Hughes.

"But the signals have to be weak . . ."

"Deep learning. It knows how to amplify them. We're the only ones using this besides Navy SEAL teams right now."

I see an outline of a suspicious metal object.

"How do I tell it to get a closer look at something?" I ask.

"Look at it and tell the URV," says Hughes.

Duh. "Get a closer look at that."

The machine moves toward the dark shape. Visually, it's just a black garbage bag wrapped around something a bit over a foot long. But little white dots are forming around it as some other sensor fills in data that tell another story.

"How far away is this from shore?" I ask.

"4.3 meters," replies the URV.

"What kind of material is that?" I ask, on a lark.

The URV reports, "It appears to be a nonbiodegradable polymer. Possibly an industrial-grade waste disposal bag. The item on the inside matches the same dimension as several metal tools found in the Grainger catalog."

"Damn, Hughes. Maybe the UIU should just be a fleet of these patrolling the canals and ocean."

"Careful what you wish for," he replies.

CHAPTER FIFTEEN
EVIDENCE

I drop the black-plastic-wrapped bundle on Gwen Wylder's desk with a loud thud. She doesn't even bother looking down at it. Instead, she makes eye contact with me, and a trace of a smirk forms at the corner of her mouth.

"So, Sloan McPherson is useful besides getting coffee. Where did you find it? Near the culvert where the body was found?" she asks. "I told them they should have done a better search."

"No," I reply.

"No? Then where?"

"Near the gas station where Michael was last seen," I explain.

"There?" She looks down at the bundle with a confused look on her face. "This could be from anything. How could you possibly connect it to Michael Lougher?"

"That's up to forensics when they examine the blood and hair samples still attached to it. The killer was smart enough to throw it away. But he wrapped it in a plastic bag before tossing it. Maybe he was afraid of getting stopped, but either way, when I pulled it from the muck, it was already sealed for us."

"Convenient," Gwen says. "You dived for it?"

"No. I used an underwater robot with a metal detector. It took a while. But I found it."

"You really think this connects to Lougher?"

I nod. "And I think it connects him to Redmond Conliff."

Gwen's eyes narrow. "I had him pegged for this, but it didn't add up. How do you think this will tie him to it?"

"I used a bright light to see through the plastic bag. There are fingerprints in the blood. If they don't match Conliff, chances are they'll match someone like him."

Gwen shakes her head in disbelief. "He was smart enough to get rid of the murder weapon but not smart enough to let the elements do their job." She reaches for the phone on her desk. "I'm going to call our forensic people right now."

I put my hand over her desk phone. "Hold up. What about Nicole Donnelly? That doesn't fit Conliff or this."

Gwen wrestles the phone from me. "I never said it did. I said it 'might.' There's a difference."

"What about the Donnelly files?"

"I'm working on them. You help me. I help you."

"Help you? I just cracked a huge cold case for you. I think I more than helped you," I say, trying to keep my temper from flaring.

"Maybe. All we have is some . . . what is this?"

"A plumber's wrench."

"A plumber's wrench with what *may* be Michael Lougher's blood and which might include fingerprints. You haven't closed anything for me yet."

"Are you kidding?"

"You want my files?" she asks, gray eyes holding my gaze steadily.

"I want to get Donnelly's killer before he does anything else," I respond.

"You got time."

"How do you know?"

"Either I know something that you want or I don't. You decide. Do you want my files?"

I let out a long sigh. "Yes."

She pushes the phone aside and grabs a box from a shelf. "Then help me with this one."

"Are you kidding me?" I groan.

"It's ninety percent there. I just need a fresh pair of eyes," she explains.

"Ninety percent? What's missing?"

"Just the suspect. Everything else is there."

"*What?* Is this a joke?"

"You're Sloan McPherson. You can get Lao's coffee even though the only way to get it is with a time machine. This should be a breeze." She shoves the box into my arms.

"Gwen—" I start to protest.

"You don't get to call me that yet. Now, go. I have to get your wrench looked at before it decomposes."

"I—"

"I'll tell them who found it. Don't worry. They're certainly not going to think *I* dived for this."

"It was a robot," I correct her.

"Whatever. Not all of us are attention-seekers. Now go. Let me handle this." Gwen walks around her desk to physically push me out of her office.

The door is barely shut behind me when I hear her on the phone.

"Robert, you lazy asshole! Get over to the lab, ASAP. I got something to shove up all your asses . . ."

If I had any question before, I now know why they put Gwen on a floor by herself.

CHAPTER SIXTEEN
HOMEWORK

I'm sitting at the kitchen table going through the box Gwen shoved into my arms while Jackie works on her laptop across from me.

Run's house is a mansion on the Intracoastal, but despite all that space, the kitchen table is where we tend to congregate. I used to call my boat my office, but I realized my effort to isolate my work from my family also had the effect of isolating me from them.

Jackie tunes out the autopsy photos I might accidentally set on the table while Run casually turns them over as he grabs something from the refrigerator. They've learned to work around me, and I've tried to be more judicious about keeping my work life separate from our home life . . . most of the time.

When I asked Run one night if it bothered him that I took my work home, he replied in his typical easygoing manner, "Better to have you looking at gunshot wounds at the kitchen table than out getting shot at."

I've had more than one brush with death. While I think I'm a more cautious person now, I don't exactly go running in the opposite direction when trouble calls.

"How's the homework coming?" I ask.

"Fine," Jackie moans. "Totally thrilling. Wish I could do it all the time. How's the murder stuff? Or do I have to wait for a podcast to find out what you're up to?"

Despite my effort to insulate my daughter from my horrible world, she's gleaned plenty of details from crime podcasts that have covered my cases. But the case Gwen dropped on me is a few years old and mostly a matter of public record, so I decide to give Jackie the broad strokes. If we can't do enough typical mother-daughter stuff, maybe this will help her understand my world.

"It's pretty graphic," I warn her.

"Don't worry. I won't tell Dad," she stage-whispers.

"Wrong answer. I'm going to tone it down." Jackie and I have a no-secrets and no-lies policy, except when it comes to Christmas presents and how I look in the morning.

"Should I get my stuffed animals down from the attic so you can do a reenactment?" she asks.

"Barbies would be a better match." I sigh. "Starting eight years ago, over a period of three years, seven women went missing and were found dead," I begin.

"Is this related to the woman on the beach?" asks Jackie.

"Probably not. This is very different. And these women were . . . in a different occupation," I reply.

"Sex workers," Jackie supplies. "That's what they're called now."

"Yes, I'm aware of the term. But there are different . . . um, levels," I say delicately.

"You mean like hookers on the street?"

"I'm not comfortable with that word or the way you just casually used it," I respond, realizing this is not the conversation I should be having with my daughter, who only just became a teenager. "Let's change the topic," I tell her.

"Sure. Because I live in a magical world where nothing ever happens to good girls and everyone gets to live happily ever after. And the guys that drive by and honk their horns at me are all nice and would never do anything bad," she says in that sarcastic way that teenagers somehow master.

She has a point. I could pretend that nobody she knows will ever be faced with a dangerous situation or that none of her friends have ever been assaulted and will never deal with that possibility.

"Okay. You win. These women worked around truck stops. Most of them had drug problems and came from really bad home situations."

"That line of work wasn't their first choice," she says.

"Probably not," I reply.

"And they didn't know about OnlyFans," she says slyly.

Why does my daughter know about a site where people get naked for money? And here I was afraid *she'd* be the one traumatized by this discussion.

"Relax, Mom. It's just a joke we use at school," she says.

"That doesn't relax me."

"You were saying that these women worked around truck stops. On the *Murder Squad* podcast, somebody said they call girls like that 'lot lizards.'"

"That's a mean name, Jackie. These are *women*. They're people."

Jackie's cheeks turn red. "I didn't mean to—"

She's quick-witted, but she's also sensitive. I don't think I've ever heard her say anything about someone in spite—other than her cousins when they push her into the pool.

"It's okay. You didn't do anything wrong. It's more about me reminding myself not to dehumanize people. That happens a lot in my work," I admit.

"Like calling the unhoused 'homeless'?"

"I guess so. I don't know if I see the difference in that particular one. But the point is the same. Don't devalue people because of things that are beyond their control. Like with these women. For whatever reason, they were in a dangerous line of work. Seven of them went missing and were found murdered."

"How?" she asks.

"That's not important."

"Come on. Ellie's dad is an ER doctor. He talks about gross stuff all the time. One time a guy came into the ER with a golf club stuck up his—"

"I got it." I need to have a conversation with Dr. Schwizer. Although he may think the same thing when Ellie recounts some police story I told Jackie.

"They were stabbed," I tell her.

"Once or multiple times? They say that can determine if it was a crime of passion or done out of misdirected anger."

Good lord. What is she listening *to?*

"More than once. Let's leave it at that. The point is that they were killed. They got some DNA from the crime scenes, but there wasn't a match for anyone in the system. So the whole case was a dead end except for one thing: someone at a radio station realized that shortly after each girl went missing, someone requested a song in their name."

"What song?" asks Jackie.

"Usually 'Killer Queen' or 'House of the Rising Sun.'"

She immediately starts tapping away on her computer, and Freddie Mercury's voice blares out into the kitchen.

"What's going on?" asks Run.

"Mom is telling me about a case where a guy would kill hookers, then call in to a radio station and request songs about prostitutes," Jackie offers helpfully.

Run takes this in for a moment as I dread what'll come next.

Instead, he surprises me.

"Probably better you hear it from your mom than one of those ghouls who does those murder podcasts you listen to."

"You know about those?" I ask.

"I recommended the one about the Swamp Killer to Dad so he could hear what you were really up to," Jackie explains.

"I see," I reply, feeling a little less guilty.

Run takes a seat next to Jackie and casually mutes the song. "Go on. Let's hear this. I'll order us some Thai food."

Some families play board games and eat pizza. We're going to eat Thai while I talk about a serial killer.

CHAPTER SEVENTEEN
The Loop

Once authorities realized that there was a serial killer preying upon women along Interstates 95, 75, and 10, they dubbed him the "Loop Killer" because those highways made a circle around the center of Florida.

The name didn't catch on, and the case received little attention after the bodies stopped turning up. This could have been due to any of multiple factors: the killer getting arrested for some unrelated crime, simply stopping and moving on, or hiding bodies where they have yet to be found.

The case was another example of people living on the margins being forgotten about the moment the evening news cut to commercial.

My conversation with Jackie about dehumanizing language was more a reminder to me. A child getting killed is a tragedy. But if we call him a gang member in Chicago, our conscience lets us casually ignore the fact that a child died.

I think it comes from that part of us that secretly wants to believe that bad things only happen to people who make bad choices. It makes us feel safer.

It's a lie, and believing it would make me not very good at my job.

Cases like the Loop Killer are hard to solve when there's no apparent connection between the victim and their murderer. Like the podcasts say, when someone's killed, it's typically by someone they know—often a person close to them.

If a man is found shot in the head in his garage, the first person police want to speak to is his wife, then his neighbors, then his friends, business associates, etc., in an ever-widening circle of suspects. Ideally the suspect is one of the first people you talk to. The problem with that ever-widening circle is, the larger it gets, the larger number of suspicious people you encounter.

Thousands of cars and trucks traveled past the spot where Michael Lougher went missing. Of the people the police contacted, plenty had criminal records or otherwise seemed like suspicious characters.

That's simply the law of large numbers. Go to a medium-size pro football stadium to watch a game and, statistically speaking, you'll be in the same space with thousands of people who have criminal records—and likely several murderers.

Amateur crime sleuths whose knowledge about police work comes from sensational documentaries and podcasts don't understand how many people we talk to in a case. One of the first things we do when we lack a main suspect is reach out to every single person with a criminal record for a similar crime and ask for their alibi.

In high-profile cases, police often interview the culprit and let them go because they don't have enough evidence, plus dozens of other people who look suspicious.

DNA evidence changed a lot of this for sex crimes. Once we could tie a person who was suspicious to a crime that happened years before, it allowed investigators to close the books on a number of cases simply by looking up who was already a potential suspect and seeing if they were a DNA match.

The Loop Killer was frustrating because the DNA found didn't match a known suspect. Nobody remembered any of the women riding off with a particular person. And there were no cameras near the pickup spots.

The only clue in the case, besides the matchless DNA, is a voice recording of a man calling in to request "Killer Queen" the night Jazmine Allegaro went missing.

A man with a somewhat cheerful voice phoned into 104.3 the Rocker on March 12, 2018, and simply said, "I'd like to dedicate <nervous laugh> 'Killer Queen' to, um, Jazmine <nervous laugh again>."

This was the only request that was aired and recorded. The others were called in to and read by DJs at other stations.

Investigators pored over the songs-played logs of other stations and found similar requests each night one of the women went missing. However, by the time they realized this pattern, the Loop Killer had already stopped his spree.

Police gave instructions to radio stations to contact them every time *any* request was made—and to log the phone numbers. The call-in clue was never disclosed to the public because of the fear of copycats. Investigators soon had listened to hundreds of hours of audio of people calling in with requests but never heard anyone who sounded like the man on the recording.

Out of curiosity, I did a search for cases in other parts of the country to see if anything like this roadside knifing spree happened elsewhere after those initial murders, but I came up with nothing.

The FBI opened an investigation on the presumption that the killer might be traveling from state to state, but they didn't find anything either. In fact, all the investigators did everything by the book. I don't have any issue with how they handled it.

Yet all we're left with is a string of murders, some call-in requests to radio stations, and DNA that doesn't match any known suspect.

Explaining all this to Run and Jackie was an interesting experience. They asked good, if slightly naive questions, along with a lot of, "Did you try this?" The graphic details of the case weren't as fascinating to them as trying to solve a mystery with so little information.

"What now?" asks Jackie after I lay out the details of the case.

I place my hand on the stack of files. "This is what we have. Sometimes there are enough puzzle pieces in the box. Sometimes there aren't."

"What do you do when there aren't enough?" she asks.

"Your mom goes out and finds new ones," says Run. "Sometimes missing dinner."

Jackie takes this in. "So, is that what you're going to do now? Go look for more pieces?"

I was planning on giving the box back to Gwen and telling her she's only allowed one miracle, and I already delivered it. But the thought of being a hero to my daughter makes me answer otherwise.

"Yes. I'm going to look for more pieces."

CHAPTER EIGHTEEN
UNSEEN

I'm standing in a patch of woods in a wildlife management area near I-4 where Jazmine Allegaro's body was found wrapped in garbage bags.

This location is a hundred yards from the highway and easy to get to if you pull over and walk on foot like I did.

Jazmine weighed around 120 pounds, so an average-size man could have carried her over his shoulder this distance without too much effort. There were no broken branches or signs that she had been dragged there. All indications pointed to someone simply stopping on the side of the road when there was a pause in traffic and hauling the body into the woods.

The biggest risk would be getting spotted by a curious highway patrol officer, but that didn't happen. All seven bodies were dumped when the fewest patrols were on the road and traffic was at a minimum.

The sun is coming up on the horizon and traffic is beginning to build, but a few hours ago, around the hour she was likely dumped here, the roads would have been deserted.

It's a strange feeling to be in a spot where a victim lay dead. And an even stranger feeling to stand in the same position where their killer stood and looked down on his victim.

It doesn't take much effort to visualize how Jazmine was found. The crime-scene photographs perfectly captured the body, bound in plastic and duct tape.

The one curiosity was Jazmine's hand sticking out from the bundle. The other victims were wrapped in a similar manner. Their killer covered them in plastic but left part of them exposed.

The behavioral experts say this might have been so he could touch them one more time before leaving them in their final resting place.

According to the records the radio stations kept for tracking song plays, the requests came in before the bodies were dumped, suggesting that they may have been phoned in from the same location where the women were killed or close by.

Police still haven't identified where they were murdered. The most recent theory was that the killer used a van or a large box truck and dispatched them inside the vehicle.

While that's a pretty good assumption, it could also be a misleading one and why we still haven't found the killer.

When the Beltway Sniper was terrorizing the DC and outlying areas in 2002, killing ten people, authorities were on the lookout for a white male with a box truck. Based on past cases and what seemed like the most likely position for a sniper to operate from, this assumption made sense. But it was only an assumption. And an incorrect one that led to the killers eluding authorities.

John Allen Muhammad and Lee Boyd Malvo were neither white nor driving a vehicle like the one the experts theorized. Muhammad had removed the back seat of a used Chevrolet Caprice and created a sniper blind in the trunk. Muhammad and Malvo could shoot at their victims while remaining completely invisible.

While a man lying on top of a truck and shooting from that position made sense at the time, in retrospect it seems hard to imagine how someone could have gotten away with that method ten times without ever being seen.

We investigators often forget to look at things from an extremely paranoid point of view. If your theory of what someone would normally do isn't helping you catch the person, you have to assume they were doing something abnormal.

The harder they are to catch, the more abnormal they tend to be.

Theodore Kaczynski lived in a remote shack as a complete recluse. It was hard for investigators to imagine how someone so isolated could be connected to attacks involving mail and technology and academia a world away.

Along those lines, what could be abnormal about the Loop Killer?

All his victims were dumped off highways. He was never seen—which suggests he never expected to be seen.

Was he merely lucky? Or was there something else going on?

I pull a folder from my backpack and flip through the records from the highway patrol and the other departments that reports came from. There's no record of a car on the side of the road or anyone calling in about, or responding to, a breakdown.

Either our killer was very lucky or somehow invisible.

Besides highway patrol, there are several county law enforcement agencies that passed through those areas, as well as Department of Transportation employees and roadside-assistance services that help people when their cars break down.

None of them saw anything.

Investigators think this might be because the killer's vehicle was dark and almost invisible on the side of the road at that time of night.

Maybe. But that also feels like "the sniper is probably a white male shooting from the roof of a box truck" theory. It's the first hypothesis that comes to mind and the only one that makes sense, all things being equal.

However, if you're a killer who doesn't want to rely on luck to avoid getting caught, you want to be invisible and mobile. The best solution would be the opposite of the first thing an investigator would look for.

The Loop Killer felt he was invisible. Maybe because he had a dark vehicle that was hard to see. Maybe for some other reason.

The killing spree could have ended abruptly for the aforementioned reasons: getting caught, dying, moving on, or a change of conscience. Or because such opportunities never presented themselves again. Sadly, the number of vulnerable young women hasn't decreased. Our highways are still filled with sketchy places where people can find trouble.

What could make things less opportune for him?

What if his killings depended on his invisibility?

How do you take away someone's invisibility?

When I walk back to my truck, there's a Florida Highway Patrol trooper parked behind me, likely running my plate. When he sees me emerging from the woods, I take out my badge and show it to him.

"Everything okay?" he asks as he steps out of his car. I can tell by his rank that Trooper Saracen is a recent hire.

"Mostly." I point to the woods behind me. "Know anyone that patrolled through here five years ago?"

"A few people. Why?"

Man, this business has a short memory. "A woman's body was found back there. Several others around the state just like it. They called the suspect the Loop Killer," I tell him.

He shakes his head. "That's a new one. When I moved here from Oklahoma, people warned me that this state is weird. I had no idea." He laughs. "I had to stop traffic two days ago for an alligator to cross the road." He laughs again. "An *alligator*. I felt like I was in Jurassic Park."

"Welcome to Florida," I say with a smile, looking at the back seat of the patrol car and imagining whether there's enough room to kill someone and wrap them in plastic.

It seems unlikely, but not impossible. And, sadly, there's precedent for law enforcement officers doing this kind of thing. Like every other occupation, we get our share of sociopaths.

While a police car parked on the side of the road might be "invisible," I don't know if one of the victims getting into one would go without notice.

Although nobody remembers seeing any of the women get into a vehicle with the killer, that's not the same as saying nobody saw that happen. If the circumstances had been unusual—like a highway patrol trooper telling a prostitute to get into his vehicle—people might have paid attention.

Saracen walks back to his vehicle. "Let us know if you need anything."

"Sure thing," I respond, then think it over for a moment. "What do you listen to out there?"

"Besides the police radio? Florida is weird with FM. The AM stations seem to stay tuned in over a wider range here."

He's not wrong. Some of our AM stations get to use overpowered transmitters to avoid interference from Cuban radio stations. WIXY 780 AM is one of those stations. Curiously enough, that station has a similar all-request evening format to the stations the Loop Killer called in to. But as far as I know, there was no record of him calling in a request to that station.

Maybe he hates AM radio?

CHAPTER NINETEEN
Snipped

Detective Waterman stands atop a ladder, inspecting the wires on a pole overlooking a roped-off area of the beach just south of where Nicole Donnelly's body was found. She has on reading glasses and is using her phone to take photographs.

"McPherson," she says as I approach.

"Any luck?" I ask.

Attached to the pole is a camera that overlooks a sea turtle nesting ground. We're hoping the dark zone's infrared wildlife camera caught our suspect.

"Nope. The feed was cut," she replies.

"When does the footage stop?"

"Day before she was found."

"Before or after she was killed?" I ask.

"Good question." Waterman descends the ladder and hands me her phone with an image of the cut cable. "I'm going to pull the whole cable out so forensics can get a better look. They should have done that in the first place."

Analysis of the cable could tell us a lot: the type of tool used to cut it, how much corrosion occurred since being severed, and potentially what else the tool was used to cut. Under a microscope, wire-cutter blades are filled with nooks and crannies where other materials can lodge. This is how you can tell that the same tools were used to make multiple bombs. Bits of plastic wire covering can get caught in the blades. Same goes for blood or other DNA.

"Any other leads?" I ask, still examining the image of the cut cable.

"Some. None promising. See it?" she asks, pointing to the image.

I zoom in on the cut. The cable was pinched on either side.

"Wire cutters?"

"Not a knife or a single blade," says Waterman.

"This person came prepared."

Waterman points to the bright sky. "New moon that night."

"The night this was cut?"

A nod. "And likely when she was killed."

I do the math. It fits: Nicole Donnelly died twenty or so hours before she was found, making it the same night the killer crippled the beach camera.

"My Google Calendar's never suggested the best time to kill someone."

"Darkest night to dump a body, but the body was dumped next day, on a crescent moon," Waterman explains in her typical abbreviated way of speaking.

I think out loud. "They came here the day before to make sure they could dump the body. And I guess they could just check online to see if someone repaired the turtle camera in between that period."

"Why not dump the body the same night?" asks Waterman.

"Maybe because she wasn't dead yet?"

Waterman pulls down the cable, cuts off the end, and wraps it in plastic to protect it from further corrosion before the forensic people examine it. As she's folding the ladder, she looks up at me. "Why put the body here if they could plan that far ahead?"

"Maybe she was dropped from a boat and this is all coincidental," I suggest.

Waterman makes a sound like a scoff.

"The new-moon thing is interesting. I'm looking into another case where the killer seems to be able to dump bodies without being seen," I explain.

"And?"

"He liked to call in to radio stations and make requests in the victims' names. It's an old case, and the investigators searched radio station logs and recordings for other evidence of his call-ins, but they came up empty. I asked my UIU partner Hughes if he could find a way to search for an AM station they overlooked."

"How's that going?" asks Waterman as she places the ladder into the back of her SUV.

"We'll hopefully know something soon. Anything I can do here?"

"Figure out why the new moon," she replies.

"Do you think it's important?"

"No. That's why I'm asking you," she says with no trace of sarcasm.

"Good to know."

I stare into the back of her SUV and try to imagine the killing and wrapping of a body like Jazmine's.

"Help you with something?" asks Waterman.

"Just wondering how hard it would be to kill someone and wrap the corpse up back here," I say, looking at the back seat and cargo areas of her SUV.

Waterman turns and faces the vehicle. "I'd put down plastic for the blood. You could dump it anywhere. Was the victim conscious or unconscious?"

"Conscious. Some struggle. But no scrapings under the nails. His first stab was always in the same place," I tell her, pointing to under my rib cage.

"Bled out fast."

"Yes. But the killer kept stabbing. Or more accurately, slashing. There weren't any fractures in the bones other than the wrists in one of the victims."

"Prostitutes?" asks Waterman knowingly.

"Yeah."

"Good luck," she says.

"Thanks. Let me know what I can do. I'm getting antsy on this one."

"Me too," says Waterman with absolutely no trace of anxiety.

CHAPTER TWENTY
FIRST-TIME CALLER

Scott Hughes has been using our exile to the FDLE as an opportunity to take workshops on artificial-intelligence techniques and cybercrime. I could have done something similar, but it only would have made me feel more guilty about neglecting my PhD work in archaeology.

"Have the robots taken our jobs yet?" I ask Hughes when I pick up his call.

"When was the last time you used the URV to pull evidence from the water?" he asks.

"A day ago," I reply.

"There's your answer."

"Well, I had to supervise. I'm still useful."

"You had to drive it to the location, McPherson. It did the rest."

"So you're saying the future of law enforcement is going to be basically working as Uber drivers bringing robots to crime scenes?"

"They'll be driving themselves too. Your job will be to sit in court and give testimony," he replies.

"I thought the goal of all this crap was for machines to do the work we hate the most. What's the point otherwise?"

"Ask the person making money selling the robots," he says.

"I don't like this future."

Before becoming a cop, Hughes was a diver in the navy who specialized in underwater demolitions. After getting into law enforcement, he started studying computer science and has become my go-to person for anything more technical than figuring out where all my saved videos are on YouTube.

"I'm not too thrilled with the present," he says. "Although I do have some interesting news for you . . . thanks to our robot overlords."

"About the Loop Killer?"

"Yep. You wanted to know if I could get WIXY's records and search for call-in requests like the other ones you sent me."

"And?"

"Nothing yet. I emailed them and even put in a request for licensing records with the music agencies. Stations are supposed to keep track of every time they play a song," says Hughes.

"So you're calling me to tell me that you did a thing, but you don't actually have a thing to show me yet. This is like Jackie wanting credit for declaring that she *will* clean her room," I tell him.

"Slow down, there. Let me explain where the robots come in. I got curious and found out that a fan of WIXY's morning radio show has been uploading the episodes to YouTube for the past eight years. The station didn't object and the shows are still up there. All six thousand hours of them. Anyway, I figured there's a chance your suspect may have called in to that show. He seemed to like radio and knew the numbers to call."

"Cool. So I have to spend the next three years listening to their archives. Did I ever tell you how much I hate morning radio?"

Hughes chuckles. "Was this what it was like when someone showed the Neanderthals fire? We're past the randomly-banging-rocks-together phase, McPherson."

"So the robots get to spend the next three years listening to the radio for requests?" I ask.

"Sort of. But it doesn't take three years. I can spin up several servers with a voice-recognition algorithm and have them go through the audio about a thousand times faster than you or I could."

I understand the individual words but not the way they were put together. "Why didn't you say so. Of course. Duh. Electricity."

"I had a computer try to find anyone in the audios who sounded like the guy in the sample you sent me," Hughes says in simple terms.

"And?" I ask impatiently.

"I've still got thousands of recorded hours to go, but I found a good match. Check your email."

"Wait? Seriously?" I quickly fumble through my screen to get to my email program and open his message.

I play a clip titled "Audio file 3322223.m4a."

Hey, Buzz and Pete. Randy Roadkill here. I think Tampa Bay's coach should be fired. <nervous laugh> Last night's game was an embarrassment.

Even though the subject matter isn't exactly Ted Bundy confessing to his crimes, a chill runs down my spine. It's the same voice. Even down to the little laugh.

"Hughes . . ." I don't know what to say.

"I know. Check the other email. You'll find out why he's called that."

I click on Audio file 7882223.m4a:

Hey Buzz and Pete. This is Randy, he says in his familiar voice over the sound of traffic.

What's all that noise? What are you doing? Out picking up roadkill? asks one of the hosts.

Randy lets out his nervous laugh. *It feels like that.*

"What do you think?" asks Hughes.

"It's somebody who works on the highway," I reply.

"We should check animal control and see who handled roadkill around those areas," suggests Hughes.

"Yes . . . but . . ." Something else lingers at the back of my mind.

The investigators spoke to different agencies and organizations whose staff would have been out there working at night. Chances are they even asked "Randy" if he'd seen anything.

However, animal control isn't usually out that late.

Then there are those roadside-assistance trucks, meant to help people when they have breakdowns. They're all over the place, but you kind of ignore them. They look like huge pickups turned into mini tow trucks. Someone driving one would have a pretty good idea of the state police's routes and where they'd patrol at night.

A roadside-assistance truck would also go unnoticed on the side of a road for a short period of time. And it'd be plenty big to kill and hide someone in.

I can think of one other case where someone doing roadside assistance killed someone. Maybe this is another. The slayings might have stopped when our killer switched jobs or was fired.

"Hughes, I got one more favor to ask."

CHAPTER TWENTY-ONE
Parlay

Gwen Wylder stares at the folder I've slammed down onto her desk. "What's this?"

"Your Loop Killer, or rather your best suspect: Randall Timmons. He did roadside assistance during the period of the murders. There's a voice match between someone called 'Randy' who called in to another radio station and the man who called in the one recorded song request we have."

Wylder stares at me, like, *And . . . ?*

"The last killing happened the week before he was fired."

Her eyebrows rise at that.

"He was fired because a woman made a credible sexual assault allegation against him when he stopped to assist her," I add.

Gwen stares at me in disbelief. "Why didn't we hear about that?"

"Timmons's uncle worked in the state attorney's office. He wasn't officially fired and he never came to our attention because the prosecutor advising on the case knew the uncle. I don't think they were trying to cover it up as much as the fact that they thought there's no way someone they knew could have been involved."

She puts her hands to her temples and rubs them. "For fuck's sake. Where is Timmons now?"

"I'm looking into that."

"Is that everything?" she says, eyeing the box of folders I set on the guest chair.

"Yes. I put all the new notes in there too."

"Okay. Leave that with me. Let me see what I can find out about Timmons and why he wasn't flagged."

"What about Nicole Donnelly?" I ask.

"What about her?"

I try to keep the edge out of my voice "Your files. Related cases. You said you were going to dig those up for me."

"I haven't had much time," she says.

"*You* haven't had much time? I've been driving all over the state the last few days chasing ghosts for you. Cases that nobody thought could be solved."

"You've given me suspects, McPherson. Maybe Timmons looks good for this and Conliff for the other one. But that's not the same as solving them. That part hasn't happened yet."

I'm on the verge of saying something very personal and very mean. "This is absurd. We made a deal."

"If you don't like the situation, then get the hell out of my office."

I stand my ground. "You've been stringing me along, Gwen. Having me do all your dirty work because you're too scared to leave this room and do real police work."

"Get the hell out of my office," she repeats.

"Gladly," I reply and storm out the door.

❦

I sit in my car for ten minutes, trying to catch my breath. When I simmer down from boiling range to cold-blooded anger, I do what I've been trying to avoid: I call George Solar.

"Gwen Wylder," I say into the phone the moment I hear him pick up.

"Hoo-boy," he responds. "Have you had the displeasure of meeting her?"

I spend the next twenty minutes going over the cases she threw at me and the progress I made.

Solar compliments me on that, but it doesn't make the sting of being manipulated by Wylder any easier to deal with. I end by telling him how she threw me out of her office.

"That sounds like Gwen."

"She's the devil. I've never done more for somebody and been treated so horribly. I don't get it."

"You know the expression that every general is fighting his last battle? That's Gwen in a nutshell."

"And what was her last battle? Helping Lucifer overthrow God?"

"That would have been an interesting sight. But no. Gwen has had a series of battles and came out on the losing side almost every time. She's argumentative, condescending, rude, and a number of other things that could maybe be said about me. But I tell you something else about her: She's smart. She's real smart. In her day, she was one of, if not the best, detectives in South Florida."

"What happened?"

"We happened. Not you, but the way things used to be. There were fewer female supervisors, almost no women working homicide. It was different. So start with a department filled with guys who aren't the most progressive thinkers and you add in a young, attractive woman who doesn't hesitate to tell them they're wrong and . . . it's not a good mix."

"I tell guys they're acting stupid all the time," I reply.

"Yes, you do. But you've also got a sense of humor, and people like you from the start. Gwen is different. And when Gwen got pushback, she got vindictive. She had every right to, but it just made things worse."

"Maybe with a different attitude, things would have been different for her," I offer.

"Perhaps. But I think that attitude got set in place when her dad was gunned down when she was a teenager," Solar explains.

I'd never heard this. "Wait? What?"

"Her father was a professor. Of history, I think. He was driving from somewhere and took a shortcut through a bad part of town. Somebody tried to carjack him and he was killed. Her mother became a bit of a drinker after that. They caught the guy, but the case was botched and he got out a few years later on a lesser charge.

"I think that stuck with Gwen," says Solar. "From the sudden loss to the cops screwing things up. She doesn't have a lot of faith in law enforcement or the people doing it."

"That's like a real origin story," I observe.

"We all have them. I remember a young girl glaring at me in the courtroom when her uncle was being sentenced and thinking to myself, *Something's happening inside that head*," Solar says, recounting the first time I saw him.

"I thought you were corrupt and Uncle Karl was being framed," I reply. "Later I connected all the dots and realized he was a liar. I still hated you, though."

"Well, Gwen Wylder isn't as into giving second chances as you are. There's also one other detail."

"What's that?"

"The Swamp Killer. She spent years trying to connect those murders. Wylder was having her meltdown around the time you found the van in the lake that connected everything. She probably believes she was on the verge of cracking it."

"But we did instead."

"Exactly. The day you walked in through her door was probably not a happy one. I suspect that she'd hoped catching the Swamp Killer would salvage her reputation."

"And I took that away from her too."

"It would seem so. To her credit, she didn't quit. She's still there doing god knows what."

"Probably waiting for a job offer to haunt a house somewhere," I joke.

"Maybe. But it looks like, despite her ill intentions, some good work came out of it."

"Good for her. I'm done with that crone. When are you getting the UIU back together?"

"I'm working on it. I've made my share of enemies too. I'm also getting loud whispers that it's time for me to retire," he admits.

"Ignore them," I say flatly.

"These are coming from places that you don't ignore."

"Like you could ever be pushed into doing something you don't want."

"We'll see," Solar replies with an uncharacteristic hint of exhaustion in his voice.

CHAPTER TWENTY-TWO
DINNER PARTY

One of the benefits of a large circle of friends and family is that a quiet evening can quickly be disrupted by a welcome visitor.

Our family's open-door policy means people drop by unannounced all the time. It could be for a beer in the backyard, to share a joke, or just to catch up.

When I step through the front door, my ears are greeted by the sound of laughter. First Jackie's infectious giggle, then Run's, followed by a warm feminine laugh.

I enter the kitchen, already smiling from the joke I didn't hear, and feel a thousand times better.

And then Satan wipes away tears of laughter as she looks up from her glass of white wine to smile at me.

"*There* she is!" Gwen announces.

What the hell is she doing here?

"Gwen was just telling us about the first time she tried to get a fingerprint and spilled powder all over her dress," says Jackie.

"I'm sure that was hilarious," I say, barely faking enthusiasm.

"You work with some interesting people," says Run as he comes over to give me a peck on the cheek.

"I sure do. Serial killers. Sociopaths. All kinds," I reply.

"I told Gwen she had to stay for dinner," Run adds, to my sheer delight.

So Run and Jackie get to call Detective Wylder by her first name after ten minutes?

"Congratulations, Mom!" says Jackie.

"Yay, me," I say without joy and give Gwen a look that is probably more of a glare than I intend.

She holds up her glass. "Yay, Sloan."

"What's the occasion, Gwen?" I ask, emphasizing her first name.

"Mississippi Department of Law Enforcement called and said they have a DNA match for our Loop Killer. And it turns out Randall Timmons is already a person of interest in a case up there. That plus the fact the walls are closing in on Conliff. This has turned out to be a career-making week for the both of us," she says.

"That's wonderful. Considering the hard work we both put in on this." Again, I say it more sarcastically than I should.

Run picks up on the tension, but Jackie is blissfully unaware.

"Come on, runt. Let's go get dinner," he says to Jackie.

"I want to hang out here," she says.

He puts a hand on her shoulder and guides her to the door. "Mom and her friend need to talk about work stuff."

I wait for them to leave before engaging Gwen.

"What are you?" I ask.

She sets her glass down. "I know things got tense earlier—"

"Tense? Who the hell said you could come by my house?" I snap.

"Who said you could barge into my office?"

"Are you serious? That's a government building. It's where you sup-posedly work. This is where I *live*. That was my family you were . . ."

"Sharing a laugh with? You never have colleagues come by the house?"

"Not usually ones that tell me to fuck off," I reply.

Gwen makes a small nod. "I know I can come across as intense at times. My shrink says I have no filter."

"Lady, you're unbalanced," I tell her straight. I want to lay even deeper into her, but I remember what Solar told me about her childhood and the circumstances that thrust her into law enforcement.

"I thought maybe we could clear the air a bit," Gwen says.

I bite my tongue and let her talk.

"I can be abrasive. And I know I gave you a hard time. We'll just add it to the list of things I'm working through." She takes a deep breath. "I don't say this often and I didn't think I'd ever say it to you, but I'm sorry. Can we start over?"

I'm not sure how to respond. Gwen clearly has issues, and she's also a clever manipulator. This would be easier to deal with if she hadn't violated the privacy of my home. After the way she treated me, this is so out of line.

However, she's clearly excited about the breaks *we* made in the cases. And sadly, maybe I'm the only one she felt like sharing the news with. It's not like she could celebrate with her colleagues . . . Gwen isn't the kind of person you root for.

"Just cut out the 'tough bitch' act," I reply. "Be straight with me. You don't have to be nice. But don't act like I'm getting ready to stab you in the back either."

"Fair enough. I'll leave before your family gets back. You can tell them the office called me in or whatever."

Does Gwen have friends? Maybe her personal life is 100 percent different from her work life, but I suspect she goes from home to the office without much socializing in between.

"No. It's fine. Stay. Clearly, you made a good impression on them," I reply.

"Your daughter is adorable. And Run . . ." Gwen raises an eyebrow. "Good job on that."

I'm not comfortable with Gwen assessing Run that way. I respond with a weak smile.

"This is good, because we can talk about the update on the case," she says.

"Timmons?"

"Huh? No, Nicole Donnelly."

Jesus! "What update?"

"A young woman was reported missing in Asheville, North Carolina, two days ago," says Gwen.

"That seems like a reach," I tell her.

"There's more to it that I can't get into. I have a friend who keeps track of these reports. Some of his methods are . . . well, let's just say that this fits. This Asheville woman, Carla Burgh, is the same age as Nicole Donnelly. Similar interests on Facebook. Similar circumstances. Same as . . ." She stops herself.

"Same as what?" I ask.

"I'll get to that. I gave my notes to Waterman and the others, but I don't think they're going to pursue this."

Maybe because you're crazy? "Why not?"

"They don't get it. They don't see things like you and I do."

"Right now, I don't see things. Why do you think she's connected?"

"Reasons. The point is, if I'm right, she's still alive. And that's what matters. Think about this, Sloan. We have a chance to save someone before the murder. How often does that happen?"

"Not often enough. Why is this connected? Is this because of your 'other files' you said you needed time to track down?"

"More or less. We can go over the details later. Right now, I need to know if you're onboard. Can I trust you?"

"Trust me? Give me your files and I'll see what I think."

"I'll share them. I'll share everything. We're going to need to."

"We? Do you want me to keep you updated?" I ask.

"Well, actually, Sloan . . . I spoke to Mazin. You're getting assigned to my unit."

This is some kind of nightmare come to life.

"What?"

"I used to have a special-crimes unit that worked with different agencies. Based on what we did with Timmons and Conliff, I was able to get that reactivated," she explains.

"When? How?"

"Actually, right after you brought in the evidence on Conliff. Timmons kind of sold it to them. That's why I came over. Well, to share the good news about the break and to let you know that we're going to be working together. Technically it's *my* unit, so you'll be working for me. But I promise to hear you out on everything."

I reach for the bottle of wine and sit down.

CHAPTER TWENTY-THREE
Lost Girls

"The moment I saw the photo you slipped under my door, I knew," Gwen says as we sit on the patio in the cool night air.

The lights of downtown Fort Lauderdale glimmer on the waves of the Intracoastal Waterway.

"You knew what?"

"She was connected to the others."

"The others?"

I recall Offerton hinting there was some similarity between Nicole Donnelly's death and other cases—at least as far as how Gwen would see it. Even though he was dismissive about it, that's what led me to her door—or rather to slipping a photo under her door.

After all her evasions, I began to think the connection was nothing more than a superficial one at best.

"You're studying me right now. Trying to decide if I'm crazy. That's fine. I'm used to it," says Gwen. "We'll see what you think after I show you the other cases."

She makes a gesture of checking her watch. "Carla Burgh has five days if I'm right."

"Five days before she's killed?" I ask.

"That's the pattern. The girl goes missing a little over a week before and then shows up dead," says Gwen.

"How many?"

"Seven that I know about. They happen in bursts. Two or three within a few weeks. Then nothing for years. The last two were almost three years ago," she says.

"Strangled?" I ask.

"Every time. It doesn't always look like that, and sometimes the bodies are too decomposed. But that seems to be the case each time. No evidence of DNA. No skin under the fingernails. They appear to have been strangled from behind," explains Gwen. "Oh, and water is also almost always an element," she adds. "But it's the girls themselves that fascinate me. They're always between twenty-two and twenty-eight. Same good looks. Same interests. It's like there's a sorority spitting them out somewhere.

"And that's what drives me crazy. They're so clearly related, but I could never find the connection." Gwen stares out at the water, lost in her thoughts.

"Where do you want to start?" I ask.

"I brought some files for you. The first crime scene was in Miami. Maybe you go there and have a look around. You're good in the field. You notice things others don't. Then I want you to take a good look at the victims and see if I missed anything. Maybe it's something obvious."

"What are you going to do?" I ask.

"I want to take a deep dive into some cases and see if there was anyone before the 'first' victim. Sometimes these killers experiment and try different things. Sometimes their victims get away and what was actually an attempted murder is filed away as an assault."

Gwen has a point. A young woman once told police in Los Angeles that a man had taken her to his house and tried to kill her, but she managed to escape. She showed the police the street where she thought it happened and even pointed out a house. The person living there didn't match the description and the woman's story was dismissed as being confused because she worked the streets.

Lonnie David Franklin Jr., aka the "Grim Sleeper," lived in the house next door. He went on to kill at least six other women.

The police were brought almost to his doorstep, but for a variety of reasons the connection wasn't made until much later.

One of Jeffrey Dahmer's victims ran from his apartment and straight to the police. Unfortunately, he only spoke Laotian and they couldn't make sense of what he was saying. When they went with him back to the apartment, Dahmer explained it was a lover's quarrel.

The police were afraid of the fallout from interfering in what they thought was a dispute between two gay men. The decided to leave the teenager with Dahmer.

Dahmer killed him immediately after.

Most serial killers don't spring out of nowhere fully formed. They experiment with different acts of violence. Often clumsily at first. So, Gwen's right: chances are there's somebody out there who has experienced some measure of cruelty from Nicole's killer and survived.

Maybe they told the police. Or they kept it to themselves because they were too confused or scared by what happened.

Gwen will have her work cut out for her, searching through cases that could be related. My head spins at the thought.

"Do we want to send out a missing-persons report in South Florida for Carla Burgh?" I ask.

"I thought about it. The problem is that if she's already being held by the suspect and they get wind of it, they might just kill her. I think we should wait a few days," says Gwen.

"That's risky," I reply.

"Professionally? Yes. If we don't find her first, then we'll have hell to pay for not putting her photo up everywhere. But if we do get her name out there, I think this person will kill her. She probably knows too much about them to keep living."

I think about this. There's no easy answer.

"Tough one, isn't it?" she asks.

"Let's give it a day or two at the most, then reconsider," I suggest.

"That's the plan."

"Tell me about the first murder."

"First, there's something else I need to point out," says Gwen. "I don't want you to think I've completely lost my mind, but this case is different."

"Different? How?"

"It's bad luck. I don't know any other way to put it. From the moment I started asking around about the first murders, things just . . . happened."

"I need more than 'things,' Gwen. What kind of things?"

"Calls with only silence on the other end. Phone numbers tracking back to people who had no connection to any of this." She sighs. "Weird stuff that will sound stupid . . . My cat went missing."

"You think somebody connected to this was messing with you?" I ask.

"That's the conclusion I came to. But everyone else thought . . . well . . . they thought that was just me trying to attract attention to myself." She shrugs. "Crazy Gwen. Whatever. Just be careful," she tells me. "You'll understand when you start looking into the Lost Girls."

"Lost Girls?" I ask.

"It's a bit dramatic, but it's how I think of them. You'll see."

CHAPTER TWENTY-FOUR
ABANDON

The undeveloped area behind the massive Buy Club store still looks like the crime-scene photos taken when Edie Elaine Pradley's body was found here four years ago.

This section isn't easily accessible unless you took the time to find the right path through the brush. Investigators think the killer scouted out the location in advance, with the intent of using it as a dumping ground.

Besides the premeditation, it brings up an interesting question: Why go through the trouble of finding a location but not burying the body or otherwise obscuring the location of the corpse?

Had Edie been buried, her body might never have been found and there would be no forensic data.

This applies to the other cases Gwen gave me. The bodies were dumped in remote locations (or attempted, in Nicole Donnelly's case), but the killer made little effort to hide the bodies themselves.

One theory is that the killer on some subconscious level had trouble accepting the fact that his victims were dead. Burying them would be an internal admission of guilt.

I think this could be true, but the bizarre circumstances surrounding Nicole Donnelly's body cloud the issue.

Of course, I have to remind myself that killers aren't completely rational people. They may be consistent at times, but they might contradict themselves and go through periods of self-doubt.

If you listen to recordings of convicted killers during interrogations, you can hear this inner drama unfold. They'll entertain any explanation other than they're a cold-blooded killer:

Investigator: Did you kill her?

Suspect: No. I would never.

Investigator: Your fingerprints were on the knife and there was blood on your clothes. How do you explain that?

Suspect: She cut herself in the kitchen. I picked up the knife.

Investigator: She was stabbed three times. Was there a fight? Did she maybe attack you?

Suspect: I told her to keep back. I didn't want to hurt her.

Investigator: But she didn't listen?

Suspect: It was an accident. I was just trying to protect myself. She was fine.

Investigator: How did she end up in the garage?

Suspect: I was going to take her to the hospital.

Investigator: Why didn't you call an ambulance?

Suspect: I don't know. I was scared.

A killer's rationale can shift as different truths are revealed. Sociopathy isn't binary. It can come in degrees. They might start with an outright lie intended to misdirect people, then play games with semantics when confronted by cold, hard facts.

In some cases, bodies have been left exposed so the killer could come back and visit them. I don't see any evidence for that here, or how it would even have been practical, but it can't be discounted entirely.

In the case of Gina Slinger, who was found dead in a motel room she had checked into a week prior, visiting the body would have been difficult because she was found the day after she was murdered.

The same for Nicole Donnelly.

I don't think the exposure was so the killer could visit them again.

Like Randall Timmons and his sense of invisibility, I think the killer thought that there wasn't enough forensic evidence to connect him to the victim—or that trying to obscure connections wouldn't make much difference.

What's interesting about Edie Elaine Pradley is that her body was moved at least once after she was killed. Investigators found embedded dirt and clay on the soles of her feet, in her hair, and on her elbows that didn't match the soil here. That means she was left for a significant amount of time in another location—postmortem—and then brought to this location.

I find that curious because the killer felt comfortable enough to leave her body in one location, then apparently decided he didn't want her to be discovered there. Edie Elaine Pradley's investigators noted it as well and tried to find a match for the soil, but the results indicated it could have been almost anywhere in South Florida.

Well, not exactly anywhere.

When I looked at the map, my many South Florida archaeology outings suddenly proved useful: the particular composition on Pradley's body came from soil found at least four feet above sea level.

That may not be significant, but I find it interesting.

The obvious answer to why she was moved was that the killer feared the original location could connect him to her.

Investigators did a brief search of other locations based on a topological map, but it covered such a large area that they gave up.

An alternative possibility isn't that the original location was physically connected to the killer but that it still could reveal something about him.

If a man killed his wife in their home, he might put the body in a different location to misdirect attention from himself.

Or if a killer lured a victim somewhere like a public bathroom, they might want to move the body to confuse investigators and direct suspicion away from that location so they could use it again.

In the case of Gwen's Lost Girls, the final resting places and the apparent murder scenes are all over the place.

Nicole was in the ocean. Edie in the woods.

There was no clay or dirt to tie Nicole to a similar initial drop. That makes sense, as she died less than twenty-four hours before her body was discovered.

The only tangible connection, besides the victims' personal similarities, is the method of death: strangulation.

Moving Edie's body was important to the killer. Otherwise, why go to the trouble?

She was moved from a higher-elevation location to this site. Why do that?

I know from the case file that the FBI labs have information on soil samples and locations. And my PhD adviser, Dr. Nadine Baltimore, has access to her own database of this information. The FBI labs could only help investigators narrow the initial location of Pradley's body down to anywhere at four feet above sea level in South Florida, which was not a surprise. I decide to email Nadine in hopes that she might have more precise data for our sample.

My phone pings. When I pull it out, I see an excited message from Gwen.

CHAPTER TWENTY-FIVE
SHELVES

The Cranny is a used bookstore in Miami. It's the kind filled with twisting sections and shelving that make it feel like a labyrinth. One moment you're staring at Robin Cook thrillers, the next you're looking at a shelf full of books on juggling and riding unicycles.

My literary tastes tended to be whatever dog-eared paperback book was drifting around the family boat. Which meant mainly the kind of things my dad and brothers liked to read. Military fiction, alien invasions, and horror.

In high school I started to read the books my friends liked—which more often than not involved vampires and werewolves.

I can remember on one or two occasions my mother taking me to a bookstore before a trip and setting me loose to find something to read. I think I chose a comic book and a story about a girl with a horse. I read both from cover to cover. All I remember about the horse book was that the girl had a horse. She loved the horse. They had fun. The end.

As I wander this bookstore, my mind is far from horses. I'm trying to determine what Nicole Donnelly was looking for here.

While we haven't yet released Carla Burgh's name and photo, Nicole has been all over the news. There are multiple alleged sightings of her, but this one is the most credible. A surveillance video shows her entering and leaving the bookstore.

She was by herself, and it was the day after she was last seen in Atlanta.

The footage doesn't establish much beyond the fact that she was in this Miami bookstore. Cameras didn't record where she went inside, nor is there a record of her buying anything.

Waterman and her unit have been scrubbing through the footage, trying to identify who else came and went to the Cranny that day. They're hoping to find someone with a criminal record who could serve as a credible suspect.

"What do you think?" asks Gwen as she steps around the corner and into my aisle.

"A lot of possibilities here."

"Bigger picture," says Gwen.

"It certainly looks like she was walking around of her own free will. Nobody came in with her." I shrug.

"And we have no idea how she got from Atlanta to here. Her car is still in her garage, and we don't have any flight records."

"I think she came here voluntarily. Did any of the other vics take time off from work?" I ask.

Gwen gives me a satisfied smirk, like she's been waiting for me to ask this. "They all quit their jobs days or weeks before." She raises an eyebrow. "What does that mean to you?"

"Harvey Carignan comes to mind," I reply.

"I can think of a few more recent examples, but that works too," says Gwen.

While Carignan's victims were primarily hitchhikers, at least one of them came across his path when they answered an ad for a job at his service station.

Carignan killed multiple women over several decades and even managed to do prison time in between for violent crimes. Guys like him are the reason the first people we consider for a crime are those who have done related bad things.

Prior to his final arrest in 1974, Carignan had been tried and convicted of murder in 1949, only to have it reversed and regain his freedom in 1951, when authorities determined that police had overstepped their bounds in getting a confession.

Cases like that are why, even though I agree in principle with programs like the Innocence Project, I don't always cheer at every case that gets overturned.

True, sometimes cops bend the rules to put suspects away.

The danger of this, as taught to me in the police academy, is first and foremost that it's a violation of someone's rights and, second, it can create a situation where someone who did the crime eventually goes free because the case was based on fabricated evidence instead of solid policework.

Carignan avoided the death penalty, served eight years in Alcatraz, then was convicted of rape less than six months after his parole.

He spent the next several years repeating the cycle of getting caught, getting paroled, and then committing more crimes, including several murders.

Did Nicole come to South Florida because she was responding to some kind of lure, like Carignan's victims answering want ads?

"Did any of them mention taking a trip?" I ask Gwen.

She absentmindedly picks up a textbook on Latin. "None. Not a single one."

"Didn't their friends think that was suspicious?"

"They'd all stopped talking to their friends and family days or weeks before. That's why I call them 'Lost.' I think these girls were going through some form of depression."

"Any medications?" I ask.

"Two had been using antidepressants. But the bottles were found in their homes. They'd stopped taking them sometime before," Gwen tells me. "And before you ask, I went through phone records and even did searches through Craigslist and other forums to see if there was anything I could connect to them."

"Nothing?"

"Zilch." She reshelves the book. "I'm sure they were in contact with the killer prior to leaving their lives behind. I just can't figure out how, or with whom. I've gone through lists of friends and acquaintances and associates, trying to find someone in common between them. Nothing. What would make *you* abruptly travel hundreds of miles?"

"A job interview? Though these women weren't the types who'd have trouble meeting a guy. I don't see them getting catfished," I say.

"You might be surprised," she answers.

"Probably."

I try to imagine what other scenarios would cause me to drop everything and go somewhere on a moment's notice. As a cop, I have plenty of reasons. But what about prior to being a cop?

"If a friend was in trouble?" I suggest.

Gwen looks around the bookstore. "I always bring something with me to read when I go to the hospital to visit someone. You often end up waiting so long."

I get the feeling there's more to her particular story, but I don't want to pry.

"We should check hospital records. If that's the case, then we might have her on surveillance video," says Gwen.

While that's not something we should ignore, I doubt it will turn up anything. I'm operating under the assumption the women were manipulated into coming to South Florida. Even if the lure were somehow medical in nature, I don't think there was anybody sitting in a hospital room.

"You don't seem convinced," says Gwen.

"I don't know." I run my finger across the spines of a row of romance paperbacks. "Maybe there's something here?"

Gwen grabs a book from a shelf and holds up the cover: a shirtless man wearing aviator sunglasses is looking off at the horizon. "You think *True Love at First Flight* may hold the answer?"

I lower my voice. "Here's the thing about bookshops—they remind me of health food stores. Half the people are walking around in a daze looking for something they think they're missing. Maybe it's fish oil. Or perhaps it's adventure."

"What do you look for?" asks Gwen.

"When I have time to read? Something that takes me a thousand miles away from whatever I'm doing at work." I keep my voice almost to a whisper. "Tell anyone this and I kill you, but I'll grab whatever book my daughter's finished."

"How's that working out?" asks Gwen.

"I've read way more fantasy books about young women and prophecies than I ever expected. But it sure takes my mind off things."

"Do you think Nicole was here to find something to take her mind off how her life was going? Or to find a part of herself?"

"If it's the latter, which part?" I reply. "How to make a soufflé? Fix a motorcycle? It's all here." I pick up a book and flip through the pages, perhaps hoping a slip of paper with a clue falls out.

No luck.

"I'm going to look around a bit," I tell Gwen.

What I really want to do is walk around a little and pretend I'm Nicole. She was only a few years younger than I am. I remember those years of my life vividly.

I was working on my PhD and making money doing evidence-recovery dives for multiple police departments. Lauderdale Shores offered me a position because it was easier to expense it that way: through some bureaucratic form of accounting, lending me to other departments helped balance their books.

I wasn't truly lost then, though. I had Jackie, and my family was always there for me.

But I was going through an identity crisis. What did it mean to be me? Not the roles I filled: mother, daughter, sister, student, diver . . .

Who was I?

What was I supposed to be?

The example I gave Gwen about people wandering the aisles of bookstores looking for an identity was really a description of the younger me.

At the time, archaeology was important to me because I enjoyed the subject and I liked having "Dr." added to my name in the event of earning my PhD.

Now that I've achieved success in other arenas, that same drive isn't there. I'm happy just being Sloan.

That doesn't stop people from bringing up every idiotic theory they saw on YouTube to me.

For an underwater archaeologist who specializes in Florida, I've had to explain to people far too many times why we think the Egyptian pyramids are as old as they are and that it's not my job to disprove every crazy idea that's out there.

Nadine has it worse with Florida pseudo-archaeology. She gets sent rocks and other items from people thinking they found Atlantis or some previously unknown ancient Florida civilization.

She also spends almost as much time in courtrooms as I do.

In her case, it's explaining why a location was or was not a sacred site to one of the many peoples who lived here before the Europeans arrived.

I realize that I've wandered into the archaeology section. Although this wasn't intentional, the hand-printed signs describing the sections on neon-colored paper undoubtedly caught my attention subconsciously.

"Gwen?" I call out.

"Lost?" she asks, poking her head around a corner.

"I think there's something we should go see."

CHAPTER TWENTY-SIX
CIRCLE

"Planning on building a pool here?" asks Gwen as she looks down into the dirt pit in front of us.

We're in a semisecluded section of woods in Miami. This location feels similar to where Edie Pradley's body was found with the exception that this area has been bulldozed and part of the ground excavated. The trees here provide coverage from the surrounding roads, and the chirping birds here could be cousins to the ones there.

Gwen looks around with a confused expression. "I don't think this is in our list of crime scenes. Was there another case connected to this?"

"Not exactly. About ten years ago, construction workers were clearing out this area when they found a large stone circle. There was evidence of a firepit along with some animal skeletons. Before an actual archaeological investigation could start, rumors began to spread that this was an ancient ritual site belonging to the Tequesta Indians—or the Atlanteans.

"A judge halted the construction project, and my professor was asked to assess the site and see if it needed further study. She came here and found melted votive candles and other signs that people were recently visiting at night to do . . . um, strange things," I explain.

"Strange how?" asks Gwen.

"Some people thought this was mystical, sacred ground. Nadine couldn't find anything of significance, and the site stayed in limbo for several years. Finally, a state historian found a newspaper article describing a Boy Scout campground that was located here, including a fire circle where the stones were located. Some people still clung to the idea that this was an ancient ceremonial location. Who knows? Maybe it was one before the Boy Scouts, but there's no evidence," I explain.

"And you think this is connected to our cases?" asks Gwen.

I point to the ground. "Pradley was moved at least once. The soil samples we found on her body could have come from this location. They're as close a match as you could hope for."

"So, what are you saying?" replies Gwen.

I think she knows but wants me to say it. "I think our killer murdered her here because he thought this location had some kind of occult significance. He didn't want to let her body be found in this location, though, because either he could be connected to it or he was trying to hide the occult aspect."

"Are you suggesting that all of these cases have an occult connection?" As Gwen asks this question, her owl-like eyes watch me, looking for the slightest twitch.

"You already suspected this, didn't you?" I ask. "Why didn't you come out and say it?"

"Maybe I brought it up early in the investigation and it was shot down. I kept noticing little things that the others didn't think were important," she tells me.

"Little things? Like what?"

"Gina Slinger, for example."

"The woman found in the motel room. What about her?"

"How closely did you look at the case?"

"I maybe spent a half hour reading the file. Not enough, apparently."

"Page 22," says Gwen. She looks up at the sky and starts reciting: "Summary of the contents of motel room 19: one ashtray, one table, two chairs, ice bucket, two plastic water cups, four white towels, one bath mat, two lamps, a Sony television, a Sony television remote control, one bed, one protective sheet, mattress cover, flat sheet, two phone books, two pillowcases, and one bar of soap. Did you get all that?" she asks. "I've read that list countless times. What does it mean to you?"

"It sounds like a motel room," I reply.

"Does it sound complete to you?"

"I'd have to compare it to another—"

Gwen cuts me off. "I'll save you the trouble. Every other room in that hotel had one more item. Care to guess?"

Of course. "A Bible."

"Exactly."

"I don't know if that's enough—"

She cuts me off again. "Glenda Baraut's body was found on April 5. The coroner said she'd been killed five days prior. That would be March 31. Do you know what holiday that fell on that year?"

Thankfully she doesn't wait for me to answer the question. "Lazarus Saturday in the Eastern Orthodox Church. The day Jesus resurrected Lazarus from the dead. And before you say 'Hey, Gwen, every day is a holiday somewhere,' let me ask you why that day? Why the missing Bible for Gina Slinger? Why the wax drippings on Monica Dean and the animal blood that belonged to a goat on Emily Poca?" She raises a hand before I can protest. "You won't see those details in the reports because they pulled them out, citing possible laboratory contamination. But that happened," she says forcefully. Her eyes burn into me. "And my question for you, Sloan: Why was Nicole murdered on the new moon?"

This woman is intense. I can imagine her making this argument to other people and coming across . . . well, crazy.

"All right. Slow down, Gwen. I brought you here."

"But you see it, right? You actually see the connection?"

"I see that it could be. Is that enough?"

"More than I've had in a while. Our lead investigator and our prosecutor had had several cases thrown out because they used a children's therapist who was exposed for leading children into claiming they were victims of Satanic rituals. The last thing they wanted was someone mentioning an occult connection. They were one hundred percent 'by the book' and only interested in hard evidence. No 'theories,' as they said. And look where that got them. Nowhere. They moved on and the cases got shelved. I'm glad you see it, Sloan."

To be honest, I thought this location was interesting because of the pseudohistorical aspect. When I showed up, I wasn't prepared to jump down the occult rabbit hole. Now I'm afraid that Gwen's pulling me down it with her, whether I like it or not.

CHAPTER TWENTY-SEVEN
WITCHING HOUR

"I met Azrael at Sanctuary. It was a club that popped up for a hot minute in North Miami. They said it used to be an old mortuary," explains Violet, a young woman Gwen asked me to speak to. "I was nineteen. He was a bit older. He seemed cool. He was into all kinds of metaphysical stuff and was a shaman."

Shaman today basically means a drug dealer who's read Carlos Castaneda.

Violet stirs her tea with a spoon. "I was kind of confused and naive. I didn't realize he was just using me."

She has an innocent grin and light-brown eyes that peer over cheeks that automatically smile to ward off hostility. She has all the signs of a woman raised in a rough environment and eager to trust the unknown danger of a stranger versus the known threat at home.

"I feel so stupid now. The number he gave me was for a throwaway phone. I never knew his last name or any of his friends. I mean, he knew people. But I didn't know them. When he asked me if I wanted to try something different, I never thought it would be . . . you know, a bad experience.

"He told me to meet him at the rock pond. That was a place near Sanctuary where people would sometimes go to get high or screw around. Only he wanted me to meet him there late and not tell anyone. So I show up, like an idiot. And he's sitting there on the rock in his big trench coat. He gives me a pill to take. So I pretend to take it. But I'd been on my period and my stomach was upset. Getting high like that always made me feel like shit.

"So I put it in my pocket when he's not looking. And while he's waiting for it to take effect, he starts talking about how nature and man are in this struggle and the only way through it is for man to understand his own nature. Something like that."

I nod for her to go on.

"He tells me 'the Visitor' will be coming. I didn't know what he meant. I was kind of zoning out until he said something about wanting to help me find an exit from all my pain. See, he'd gone on before about how modern cultures embrace suicide and people 'moving to the next level.' I think he even said once that he wanted to go work in Europe to help people end their suffering." She looks up at me and blinks. "To be honest, I didn't know what he was talking about most of the time. He was just interesting. You know what I mean? Some guys are like that."

I want to point out that there's "good" interesting and there's "bad" interesting, but I keep silent and let her tell her story.

"Anyway, he asks me how I'm feeling. Since I didn't know what he gave me, I just said 'weird.' That's usually a good one, you know."

I nod.

"The next thing you know, he's lifting my shirt up. I tried to pull it down, but he tells me to relax. Then I see he's naked under his coat. That's when things got weird," she says.

That's when it got weird?

"We'd done stuff before. I figured he was just horny or whatever. But then I noticed the others."

"The others?" I ask.

"The other people watching. There were five or six, I think. I was about to say something, but then he grabbed me around the neck and the next thing I know, he's choking me.

"At first I think he's just messing with me. Then I see his eyes and realize he's high. So I start struggling, trying to get away.

"He wouldn't let go, so I kneed him in the you-know-whats. Then I ran. I kept going until I was in the street and a garbage truck stopped.

"I was too scared to think, but they said I had to call the police. When the cops showed up, I took them back to the rock pond, but there was no Azrael. No people.

"The cops searched my clothes and found the pill. They asked me if I was high. I said no. They told me that if they made a police report, they'd have to put in the part about the pill.

"I decided not to. Maybe it was a mistake. Anyway, I never saw Azrael again, and it never came up until Detective Wylder asked me about it a couple years ago.

"She said one of the deputies who was there told her about it. She said she believed me and wanted a description of Azrael and anyone else I could remember. I didn't hear from her after that. Not until she called and said I should talk to you," explains Violet.

Gwen told me Violet's story would be interesting. I don't have a reason to doubt any part of it.

Maybe this "Azrael" wanted to kill her. Or it could have been a sick prank. I've heard of worse.

I thank Violet for her story, then go back to Gwen's office, where she's reading through a new stack of files that have been dropped in the middle of the already cramped room.

"What did you think?" she asks.

"Crazy story," I reply.

"Did you believe it?"

"She seemed sincere."

Gwen grabs a stack of thin folders from the side of her desk and starts tossing them in front of me.

"Annadette Wilmer met a man named Nakir who took her to a secluded spot and tried the same thing. She clawed at him and got away.

"Britley Steinman met a man named Samael, similar story.

"Including Violet, that's three women who don't know each other who meet a mysterious man who tries to strangle them. In each case, the man makes occult references and happens to be using the name of an angel. Either a fallen one or an angel of death."

"And you think this Azrael or whoever also killed our girls?" I ask.

"Not a chance," Gwen says, shaking her head. "Our killer knows what he's doing. This guy is a complete screwup. Three vics got away. Plus, this idiot was sitting in jail when two of ours were killed. His real name is Robert Gisberth. He's currently serving time for nearly fatally stabbing his girlfriend. All his victims said his photo matched the man that tried to kill them. We even have DNA from one that we could use to connect him," says Gwen.

"I don't understand," I reply. "Why bring this up if it's not connected to our case?"

"Two reasons. One, I want you to see the patterns, Sloan. Gisberth isn't our killer, but lunatics like him talk to other lunatics and give them ideas. John Wayne Gacy read about how Dean Corll liked to kill people and changed up his methods.

"Second, it's the occult thing. Nobody wanted to touch it. This is what we're dealing with, Sloan. It's almost as if . . . someone higher up is trying to avoid anyone looking too closely at crimes involving occult aspects. I know I sound crazy," she adds, confirming the fact that she sounds crazy.

It's enough already to deal with the fact that there's a ticking clock for Carla Burgh; now I have to worry if I might be enabling something self-destructive in Gwen. She's clearly brilliant and has unique insights, but I don't know how much I can trust them—or her.

CHAPTER TWENTY-EIGHT
CLEANER

Esmerelda Quintana stands near the closed doorway of the motel room with a nervous look on her face. I can't tell if it's me, the room, or both.

Surely she's had to clean this room a thousand times since she found Gina Slinger's body here. Maybe my presence resurfaces the trauma.

I decided to visit room 19 at the Sun Palms Motel to see if there was anything else that stood out besides the missing Bible. Not that I didn't find that interesting, but like Gwen's other clues, it's circumstantial.

I'm curious whether Gwen's focus on the occult might have caused her to miss other details. While I think she's smart and thorough, the time she spent trying to convince others to consider that angle could have come at the cost of overlooking something critical.

"Did you see the deceased before she checked in?" I ask Esmerelda.

"No. The first time I ever saw her was when I found her there." Esmerelda points to the bed.

I check my notes. "It says the manager, Rosalee Lagan, checked her in? But she had no recollection of the woman?"

"I believe that's correct. Mrs. Lagan didn't see so well. She went to the retirement home not too long after," Esmerelda replies.

"So Ms. Slinger checked in and then the next time she was seen was right here?" I say this more to myself than as a question.

"I guess so," Esmerelda responds, unsure if I was asking her.

According to the file, there were no other witnesses. None of the guests or staff they contacted reported seeing her.

Part of the problem is that the Sun Palms Motel is the kind of place people go when they don't want to be seen or have to talk to the police. At least three of the motel rooms here are rented to apparent sex workers. The MPD vice squad has even used this motel to do undercover drug buys on multiple occasions.

It's that kind of place.

While the report indicated that Gina Slinger was probably killed here, I have my doubts.

The other bodies were moved post-murder. Why not this one?

On the surface there's no connection to the killer. Gina paid in cash, and nobody saw anyone else enter or leave this room, but that's looking at things after the fact.

Assuming these cases are all connected, the killer is cautious, but that doesn't mean he wasn't taking other precautions as well. But then again, I saw this pattern in Gwen's other cases: investigators assuming the killer was eluding detection because they were simply lucky.

I didn't buy it with Randall Timmons, and I'm skeptical here.

The killer might not have known the police make frequent stops at this motel, but he would certainly know there's a chance someone could happen by and hear a scream or a struggle.

Killing Gina here was risky. Why go through the effort of moving the others to remote locations while killing and leaving Gina here?

Why remove the Bible?

Was that an accidental tell that this was an occult murder? Or intentional misdirection?

Assuming that Gina wasn't murdered in haste but as part of a premeditated plan, leaving her body in this motel room was intentional—it was meant to misdirect us from somewhere else.

This part of Miami is fairly well developed. While there aren't many wooded spaces to leave a body, there are plenty of dumpsters and canals where other bodies have been disposed of.

Leaving Gina here placed the focus on this location. Investigators didn't look for another murder scene because they were confident this was it.

Had she been found in an alley or behind a building, potential local eyewitnesses would have been canvassed, security camera footage checked, etc.

Since they presumed where she was found was also the scene of her murder, the forensic investigation was limited to identifying who could have done this and not much else.

The crime-scene report did a fair job of looking at Gina's clothing for clues. The only suspicious evidence it found was oil stains on her socks. These were attributed to her having stepped into the parking lot without her shoes.

That's a perfectly reasonable theory, but the photographs taken in this room tell a different story.

I wouldn't expect the investigator or even the forensic specialist to notice what I saw. You'd either have to be a tribologist—an expert on formulating oil mixtures—or a young woman who has ruined more than one pair of socks on a boat.

The oil lubricants in marine engines are designed to minimize corrosion and last for long periods of time between use. They also look different when they stain certain socks, as I've discovered, because the additives seep through the fibers like filter paper, leaving a pattern different from car oil I've stepped on in the driveway.

There are thousands of different kinds of oil mixtures used in cars and trucks. And it's possible that Gina's socks were stained by an automobile oil I've never seen before, but to my eyes they looked like my socks stained by marine oil.

While it would be understandable to jump to the conclusion that Gina was killed in a boat or at a marina, that would be too simplistic.

The vast majority of boats in South Florida sit in driveways, back-yards, or warehouses.

Gina could have stepped in that oil anywhere that you could park a car with a boat trailer—which includes the parking lot outside the motel.

So it's not an earthshaking discovery. But it is a detail that makes me suspect Gina was killed at another location.

"Is there anything else?" asks Esmerelda.

I'm about to let her go, then decide to ask her one more question. I take the list of motel room items from my folder and show them to her. "Is anything missing from this list?"

She studies the inventory for a moment. "No. I mean nothing was missing from the room. But not everything is on this list."

"What do you mean?"

She points to the sink at the far end of the room. "There were three rolls of toilet paper there. Plus the one in the bathroom. They weren't on the list. But they were here. Even the one in the bathroom. It still had my fold from when I cleaned the room the morning she checked in."

"The toilet paper?"

"Yes. It was all here. I thought that it was weird that she never used the bathroom. I guess she didn't spend much time here."

Indeed.

CHAPTER TWENTY-NINE
AREA CODES

"What makes you sure she wasn't killed there?" asks Gwen over the phone.

"It doesn't fit. The killer was cautious in the other places. This place is a bit public," I reply from my truck in the Sun Palms parking lot.

"Public? People go there because it's *not* public, Sloan. That's the whole purpose of sleazy motels like that. Sweaty encounters with strangers, and privacy," she explains in her lurid way of describing things.

"But for murder? What if the victim screamed?"

"I don't think anyone would care. It's that kind of place. Plus, the Bible. Don't forget about the Bible," she insists.

This brings me to another point that's hard for me to discuss with her, given how sensitive she can be.

"I spoke to the cleaning woman. She says several of the rooms don't have Bibles. It's not that unusual. The Gideon people don't always keep them in stock," I explain.

"All the rooms had them when I was there!" she shouts through my phone.

"Did you check all the rooms? Even ones with guests?" I ask and immediately regret it.

"Yes. As a matter of fact, I did. Check the file. I went door to door to interview the guests. I also checked for Bibles. Do you think I'm stupid or a liar?" she asks coldly.

"Neither. I just—"

"Think I'm making things up? It's fine, Sloan. Think what you want."

"Would you stop that? I get that you've been screwed over and ignored. I'm hearing you out. You can't expect me to accept everything uncritically, Gwen. What good would I be to you if I did?"

I can hear Gwen exhale on the other end. "Fine. Apology accepted."

"I don't think I made one," I tell her.

"It was a joke. You remember those, right? We're good."

Gwen is like a feral child, except she's actually an adult who's been locked away in an office with stacks of unsolved murder cases.

"My point is that I think Gina was killed somewhere else. Just like Nicole. Just like Edie Pradley," I explain.

"And you think that other site is where Carla Burgh could be right now?"

"I don't know. I really wasn't even considering that," I reply.

"Well, you need to. Her hourglass hasn't got much sand left in it."

"I know. I know. The oil stains on Gina's socks might be important. She was moved for a reason. Just like the others."

"Yes. But they were probably moved from different locations," Gwen says. "I don't know if finding Gina's murder scene is critical right now. We know why the bodies were moved."

"We do?"

"Yes, Sloan. To hide the occult connection. Isn't that what we decided earlier today at the ritual circle?"

"I think we agreed there might be an occult connection. I don't know if it's being hidden or not. It's kind of hard to change the dates that have occult significance," I respond.

"They can't hide that. But the other details. They don't want us to know about them. Anyway, I've got a list of suspects I want you to talk to. One of them could be involved."

"What's the source of this list?" I ask.

"I pulled the files on anyone with a criminal record and tattoos or other markings of an occult nature who's been arrested in South Florida in the last five years," she explains.

Good lord.

"And how long is this list?" I ask hesitantly.

"Don't sound so worried. I ranked them in order of priority. With any luck our suspect could be in the first ten or so."

Ten suspects she selected because of body art? Setting up interviews could take weeks.

"Gwen, I don't know if that's the most efficient use of our time right now."

She responds with silence.

"Gwen?"

Finally, she replies, her voice flat and cold again. "And how would you suggest we focus our investigative efforts?"

"I'd like to chase down any other leads I can find on Gina. Then there's Monica Dean, who was found in an abandoned swimming pool. That sounds a bit like Nicole Donnelly," I speculate.

"Hmm. That sounds like a familiar approach. How did that work out the last time?"

God. I suddenly wonder why she's the one who ended up in the loony bin and not her poor coworkers.

"This is different. I'm not ignoring anything. I'm just following the things that stand out as unusual," I tell her. "Or connected."

"Right. Got it. You're Sloan McPherson. I keep forgetting."

"Gwen—"

She cuts me off. "You go do your thing and I'll do mine. How about that? And Carla, god help her. How does that sound?"

She ends the call before I can respond.

CHAPTER THIRTY

GWENTUITION

The sun is setting and I'm driving around industrial areas in some of the sketchier parts of Miami, comparing locations from Google Maps to how they appear on the ground.

It's not the most focused search, and the setting sun is a reminder that time keeps slipping away for Carla Burgh—assuming she's actually connected to all this.

Gwen's explanation that she fit the profile of the other victims is beginning to feel a bit more . . . intuitive than grounded. I'd still rather err on the side of caution. Better I drive in circles and chase down a few of Gwen's shadows than do the opposite and end up with another dead woman.

My phone rings and I answer it on speakerphone.

"McPherson."

"Hey, McPherson, Suarez here."

"What's up?" I ask the detective.

"Not too much. I've been assisting Waterman on the Nicole Donnelly case," he replies.

"How's that going? Her briefings must be . . . um, brief."

"Just don't get her started on the Red Sox. You'd be surprised. Anyway, I wanted to see how things are going on your end. I heard you're doing some background work."

This is a little uncharacteristic of Suarez. He's not the type of person to randomly check in unless there's an ulterior motive.

"I've been helping Gwen Wylder with some old cases," I tell him.

"Huh." He responds as if I just told him I was planning on skydiving into an active volcano. "How's that been going?"

"We've made some progress on a couple of them," I reply.

"I heard. Actually, I heard *you* made some progress."

"Gwen pointed me in the right direction. I never would have known about them if she hadn't put them in front of me. She's got good instincts," I tell him, improbably defending Gwen Wylder.

"Yeah. Her 'Gwentuition,'" says Suarez.

"What's that?"

"Just a thing the guys down in Miami used to say. Kind of a joke. Nothing," he says, trying to backtrack.

"Tell me more," I say.

"Is she there with you?" asks Suarez.

"Yeah, she's right here. We're doing our nails and watching *Sex in the City*. No, you doofus. She's not here," I snap.

"Sorry. I just—"

"Don't want to get caught talking behind her back?" I ask.

"Hey, I don't have anything against her."

"But she's crazy," I supply.

"I don't know if we're actually supposed to use that word to talk about her. But, yes, Gwen can be vindictive.

"The reason I called you is that I just wanted to make sure you were keeping both eyes open. What I said about her Gwentuition? She's smart. Very smart. The guys in Miami all made that clear. But if she gets something in her head, you can't talk her out of it. That became a bit of a problem."

"I've seen a little of that," I confide.

"That Gwentuition can backfire too. They've pulled the wrong guy in and made people's lives hell because Wylder was adamant that they had the right person."

"Oh?"

"Yeah. They stopped letting her into the interrogation room because her temper could get a case dismissed."

"I'll be careful," I assure him.

"I know. There's another thing. I've heard allegations that in some of the cases she was working on, if the evidence wasn't there, sometimes it would magically appear."

"Really?"

"Yep. A fingerprint card showing up that the techs didn't remember getting at the scene. A victim's driver's license appearing in a suspect's car. That kind of thing."

"Are you saying Gwen planted evidence?" This a major accusation.

"I'm not saying anything like that. I'm telling you what other people told me. I don't know if it's true, but between me keeping this to myself and you getting burned down the line or me telling you now, I'd rather you not get burned."

"Okay. I appreciate that."

"Look, I don't know Wylder. I don't have a grudge against her. I also don't think the guys I know would make this kind of thing up. So I'm just telling you."

"I get it. And I appreciate it."

"All right. Let me know if you need anything," he offers before hanging up.

CHAPTER THIRTY-ONE
Oil Stain

I'm not sure what the *n* stands for in E-n-Z Storage. From the looks of the rusted barbed wire and graffiti-tagged black metal fence that conceal the darkened facility, my first guess would be "nope."

In my list of suspicious places to check out, this was close to the top. It's located between the highway and the Sun Palms Motel. On Google Maps I saw a section at the west end where boats and RVs are parked across from a row of storage units.

I pull up to the gate and eye the keypad. In most circumstances you'd call the owner of the facility and ask for access. The problem is that locations like this in this part of town are often owned by people who don't like the police in their business or that of their clients.

This kind of storage facility probably has a cash and no-questions-asked policy.

If I call them and ask for permission to inspect the premises, there's a good chance I'd be told to pound sand, as Dad likes to say.

No judge is going to give me a search warrant on a whim. Which leaves this in a vague area of the law. A police officer can't walk into your home without probable cause. But they can walk into your restaurant if you're open to the public. You can then ask them to leave. But up until that point, there's no trespassing.

Bolted to the gate is a sign that says, ASK AT THE MANAGEMENT OFFICE ABOUT VACANCIES.

Presumably the gate is open during the day and this can be done without a gate code. Just like walking into a restaurant.

Presumably.

The sign offers no instruction for what to do at night when the gate is locked.

I call this situation gray. A lawyer might say otherwise.

They could point out that the presence of a keypad indicates that this is private property. But what if numbers 1, 2, 3, and 4 were worn to the point of being invisible along with the pound symbol and the asterisk?

They'd probably maintain that this was private property.

But that would be moot, because I've already pressed those buttons and the gate has opened.

I drive into the facility and park in front of the management office. There's a camera with a conspicuous red light watching this part of the facility, but I see no other security measures. It's as if the only thing they cared about was making sure that nobody broke into their office . . . or avoiding having a record of anything else that goes on in this facility.

It's a safe bet that this tape gets wiped every day if nobody has broken in.

That said, I make a point to knock on the door as if I want to speak to the manager. This sets up my alibi for when I decide to walk around and see if they're somewhere else conducting maintenance or whatever managing this joint at night entails.

While waiting for an answer, I take another look around. The facility has four buildings containing rows of storage units concealed by roll-up doors. Some have standard doors as well. Floodlights, placed almost at random, illuminate some sections and cast others into shadow.

Around the corner I can see the flicker of an arc welder as someone works with metal in a storage unit.

The boats are in the opposite direction of that unit, so I don't bother investigating. If it's a chop shop breaking down stolen cars, it's not my problem right now. Miami police drive by this location a dozen times a day. I wouldn't be stumbling upon anything they don't already know—if they care to know.

Still no answer, so I take a little stroll. At the end of a row of units, the asphalt comes to a T intersection. To my left there's a unit facing the parking lot where boats and RVs under tattered tarps are lined up.

In the beam of my flashlight, I can see where a large puddle forms when the storm drain overflows. The rainbow hues of motor oil stain the wet asphalt.

There's one storage unit facing the drain. It has a roll-up door and a standard one. It also has a pile of wooden pallets stacked up against the wall to the side of the big door.

I walk toward it and spot a padlock a foot above the door handle. The lock is covered in grime and doesn't appear to have been opened in years.

This is a wild shot, but the motor oil from the derelict boats feels like more than a coincidence.

I don't know how I can get a warrant, but I do know how I could get a peek into the window high up on the side wall. The stacked pallets reach halfway up. I could probably pull myself up on the window ledge the rest of the way and have a brief look.

I test out the sturdiness of the pallets by placing a foot onto the stack.

Nothing collapses beneath my feet. Although I do hear the skittering of things moving around inside the pallets.

"Sorry, guys. I'll just be a moment," I say to the rats in the hope that they'll reciprocate my politeness by not jumping out at me.

I grab the top edge of the pallets and ladder myself onto the top. As my weight falls onto the stack, there's a cracking sound somewhere below.

I can also smell rotting wood and dead things.

This was probably not the smartest idea, but the hard part is already over. I'm on the stack of pallets. Now it's just a matter of carefully balancing my weight as I move toward the wall. I reach up and my fingers miss the ledge by inches.

Okay, I underestimated the height of the window and overestimated my reach.

It's all right. It won't take a giant leap. Just a small one to get my fingers onto the ledge.

I leap and grab hold. I kick my feet at the wall and manage to pull myself up and lock my elbows.

I have a perfect view of a completely dark interior.

Good one, Sloan.

With just a little effort I can probably get my light from my pocket and see inside. I reach down, trying to keep myself balanced.

I fail.

I fall.

I don't hit the pallets.

I go through them like a meteorite crashing through a multistory building.

I feel sharp pain and find my right hand pinned to my back. I think I hit my head on the wall, because I'm seeing stars.

I'm calm. I've been in worse situations.

I think I'm getting dizzy.

I hear footsteps.

Voices.

"Oh, shit. Some meth-head bitch got stuck trying to break in," says a voice.

I try to fight back the dark silhouettes at the corner of my vision pushing me into unconsciousness.

Blurry faces come into focus. Tattooed faces. Not just any tattoos. The facial markings of an El Salvadoran gang known for their brutality.

"Having a rough night, bitch?" says the one nearest to me. He grins and his metal teeth reflect the floodlight in the distance.

I can't get to my gun, and I think I'm bleeding somewhere.

"I'm a cop," I manage to say between gasps of air.

He laughs. "You're fucked is what you are."

CHAPTER THIRTY-TWO

INTERVENTION

In police training they try to teach you how to de-escalate situations. Part of this training involves cops and actors role-playing the parts of aggressive people while you try to find a solution that minimizes the chance of a violent outcome.

If you use deadly force when there was an obvious alternative, you lose. If you don't use adequate force and the suspect takes your life, you also lose.

The only way to learn how to handle these situations is through experience. Armchair observers with theories on how to de-escalate and read the room generally fail in these scenarios.

The actors don't conform to how suspects actually behave in real life.

The angry drunk with a knife might become a docile child the moment you confront him and tell him to sit down.

The amiable man who was cracking jokes with you a minute ago might pull a gun when he realizes his charming personality won't stop you from seeing if he has any outstanding warrants.

Right now, I'm surrounded by three gang members indicating that they want to do harm to me. I've told them that I'm a police officer, but

I can't readily reach my badge or my gun. Training never put me into this exact situation, but hopefully life experience can see me through to a good outcome.

Step one is for me to assess the situation. Yes, they're gang members, and they're threatening me. They're also young men who might behave completely differently in another situation.

I make eye contact with the one closest to me, who also seems the most aggressive.

"I'm such a klutz. Could you do me a favor and hold on to the edge of the pallets?"

I don't wait for a response. I turn to the smallest of the other two men. "If you're careful, I think you can get up on the edge and help me outta here."

The closest, the one with silver teeth, grabs the edge of the pallets. He clenches them and makes a menacing face as he's about to say something.

"That's perfect. Thank you," I reply.

"Hey, Brio, hold on to the side while I climb up," says the smaller man, who has half as many face tattoos as the others.

Silver Teeth, Brio, and Half Face is how I tag them.

I start to pull myself up. Half Face holds out a hand.

"Thank you." I wince in pain as a splinter moves in my thigh.

"Didn't you say you're a cop?" asks Brio.

Damn. I didn't assign him a task. I have to let them know I'm not a threat.

"Yeah. I was checking out this building for a missing girl," I reply.

"You almost became a missing girl," says Silver Teeth.

"No kidding. If it hadn't been for you guys finding me, my partner would have come along and found me bled out."

I pull myself fully out of the hole I fell through and sit on the edge of the pallets so I can check out my leg.

Silver Teeth grabs Half Face and whispers fast into his ear. The younger man takes off running.

"Can you bring back some towels?" I call out to him.

The other two watch me, but I keep my focus on my thigh and the blood coming from the rip in my pants.

"This doesn't help," I say as I pull my gun from my back holster and tuck it into the front of my waistband.

I don't make eye contact. I don't threaten.

"How long you been a cop?" asks Silver Teeth.

"Five years. I started as a police diver," I reply.

I'm not strong enough to start walking. I also want to wait for the blood to stop gushing. There's a first-aid kit in my truck, but I'm not about to give either of them the keys.

"A diver? Like with sharks and stuff?" asks Brio.

"Sometimes."

"Damn. You're crazy, bitch," he exclaims.

I make eye contact. "McPherson or Special Agent McPherson. Don't call me bitch."

"She got a gun, brother. Manners," says Silver Teeth.

"Sorry, ma'am," says Brio.

"This missing girl, you think she was here?" asks Silver Teeth.

I suspect that they're stalling me while Half Face tells the guys in the chop shop to stop whatever they were doing.

Fine by me.

"I don't know. I was just chasing down a lead. You ever see anyone using this unit?" I reply.

"Michael Myers," says Brio.

"Oh, shit. Him." Silver Teeth nods solemnly.

"Michael Myers?" I ask.

"There's a dude we see here sometimes. Big white guy. Older but thick. We call him Michael Myers because he looks like the big dude from *Halloween*."

There's a high probability that they're messing with me, but I keep talking in case they're telling the truth. I can hear the sound of cars starting and a roll-up door closing in the distance. Probably the chop shop closing for the night.

"Does he have any facial scars?" I ask.

"No. Just a big white dude. He wears those overalls when he loads the truck," says Brio.

"A truck? What's he loading?"

"Just boxes. I haven't seen him in months. You see him?"

"Not in a while," replies Silver Teeth.

Half Face's footsteps echo along the alley as he comes trotting toward us. He's clutching a roll of paper towels and some duct tape.

"Does this help?" he asks.

"Perfect," I reply. I can disinfect the wound when I get to the truck. I just need to avoid bleeding out before getting there.

I dab the wound with a paper towel. The end is covered in red. Silver Teeth turns away.

"*You* ever see the guy who owns this unit?" I ask Half Face, now that he's back.

"Michael Myers? That dude is one big mother."

Okay. So they weren't making up the story about a man who resembles the killer from *Halloween* owning this storage unit. That does not make me feel relieved.

I push a wad of paper towels over the wound and wrap my thigh in tape. Once I'm sure it's tight enough, I slide down off the pallets.

"Let's see if I can make it to my truck before my partner gets here and I have to explain how this happened."

Half Face whispers something to Brio. He seems nervous.

I don't wait for their permission and start walking back down the asphalt. They follow behind. More whispering. They're agitated about something.

I keep one hand on my stomach, next to my gun, but don't make it look like I'm trying to grab it. I also keep my limp to a minimum so I don't send off helpless-animal vibes.

They continue to follow but keep their distance.

When I reach the office, there's a tall, heavyset man in his late forties leaning on my car. Dressed in slacks and a silk shirt, he doesn't resemble a common street punk. He has tattoos on his neck, but none of the facial ones like the younger men have.

A black SUV with three men inside is parked directly behind me, blocking my vehicle from leaving.

"What are you doing here?" he asks.

I walk right past him. "I'm about to get the first-aid kit out of my car and dress this wound. It would help if you had your friends back up."

"Lady, I think you're trespassing," he replies as he follows me to the back of my car.

"Cool," I say as I open the back hatch and reach for my first-aid kit.

"What department are you with?" he asks.

"Florida Department of Law Enforcement."

I drop the tailgate and it falls within inches of the passenger door of the black SUV.

"I don't know who you are and you haven't shown me any identification," says the man.

"That goes for the two of us. Are we done here? I need to either dress this wound myself or call an ambulance. At this time of night that'd mean more cops," I explain and point a bloody thumb behind me. "I was looking for a missing girl. I didn't find her. I'm ready to patch this up and call it a night. Unless you know anything about a missing girl. Then I'm all ears."

He turns to the SUV and calls out, "Back it up."

He climbs inside while Silver Teeth, Brio, and Half Face get into another car and drive off.

I take the first-aid kit to the front of my truck, climb inside, lock the door, and let out a long, pained breath.

CHAPTER THIRTY-THREE
Rogue

"What's this about?" I ask Jennifer Mazin as I enter the conference room at the FDLE office where she told me to meet her first thing in the morning.

"Let's wait a few minutes for the others to get here," she replies. Her face is aimed at her laptop, and she simply points to an empty chair at the far end of the table.

I take the seat and try not to wince from the pain. Run did a good job of patching me up, but the sting is still there. He said the bruises on my head, back, and side made me look like the loser in an MMA fight.

I've suffered worse. But this doesn't feel good. The worst part is how stupid I feel.

I drank a beer and went to sleep early, then filed my report first thing after I woke up.

Mazin texted me ten minutes later, telling me to meet her here.

I was surprised she'd read it. She'd been ignoring everything else I'd sent to the working group email address for the case. In fact, everyone has pretty much been ignoring my reports.

I don't take it personally. These cases can quickly overwhelm you with email and documents. Technically I'm working under Gwen—*shudder*—so informing Mazin was a courtesy.

The door opens and a man in his midforties wearing a high-end suit with a haircut to match enters the room. He gives me a long look, then nods to Mazin.

"Is Detective Gonzalez coming?" she asks.

"He's parking."

"Hi, I'm Sloan McPherson," I say to the man, trying to overcome the awkward lack of introductions.

"Oh, I know who you are," he replies.

"Care to return the favor?"

Mazin glares at me.

Screw her. This is feeling weird.

"Jase. Miami Police Department," he answers.

The door opens and a second man enters. But not just any random man. It's the dude in the silk shirt from last night—the guy bossing the gang members around.

"I believe you already met Detective Gonzalez," says Jase.

Damn.

"Care to explain why you were fucking up my operation last night?" Gonzalez asks, his voice tight and angry.

"I didn't—"

"Didn't have a warrant? Didn't notify Miami PD that you were going to be sticking your nose in places it doesn't belong? Do you know how long I've been working undercover with that gang to build up trust? You could have got me killed. You could have got us both killed!" His voice has risen to a shout, his knuckles flat on the table like a gorilla, ready to pounce.

"Good thing we're both professionals and know how to handle ourselves around juvenile delinquents," I reply.

"McPherson." Mazin's way of telling me to back off.

I shut up to let Gonzalez talk himself down from his rage. Except he only seems to be getting angrier.

"Juvenile delinquents? Two of the ones you were talking to are killers! Things could have gotten really messy. The others were talking about killing you. *I* had to talk them down! Putting myself at risk!"

"I understand your point of view," I reply.

"McPherson, this is serious. Let him talk," says Mazin.

"Yeah. Maybe rest your mouth," says Jase. He tries to flash a "just joking" smile. All it makes me want to do is punch him.

This was an ambush, and Mazin is sitting there letting it happen. I'm helpless because if I put up a verbal fight, she can spin it however she wants.

Gonzalez holds his fingers an inch apart. "You and your mouth were this close to me having to tell your supervisor that you were killed. How does that make you feel?"

"Like I—"

I'm cut off by a voice coming from the doorway.

"Irresponsible!"

My shoulders clench because I can tell without looking that it's Gwen Wylder.

"Insubordinate! Reckless!" she yells as she enters the room.

Gonzalez, his finger pointing at me as he's about to let loose another tirade, is stunned into silence.

"Unprofessional!" Gwen barks as she leans on the table like a dragon perched on a castle wall, ready to devour a peasant girl.

Except . . . the peasant girl isn't me.

She's staring at Mazin.

"How dare you call in my subordinate for a meeting like this without notifying me!" Gwen upbraids my actual boss, then turns to Jase before Mazin can respond. "And *you*. Letting your detective berate someone like that. And not just anyone. Sloan McPherson!"

Gwen puts her face nose-to-nose with Gonzalez for his dose of whatever this is she's doling out.

"I came in late, but you were in the middle of telling a woman who's put cartel assassins in the morgue and Navy SEALs in the hospital how scared she should have been. Please go on about how lucky she was that a big, strong man like you was there!" She doesn't let him answer. "You wouldn't last a second doing what she does."

"Wylder," Jase sighs.

"Jase," Gwen responds.

"Why are you here?" he asks.

"Why the fuck are you here?" She points to Gonzalez. "This dipshit is too busy screwing strippers while working 'undercover' that he can't build a case and comes crying to you with someone to blame?" She shakes her head. "Nope. Not happening."

Finally, she turns to me. "Come on, Sloan, we're leaving."

"I'm McPherson's supervisor," says Mazin. "You're not even FDLE."

"My unit. My responsibility," Gwen fires back.

Mazin stares at me. "Don't do it, McPherson."

It's a choice between the devil I know and the devil I also know who's batshit crazy but sometimes gets shit done.

"Fire me," I reply and get up.

"This is a big mistake," she warns.

Gwen rolls her eyes. "Oh, give it a break, Jennifer. Do you really think you can fire her? You're a fucking paperweight."

"And what are you?" asks Jase.

"I'm a goddamn hand grenade."

Gwen is pacing around the top of the parking garage, sucking on a vape pen I'd never seen her use before. She's still worked up and muttering to herself.

"Those Neanderthals. Those corrupt, side-dealing mothers," she growls.

I lean against the wall and let her work this out.

She raises a middle finger at a heavyset man getting into an unmarked police car.

"Fuck you too, Gwen," he shouts back at her.

She breaks into a smile. "That's John Lacroix. One of the only good ones," she tells me.

It seems there's a fine line between friend and enemy with Gwen.

"Here's the way it's going to work," she explains. "I'm going to yell a lot. Sometimes at you. I might kick you out of my office or hang up on you. And maybe you'll yell back at me and call me psychotic. But I'm always, *always*, going to have your back."

"Unless you think I screwed you over," I reply.

"Well, of course."

"That's the problem," I tell her. "You can stand here and tell me that you're going to trust me—but what about when you're . . . angry?"

"You're different, Sloan. You get me. Nobody else does," she says.

"Do I?" I ask hesitantly.

Gwen fixes her gray eyes on me. "We're more alike than you realize."

Take it back! I scream inside my head.

"Okay. Maybe I'm a little more intense," she concedes. "You have more restraint."

"Solar might say otherwise," I reply.

"Solar . . . there's a cop," says Gwen. "And a man."

I'm a little uncomfortable at the way she says the last line. I'd feel the same way if she'd said it about my father. Which probably explains loads about my interpersonal dynamics with Solar.

"I promise you, Sloan. I'll do better," she says.

"I think we've had versions of this conversation," I remind her.

"Yes, but you keep forgetting something."

"What's that?"

"I'm crazy. I know this. You know this. Well, everyone knows this. The difference is they're afraid of me and you're not," she explains.

"Don't be so sure about me not being afraid of you," I reply.

"We can make it work."

"Not if we're always at each other's throat. Carla Burgh has maybe three days left. I don't know if we're any closer to finding her," I respond.

"Let's at least try. We'll figure it out," she says.

"We don't exactly have the support of everyone else," I point out.

"It's better this way. We can move faster and . . ."

I think she's about to say "break the rules."

". . . get things done," she finishes.

CHAPTER THIRTY-FOUR
STORAGE

My suspicion that Gwen was about to say "break the rules" is affirmed by the bundle of cash clutched in Gordon Fernandez's fist.

Fernandez is a short man with a silver mustache, oil-stained knuckles, and pants covered in paint.

The cash came from Gwen's purse and was dropped onto Fernandez's desk in the manager's office at E-n-Z Storage.

Whatever romanticized ideas I had about the owners of the storage facility looking out for their fellow hoodlums when it came to the long arm of the law evaporated when Fernandez grabbed the cash and grunted, "Follow me. I've been meaning to cut the lock anyway."

We follow Fernandez and the large pair of heavy-duty bolt cutters he kept in his truck to the storage unit I'd visited last night.

"What do you know about the owner of the unit?" asks Gwen.

"Whoever set it up did it before I started here. Every couple of months an envelope with cash would be shoved into the slot along with the number of the unit," he explains.

"But you never saw the owner of this unit?" I ask.

"I don't really pay attention. If there's cash, what do I care? When there's not, then there's a problem."

As we walk past the pile of pallets I'd fallen into, he glances at the drops of dried blood and mutters, "That must've been one fat raccoon."

I remain stoic but catch Gwen smirking out of the corner of my eye.

Fernandez cuts the lock, lets it fall to the ground, then turns away without opening the door.

"Don't you want to look inside?" I blurt out without thinking.

"Why? If it's something I don't want to see, I don't want to be the first to see it," he replies before walking away.

The man's logic is unimpeachable.

Gwen reaches for the door handle. I give the rows of storage units behind us an anxious glance.

"Are you afraid of Gonzalez?" she asks in a mocking tone.

"I just don't want to go through last night again," I reply.

Gwen points to the hole in the pallets. "You almost gutted yourself and bled to death alone out here and you're afraid *now*? I thought you were fearless, McPherson."

"I have my limits."

"Yes. Approval. You know that about yourself, right? That's what motivates you. Not fear of physical harm. Not status. Just approval," she explains.

I don't bother putting up a defense.

Gwen pushes against the door but it doesn't budge. Before I can step in to help, she rams it with her shoulder and it swings inward.

The interior is illuminated only by the light through the door and a sliver through the upper window I tried to look through last night.

Gwen flips a light switch, but the only thing it does is create the sound of an electrical element fizzling out.

I turn on the flashlight I carry around for these occasions. The beam reveals a dirty concrete floor. No body bags. No workbench with a selection of serial killer tools. Not even a collage on the wall of photos cut out from magazines and ransom-note-like musings on sex and subliminal messages in YouTube videos.

It's just an empty storage unit.

"And you said the kids all claim they saw a large white guy moving boxes in and out of here?" asks Gwen.

"Yes. Michael Myers," I reply. "In the build. No mask."

Gwen steps inside but keeps to the outer perimeter. She takes a small light from her purse and inspects the floor.

"It'd be helpful to get the forensic folks here," I point out.

"It would. But you only found this location on a whim, and there's no chance in hell anyone will send a full team out here based on that."

"I might be able to twist a few arms," I reply.

Gwen doesn't take her eyes off the floor and replies under her breath, "I keep forgetting. You're the famous Sloan McPherson."

"You know I can hear you when you mutter like that?"

She gives me a sidelong glance. "Yes, I'm aware. I'm still working through my resentment issues with you."

"I never meant to take anything from you or anyone else. I just wanted to help people," I tell her.

"That only makes it worse. I'd like to have an excuse to vilify you."

"If we don't find Carla Burgh in time, you'll have a very good reason."

"Okay, I'm sick of this."

"I had my doubts about us working together," I respond.

"Not that. I mean this unit. We don't have time for forensics, and this flashlight bullshit isn't working. We have to get down and dirty."

"How do you propose we do that?"

Gwen reaches into her purse and tosses me a pair of surgical gloves. She takes out a pair for herself and slips them on.

"I studied forensic science under Dr. Heslin. Ever heard of him? Probably not. Before your time. Heslin was considered one of the best crime-scene specialists—even though he was legally blind." Gwen gets down on all fours. "My knees are not meant for this. But that's why god invented Tylenol and gin. Come on, Sloan. On all fours."

My knees aren't in much better shape at the moment. But if she can do it, I can too. At least the dirt stains won't be obvious on my dark workout pants. Gwen is not so lucky with her light-tan slacks.

"Just use your hands to feel the floor. Don't worry about what your eyes see. It's mostly shadows and tricks of the light," she explains.

I don't argue and start sweeping my hands across the floor for anything other than dirt.

"Toss anything unusual into the center of the room," says Gwen. "We can examine it later. Let's just get whatever we can."

As an archaeologist, I'm a bit aghast at this approach, but I get the efficiency. Rather than spending ten minutes scrutinizing a paper clip, we can find most of the larger objects quickly.

I feel a scrap of cardboard and toss it into the center along with a few other items.

"You know, a shop vac or a dust broom might be better for this," I suggest.

Gwen aims her light at the pile. "Where did you find the torn cardboard?"

"A yard from the door," I reply.

"Would a vacuum cleaner tell you that?" she asks.

"In a properly gridded examination, yes. I'd have each section bagged and labeled," I reply.

Gwen sweeps her hand across the floor in a wide gesture. "And how long would that take?"

"Probably too long," I admit.

She gets up and dusts the dirt from her knees in a futile effort, leaving grimy palm prints on her thighs.

"Let's see what we got," Gwen announces as she leans over the small pile of debris.

I realize there's no lock on the latch for the roll-up door. I pull the mechanism out and pull on the rope, raising the door and flooding the interior with sunlight.

Gwen squints at the bright light and glances at me. "I guess we could have opened that first. How long have you known that we could do that?"

"I just realized," I admit.

"Okay. Um, let's not tell anyone about our fumbling around in the dark. Agreed?"

"Agreed," I reply without hesitation.

Gwen squats to inspect the pile of torn newspaper, box shreds, and splinters.

She holds up a small, thin wooden stick. "Care to guess?"

"It looks like a kebab skewer," I reply.

Gwen holds it under my nose. "Smell."

I catch a powerful scent. "Incense."

"Correct. Dr. Heslin would have spotted that from the door."

Gwen pulls out a small charred piece of cardboard no bigger than a postage stamp. One side is glossy brown with a gold loop printed on it.

"Burnt matchbox?" I ask.

"Correct again. I even know the store. It's an occult bookstore called Sacred Angel in Hialeah that sells ceremonial candles and other items for spiritual rituals. Look it up."

I take out my phone and search for the store. Sure enough, the website pops up with a gold-on-brown logo. The loop was from the fancy *g* in "Angel."

"Damn," I say under my breath.

Gwen slips the items into a plastic bag. "We see if there's a partial print on that. Unfortunately, only you and I see the occult connection and can draw the line from the incense and that store to what happened to Nicole Donnelly and the other girls," says Gwen.

"I like how you just assumed I agree with every logical leap you made there, Gwen."

She places the bag in her purse and stands up. "Okay. Which part do you have a problem with? We're in this storage unit because of your gut instinct about the oil stain." She pats her purse. "Are the incense and matchbook just a coincidence?"

"I don't know. I just—"

"Have a habit of second-guessing yourself. Let's just follow this thread and see where it goes. Your instincts have been spot-on before. Don't question them now."

"Fair enough," I reply. "What now?"

"We go to the Sacred Angel and ask if anyone matches the description of the man who rented this unit. What do you think?"

"I've been putting some thought into this. This unit wasn't the big lead I was hoping for. It could be connected, but there's nothing much else to go on. I think we have to release Carla Burgh's photo and info to the press. We also need to put out a description for our 'Michael Myers,'" I tell her.

"He might kill her," points out Gwen.

"I have a hunch he won't. Nicole and the other girls didn't show any sign of restraint or being bound. It's weird, but it suggests to me they didn't know they were in danger until it was too late."

"That sounds like borderline wishful thinking," replies Gwen.

"Maybe. But if he has Carla locked down somehow and secluded, then there's no point to killing her now—unless he's convinced we can reach her or catch him. Which clearly we can't."

"Okay," says Gwen.

"And I'll take the blame if it goes badly," I add.

"That's just words," she says. "Trust me. You don't want to know the difference."

CHAPTER THIRTY-FIVE
UNMISSING

The decision to release Carla Burgh's photo as a person of interest in relation to Nicole Donnelly's murder wasn't Gwen's and mine to make alone. To get authorization to do this required a conference call with the Fort Lauderdale assistant police chief, the Miami assistant police chief, the district supervisor for the FDLE, as well as Waterman, Offerton, and the other detectives on the case.

"Explain to me again why you think Carla Burgh is connected to this case?" asks Monica Kirch, the FDLE supervisor to whom both Mazin and I answer.

"There are similarities between her and the Donnelly case as well as some other potential victims," explains Gwen.

"And how do we know Burgh's a victim?" asks Kirch.

"They haven't issued an official Be on the Look Out, but a friend of hers made an inquiry," Gwen responds.

"Hold up," says Gordon Bennett, the assistant Miami police chief. "No BOLO?"

"Correct. A friend made an inquiry with the Asheville PD," Gwen repeats.

"North Carolina?" asks Bennett.

"Correct. All of the victims are from the southeastern United States and go missing a week or more before they're found," says Gwen.

"What victims?" asks Bennett. "I'm only aware of Donnelly."

"I sent the details on the other cases I think are connected," she replies.

"Hold on, Wylder. You've sent me these before. I still don't see it."

Offerton speaks up on the line. "We don't either. This seems like a big leap and waste of effort."

"We only have a few more days," says Gwen. "I can go into greater detail, but time is limited."

"Is McPherson on the line?" asks Kirch.

"I'm here," I reply.

"What's your take on this?" she asks.

"Well, I'm with Detective Wylder. In fact, I suggested we have this call."

"And what's your take on the evidence?"

Yikes. A lot of this is Gwentuition and Sloanology. "I think there are a number of suspicious factors that make the risk worth it. Our main concern is that this might tip off the killer and he might get rid of Carla Burgh," I explain.

"I think that's putting the cart a mile ahead of the horse. We don't even know that Burgh is actually missing or connected to the case. I wouldn't worry about her getting killed," says Offerton.

"So you have no problem with us going to the media and having them release her photo?" asks Gwen.

"Just as long as you keep it to Miami and don't mention Donnelly," he replies.

"I have a problem," says Bennett.

"Same here," adds Kirch.

Bennett goes on: "This is flimsy. Real flimsy. If we announce this and it turns out that she just shut off her cell phone, we're going to look like idiots and it will be that much harder to get attention for the next case when we really need it."

Gwen and I are sitting in her office, and I can see her grit her teeth. This is coming from an assistant chief who's held press briefings to announce that his department reunited lost pets with their owners. They usually do this when they're under intense media scrutiny and need a soft story. I hope Gwen can keep her composure.

She can't. "Would it help if we told people she owns two shelter dogs?" she asks Bennett.

Someone laughs on the line.

"Wylder . . . ," sighs Bennett. "I'll tell you what. If Agent McPherson is signed on to this, you have my blessing. There's one condition: this comes from you, not the Miami press office. You send it to the media using our template, but it gets sent from you. Understood?"

This is an unusual move. Normally these bulletins go through the press office at the respective department. The only explanation is that Bennett wants it to backfire on Wylder.

"And no mention of Donnelly," adds the Fort Lauderdale assistant police chief—probably at the urging of Offerton or Waterman.

"Fine," says Gwen. "It'll be a standard request-for-information bulletin. Would you like me to use my personal phone number too instead of the tip line?"

I know she's joking, but she's also trying too hard to push back.

"The tip line should be fine," replies Bennett.

"McPherson should have her name on it too," says Mazin.

Damn it. I forgot that she was on this call.

She continues, "It only seems appropriate. Don't you agree, McPherson?"

She's out for blood after what happened in the meeting earlier. Bennett sees this as a chance to freeze out Wylder, and Mazin would be delighted for it to take me down a peg.

Gwen shakes her head and puts her hand over her phone. "You don't have to do this," she whispers.

It's kind of her to offer, but this was my idea.

"I think that seems fair. I'm glad the FDLE is getting behind this," I tell my supervisor.

Take that, Mazin. I just connected this to the FDLE in front of your boss. If I go down in a blaze of glory, Kirch will remember whose bright idea it was to invite the press to the bonfire.

"I think we're all good here," says Bennett.

I've never met Bennett, but I am imagining him twirling his mustache at the thought of this blowing up in Gwen's face. If Carla Burgh's dismembered head showed up on the steps of Miami city hall tomorrow morning, he'd probably consider it a personal victory over Gwen.

I don't want to be too judgmental, but some of that may be Gwen's fault. I worry that prolonged exposure to her could warp anyone, including me.

"Those fuckers," says Gwen as she slams the phone down.

"Yeah," I reply weakly.

"You good with this?"

"Okey doke," I reply.

"Good." She checks her watch. "It's almost five p.m. now. We can get this out to the news in the next twenty minutes. With any luck we could hear something encouraging in the next few hours."

"Unless it blows up in our faces."

"It won't blow up," she assures me. "Don't worry. You made the right choice."

CHAPTER THIRTY-SIX
BLOW UP

It blew up.

The bulletin with Carla Burgh's photo went out on the evening news in South Florida within the hour. Gwen understood the TV game well enough to include one photo of Carla that resembled how she'd normally look in person and another taken from her Instagram account in which she's wearing a small bikini, throwing up a peace sign, and winking. Pure hormone bait.

The news stations ran both images but used the bikini photo in the commercial bumpers.

Gwen understood that what would have been a minor public service announcement could get promoted to prime time if the subject were attractive enough.

While it would help get our word out, it underscored the sad reality that if you're not attractive enough, society—or more precisely, news producers—won't care. (The morning edition of the *Sun Herald* also had the bikini photo, proving this wasn't only a TV journalism problem.)

We spent the evening going over case files and trying to find anyone that matched the description of "Michael," the large man who rented the storage unit.

By the time I went home, we'd identified twenty-two persons of interest who had been spotted or pulled over near the crime scenes. Two of them appeared to be the same person. The files were incomplete, so we had to put in a request for the police reports—which meant waiting until morning.

Gwen kept checking the tip line, hoping for a break. And while there were dozens of calls, the majority seemed motivated by the salacious nature of the photograph. There were alleged sightings of Carla in strip clubs, on pornography sites, and several wishful-thinking scenarios about Tinder hookups.

Still, we followed up on even those tips and were able to quickly dismiss them with a check of Carla's social media timeline.

What we didn't receive was a single credible sighting that we could act on.

I went to sleep sometime after midnight. I suspect Gwen was up later, still checking the tip line.

We spoke via phone in the morning and were both working from home, since it was a Saturday.

Things finally blew up at eleven a.m. Mazin called me to deliver the news.

I hesitate to call it "bad" news because it was in fact very good news—just not professionally for Gwen and me.

Apparently, Carla Burgh was alive, well, and very confused by why her name was all over the South Florida news.

Mazin's call was abrupt and to the point. "The Asheville Police Department just got a call from Carla Burgh. She says she's fine and had been away at a yoga retreat. See me in my office Monday morning."

"Do they know it was her?" I asked.

"They seem convinced. Do you want to cling to the notion that this was an impostor?" she replied.

"No, it's great news. I'm glad to hear it," I told her, truthfully.

"We'll talk on Monday and see how you feel then," Mazin responded before hanging up.

❧

"You heard?" asks Gwen as she picks up.

"Just got the good news."

"Right. Good news," she scoffs.

"Would you rather she was dead?"

"No. Of course not. I just want proof. All we have is the word of some yokels in North Carolina. They haven't even *seen* her. How are we supposed to know this is really her?" asks Gwen.

"I'm sure it will come out. Mazin seemed convinced that they were convinced," I reply.

"She and Bennett are probably giggling themselves silly as they write their own press releases calling us buffoons," she growls.

I can't say she's wrong. Both of our supervisors seem to take great joy at the idea of us falling flat on our faces.

"Mazin's taking me to Kirch's office on Monday. I'm pretty sure I'm going to get read the riot act. I wouldn't be surprised if she pressures me to resign."

"You gonna let them run you out like that?"

"I'm tired of this bullshit. I'm sick of working for someone who wants to see me fail. If I can't have my old unit, I just want out," I admit.

"Just like that? On their terms?"

"Is there another option?"

"There's always other options. Bennett wants to talk to me on Monday too. That gives us almost forty-eight hours," says Gwen.

"Forty-eight hours to do what? Update our résumés?" I look at the kitchen stove and think now might be the chance to learn how to cook something besides grilled fish and hamburgers.

"I'm already packed," says Gwen.

"Packed? For where?"

"Asheville. There's a flight leaving in a little over an hour. I want to talk to this Carla Burgh myself. I'm not buying any of this until I see her face-to-face."

Typical Gwen.

"Isn't that a little extreme? We're already on thin ice."

"Screw the ice!" she shouts. "I don't care. I want to see this brat up close."

"Gwen . . ."

"What?" she snaps.

"What if it *is* her? What if we were wrong?"

"Then yippee. I can fade off into the sunset or whatever. I'm not letting Bennett and those ghouls have the last word. See, this is it for me, Sloan. They'll cut you down a size or two, but they're not going to get rid of you, no matter how much Mazin wants to. But me? This is my last chance to ram it up . . . You know what I mean."

Gwen is serious. While I'm merely exhausted from all this, she's trying to cling to some last shred of dignity. After this case is over, she'll be nothing more than a cautionary tale.

"Everything okay, babe?" asks Run as he walks into the kitchen and sees me nervously rapping my nails on the counter.

"Tell Run I said hi," says Gwen.

"Back up, sister." I turn to Run. "I have to fly to North Carolina. I should be back tomorrow. You'll be okay with Jackie?"

"We'll be good," says Run. He senses my anxiety, pats my nervous hand, and gives me a kiss on the cheek.

"You don't have to do this," says Gwen.

"In for a penny, in for a pound," I say with a sigh.

While part of me wants to be supportive of Gwen, the other part wants to make sure she doesn't attack Carla Burgh and try to rip her face off like a rubber mask in a Scooby-Doo cartoon.

CHAPTER THIRTY-SEVEN
Retreat

Detective Arthur Mathers meets Gwen and me at the reception desk of the Asheville Police Department. He's in his early thirties but has gray streaks at the edges of his temples, giving him some of the gravitas of an older man.

"You're the two Florida detectives?" he asks us.

Gwen indicates our badges sitting on the counter.

Mathers gives them a passing glance. "We asked Ms. Burgh to come in and make a statement."

"Is she here now?" asks Gwen.

"Yes. She's very confused by all of this. As am I. Care to explain how her name ended up all over the news? Her parents were scared half to death," says Mathers.

"It's part of an ongoing case. We'd like to speak to her," replies Gwen.

"She's pretty rattled by all of this. Not used to all this attention. She was practically in tears."

"Tears or not, we'd like to speak to her," says Gwen.

"I can ask Ms. Burgh. But it's up to her."

"And you're sure it's her and she's not under duress?" Gwen asks a little too hastily.

"I think we know how to make sure we're talking to the right person and if there's a gun to their head," Mathers says. He walks back down the hallway, leaving Gwen and me alone at the front desk.

"Jerk," she mutters under her breath.

"And if it's her?" I ask.

"And what? I don't know. It just feels wrong. Why did she take all day to get here to give them a statement?" replies Gwen. "Doesn't that seem odd?"

"Honestly, no. When my face is in the news, the last thing I want to do is talk to anyone. I don't know if I'd read anything into this."

Gwen is agitated. She starts to pace around the lobby, looking at everyone in the room—mostly uniformed officers and plainclothes detectives.

Mathers returns from the back. "She says she had enough for today."

"We just want a minute or two," Gwen pleads.

Mathers holds his hands up. "She's not a suspect. She's not a person of interest as far as we're concerned. We really can't hold her or ask her to stay."

Gwen eyes the hallway where Mathers came from. "But there's nothing saying we can't talk to her when she leaves?"

"No. Other than the fact she used the rear entrance to go to the parking garage."

"Damn it." Gwen grabs her badge off the counter and heads for the door in a brisk jog.

I snatch mine and follow after her.

"Your friend's intense," Mathers says as I leave.

"You have no idea," I call back.

I chase Gwen out the door and down the block along the old brick police station.

169

A young woman who looks an awful lot like Carla is crossing the street toward the parking structure.

"Carla!" shouts Gwen.

The woman is startled and stops as she's about to step on the curb. She's wearing yoga pants and a track jacket. A small backpack hangs over one shoulder.

This is the woman in the photos.

"Carla?" asks Gwen, a little more calmly.

"Yes?" she replies.

"Carla Burgh?"

The woman is almost as confused as Gwen. I realize now that Gwen was expecting an impostor and not the real Carla Burgh.

"How are you?" Gwen says as we near the young woman.

"I'm okay. Who are you?" asks Carla. Her eyes are red, and she looks like she hasn't slept in days.

"I'm Gwen Wylder. This is Sloan McPherson. We're detectives. We just had a couple of questions."

"I said everything in there. I don't have anything else to add. This entire thing has been personally embarrassing for me," she tells us.

I'm still processing the fact that the woman I was afraid was trapped in a secret basement or locked inside a shipping container is having a conversation with us in broad daylight, apparently no worse for the wear.

"Where were you?" asks Gwen.

"I was meditating," replies Carla curtly. "I'd like to go."

"Where?"

"In the mountains." Carla glances at me.

"We're just trying to get things right for our report so we can leave you alone," I explain.

Gwen gives me a sharp look but doesn't say anything. Instead, she focuses her intense owl eyes on Carla. "Are you going to your car?"

"Yes . . . ," Carla responds nervously.

"It was at your apartment. How did you get to the mountains?" asks Gwen.

"A friend drove," replies Carla.

"Who? What was their name?" Gwen demands.

"I don't have anything else to add. This entire thing has been personally embarrassing for me," Carla repeats.

"You just said that," Gwen points out.

"If you have any other questions, talk to my attorney."

"Okay. What's his name?" asks Gwen.

"I'll have him contact you." Carla turns and heads toward the garage.

Gwen is about to follow her, but I grab her elbow.

She tries to jerk it away, but I clench it tightly and whisper to her, "Mathers is watching us."

I caught him out of the corner of my eye standing next to the police station. His body language reads like he was considering intervening.

Gwen relaxes and turns around to me. All the tension vanishes from her face, but I can tell she's faking.

"Pretend we're having a casual conversation," says Gwen.

"It's a perfectly casual conversation," I reply with forced joviality. "Let's go pump Mathers for information instead."

"Fine. But I'm not done with her," Gwen says under her breath.

"Everything okay?" asks Mathers as we approach him.

"Just had a couple questions," says Gwen.

"I could see that."

"Did she happen to mention how she got to and from the retreat without her car?" asks Gwen.

"She said a friend drove her."

"Did she say who this friend was or the name of the retreat?" Gwen replies.

"She's not a suspect so we didn't pry. It's not how we do things around here. Speaking of which, do you two plan on being here much longer?"

Mathers isn't exactly hiding his disdain for us. In fairness, from his point of view, we come across as two pushy outsiders badgering one of his locals. I don't know if I'd act much differently in his shoes.

"I think we're good here," says Gwen. "We just need to wrap a couple things up."

"Great. Can I take you to the airport?"

"I don't know if you're being polite or telling us to leave town. But thanks, we have a rental car."

"I was being polite," replies Mathers.

My vote is both.

"Thank you anyway," says Gwen.

"Did Carla mention a lawyer?" I ask.

"Yes," says Mathers, not offering any information.

"Could I have their contact information?" I ask.

"I'll get it," he replies. "Wait here. And try not to accost anyone else."

"We'll try," says Gwen.

She waits for him to get out of earshot, then mutters, "Asshole."

"Look at it from his point of view," I tell her.

"We're cops trying to do our job. He's not helping," replies Gwen. "He's only trying to white-knight for her because she's attractive."

"Maybe. But we're coming across a bit intense."

Gwen flashes a look that is 100 percent intense. "Fine."

Mathers returns and hands me a slip of paper. Gwen looks over my shoulder as I open it.

"This is just an email address," Gwen observes.

"That's all she gave us. Anything else?" he asks.

"We want a copy of her statement," says Gwen.

"Once it's processed, I'll be sure to send it to you. If that's it . . . good day."

Mathers heads back into the police station, leaving us alone again.

Gwen turns to me with her arms folded. "Well?"

"Well what? She's alive and doesn't want to be bothered."

"That's it? You have no more questions? You're completely satisfied? She didn't sound at all like she was being evasive?"

"Maybe she was. But maybe it was something else. Maybe she was off with somebody and she doesn't want anyone to know."

"Why not?"

"Maybe she's seeing a married man. I don't know."

"That's a better explanation than the one she gave," Gwen responds. "We need to talk to her."

"We did. We're on the verge of getting a restraining order."

"I don't think so. Contact that lawyer and see what he says," she suggests.

"Actually, I will."

"In the meantime. Let me talk to her again. Just a couple more questions. Maybe somebody contacted her. Maybe she knows something and doesn't realize it. Hell, maybe girls get kidnapped from that meditation retreat."

"Seriously?" I roll my eyes.

"Just give me five more minutes," Gwen pleads.

"Gwen . . ."

"I don't need your permission," she adds. "But I'm asking politely."

"Okay," I sigh. "But we play nice."

"Of course. Don't I always?"

CHAPTER THIRTY-EIGHT
SOUL SEARCHING

The Oak Tree Manor apartment complex is in a wooded area of Asheville. Each unit has a set of wooden steps leading to a deck with parking underneath.

It's night now, and the lights are on in Carla's apartment and her car is in the garage. She apparently drove straight here from the police station.

Gwen had me drive around the block to make sure that nobody was watching Carla's apartment. It might be a bit paranoid, but I have to admit I'd get into less trouble if I took precautions like that more often.

I pull on to the side of the road and kill the lights. Gwen is in deep thought.

"You okay?"

She holds up a finger to shush me.

I realize that this is make-or-break for her. Not just the case, but her career and her life.

She fought as hard as she could to keep them from pushing her out of the police department. Staying isn't about ego; it's her identity. It's who she is as a person.

Either they were right and she was just Crazy Gwen, or they were wrong and there was more to her than an opinionated know-it-all who's always ready to use the nuclear option.

Gwen turns to me, looking almost at the point of tears. "What if I have it all wrong?"

"With this? What does it matter? We tied up two other career-making cases, Gwen. We wrap them up in a bow, give Waterman the notes on this, then move on. If Bennett wants to be a dick about it, we make sure the press knows that your tireless efforts are why the Loop Killer case now has a suspect. He can try to bury you in the department, but we can set the story straight. You're one podcast interview away from being the star of a Netflix show. Instead of casting you aside, he'll learn 'Gwen Wylder' is tattooed across his forehead because that's all people will ask him about."

"Reminds me of a certain someone," says Gwen.

"So you know what he's in for."

"You're good people, Sloan." Gwen grabs my hand tightly.

"I'll never understand that phrase. Anyway, here's what I'm thinking:

"Situation A: This is all a misunderstanding and Carla really was just a random match. Situation B: Carla was a target and maybe was in the presence of our killer and doesn't realize it. Or situation C: Carla is in on it."

Gwen ponders this for a moment. "There might be another scenario. But I'm still thinking it over." She reaches for the door handle.

"Are you sure you're ready?" I ask.

"Nope. But that never stopped me."

We get out and head up the steps to Carla's apartment.

Before we reach the door, Gwen stops me. "You do the talking. I'm afraid I might be a little too . . ."

"Intense? No problem."

I pretend like this is no big deal for me, but I'm filled with anxiety as well. We may be crossing into harassment—something I've done before. And I might be a little more restrained than Gwen, but not by much when I get my teeth into something.

I knock on the door. No answer.

We wait a minute and I knock again.

Gwen and I are both trained to listen while doing this. She nods at me when she hears the sound of someone walking around inside.

I call out, "Ms. Burgh, this is Special Agent McPherson of the Florida Department of Law Enforcement. I just need five minutes of your time and then I'll be out of your hair forever."

No response.

"I know this is frustrating. We just want to wrap things up and catch our flight."

Still nothing.

Gwen raises a fist and starts pounding the door. "Carla Burgh, answer the door!"

"You'll scare her," I whisper under my breath.

"We know what's going on!" Gwen shouts so loudly that the neighbors can probably hear us.

"Gwen!" I whisper.

She turns to me with fire in her eyes. "Don't tell me how to play the game! You don't control me! You're not even into this!"

Oh god, she's flipping out.

As she shoulders me aside, she whispers loudly, "I need this. Let me play my part and then move on. Just back off with your toy badge."

Now I'm beginning to panic that Carla will call the police on us.

"Gwen . . ." I use her name soothingly, trying to calm her down.

All the anger vanishes from her face. "She gets it. I knew she would. Tell him I did what I was supposed to. All right?"

"Are you okay?" I ask.

"Yeah, I'm good. I just don't think you understand sometimes. You're always sticking to the rules. But the real secret is we have to make our own. That's what it's about. I figured it out," says Gwen.

"I know, I know," I reply, knowing nothing.

"I have to use the bathroom really bad," replies Gwen.

There's a sound of a dead bolt being unlocked. Carla opens the door and peers out at us.

"You can use my bathroom," offers Carla.

"Thanks," says Gwen. "I don't know how much longer I can keep this up."

"Tell me about it. Down the hall on your right." Carla opens the door for us to step inside.

Her apartment is fairly spartan except for a nice couch, a kitchen table, and a coffee table with scattered books. There's no television, just an old iPod sitting on the books.

Gwen walks past her, then spins around and makes a stretching movement with her hands behind Carla's back.

I have no idea what the hell is going on.

I smile at Carla. "Thanks."

"Of course." She sits on the edge of her couch and stifles a yawn. "You guys are really good at this," she says after an awkward silence.

"Not as good as I'd like," I reply.

Gwen returns from the bathroom. "When did you start?" she asks Carla.

"Two months ago. You?"

"Three. Same as Sloan. We were comparing notes on how different it is," replies Gwen.

I have fleeting thoughts about what's going on, but I'm far from sure.

"Are we allowed to do that?" asks Carla.

"The secret is to make your own rules. Or did you get that far yet?" says Gwen.

"Not yet. Dr. Isaac says I still have to learn self-control. He says part of that is obedience."

Gwen lets out a laugh. "I remember that phase. I fell for it too. Dr. Isaac and his contrarian lessons."

Carla gives a nervous nod.

Gwen checks her watch. "Hurry up and get your things, Carla. It's time for the next lesson."

"The next lesson?" she asks. "What happens now?"

Yes, what happens now? And what the hell just happened?

"Can I use your phone? My battery is almost dead," asks Gwen.

"Which one?" replies Carla.

"The secret one. Of course," replies Gwen.

Carla reaches down into the cushions of her couch and takes out an iPhone. "Passcode is 'karma,'" she says, handing it to Gwen.

"Thanks," Gwen tells her.

Carla stops. "Oh, I need to—"

"He already knows. You're in our hands now."

Carla smiles. "I'm just glad to have somebody to finally talk to about the game."

Aren't we all.

CHAPTER THIRTY-NINE
THE GAME

Gwen uses Carla's key to lock the door to her apartment. Carla is already in our rental car, curled up in the back and sleeping.

"What's going on?" I ask Gwen.

She looks out at our car. "Haven't you figured it out yet?"

"Maybe. But I'm going to sound really stupid if I explain what I'm thinking. Why don't you enlighten me."

"When I was younger, I had a bit of a personal tragedy. I found myself reaching out for answers and support. Some conventional. Some not so conventional. I also came across people and groups that didn't have my best interests in mind. I was a pain in the ass back then and not worth the effort, but I got a pretty good idea how those types operate," she explains.

"Like a cult?" I ask. From her inquisitive yet brusque manner to dealing with the tragedy of the loss of her father, I get the sense that Gwen has spent a lot of time searching for answers about the world. And probably hasn't been satisfied with any of them.

"Put that word aside for a moment. There's a lot of baggage that comes with it. Think instead about a charismatic person who feeds on attention and control. It could be a preacher in a church. A school teacher. A therapist. A politician. You've met these personalities before."

I nod uncertainly.

"I don't know for sure what's going on with Carla, but I think this Dr. Isaac has been pulling her strings," Gwen tells me.

"Maybe we can ask her to give us a description?"

"See, I'm not sure she's ever met him. The 'secret' phone? The game? This is grooming behavior. What's the word kids use? 'Catfished.' I also don't know if it stops at Dr. Isaac. Carla could be in some kind of online support group and everyone she interacts with is the same person," explains Gwen.

"So, what now? She thinks we're part of this? Technically, this could be considered kidnapping."

"Do you have a better idea? Do you think this Dr. Isaac is just going to let her go? She might know too much."

"Then why not have her go to the police?" I ask.

"You saw how the Asheville police regarded this. They weren't even slightly curious. For all we know, a week from now she could disappear for real. If we don't help her out now, there might not be another chance."

Gwen has clearly thought this through and is speaking from experience that I don't have. I'm not comfortable with the lies we've been feeding Carla, but it was the only way we got her to open up.

"So, what's the plan? We drive her back to Miami? How do we get her into a police station without her realizing she's been lied to?"

"One step at a time. We got a sixteen-hour car ride ahead of us. That might be enough time to deprogram her, or at the very least get her to start externalizing her doubts," says Gwen.

"And what if she realizes we're lying to her and she wants to make a run for it?" I ask.

Gwen shrugs. "Whatever happens, we have to keep her from contacting Dr. Isaac. That could ruin everything."

🦋

I climb into the driver's seat so Gwen can focus on talking to Carla. She's exhausted and still fast asleep, but now is actually the perfect time to start interrogating her, as cruel as that may be.

"Hey, Carla," says Gwen as she gently nudges the young woman awake.

"Yeah?" she says, wiping at her eyes.

"How did you find Dr. Isaac?" asks Gwen. "It was different for Sloan and me. I want to hear your story."

I spot Gwen turning on a digital recorder from the corner of my eye.

"I met him through Instagram," says Carla. "He DM'd me from his personal account. I wasn't sure who he was, but then I saw all the people praising him in his posts. He seemed so interesting. His kids, his wife, everything was just so perfect. I realized that I wanted that kind of balance for my life. When his wife, Brenda, reached out to me and told me he wanted me to be part of his new research project for the Harvard study, I couldn't believe it. Good things like that never happen to me."

Good lord. Carla thinks Dr. Isaac is her savior. How the hell is Gwen going to break her free from that?

"I don't know about you, but I was weirded out about the nude photos," says Gwen.

I focus on the road and don't flinch. Hopefully Gwen knows what the hell she's doing. I certainly don't.

Carla yawns, then laughs. "Yeah. Dr. Diane explained that one to me. I was like, 'Why do these researchers need nude photos of me?' Then I realized it was about trust."

Gwen taps something on her phone and shows me the screen. It's one word: "Filter."

"Filter," as in not every woman who "Dr. Isaac" and his totally-not-imaginary female coworkers ask for nude photos will send them. The ones who do make for the best targets. They're overly trusting and willing to convince themselves of something even when the explanation is lacking.

Gwen turns to me. "I never asked you this, Sloan, but did Dr. Isaac ever ask you to do anything you were uncomfortable with?"

I'm afraid to make up an answer. I assume Gwen is trying to make me part of the conversation so it isn't obvious to Carla that we're interrogating her. She's half asleep, so maybe I can make up something convincing.

"I had to go skinny-dipping in the ocean at night," I reply.

Actually, not something I have to be dared to do.

"That sounds fun," says Carla. "I could hear the ocean in the condo, but I never got to see it."

Gwen and I exchange glances.

"Did you stay at the condo?" Gwen asks me.

"No. I guess I wasn't special enough," I reply.

"It wasn't as nice as Brenda made it out to be, honestly," says Carla. "And I hated not being able to leave. But I get the point of it all. I just wish I didn't have to leave before the end of the program."

Poor dear . . . you should be very glad you left before you found out what happened at the end.

"Wait a second," says Carla as she bolts upright. "I get it."

Damn it. And we're not even on the freeway.

"What's that?" asks Gwen as casually as possible.

"This is still the program. Duh." She lets out another yawn. "I'm sorry. I'm very slow tonight. The car ride back from Miami exhausted me. I spent half the trip on the phone with Dr. Isaac going through the next steps."

"Did he let you drive yourself?" asks Gwen.

"No. He sent one of his personal drivers for me. The whole no-airplane thing for the study," says Carla. "You know."

"Mm-hmm. Same driver who brought you to Florida?" asks Gwen.

"I see why he had you play a cop. You're good at asking questions," replies Carla as she kicks the seat.

"Sorry. Sloan will tell you I did the same thing with her. I still can't get over my self-doubts. They're really holding me back," says Gwen.

"I just learned to let go."

You have no idea where that almost took you.

"Anyway, it was a different Mexican guy. Not much English, like the other one."

Interesting. Isaac may be hiring men who don't speak English to drive the women to Florida. It would guarantee minimal interaction.

This also suggests that Isaac is bilingual.

The real burning question for me is, Did Carla ever actually *talk* to anyone or was it all through text? "Talk" doesn't mean what it used to. She may never have seen, let alone spoken to, Isaac. If he's as savvy as he appears to be using text messages and online communications, we might not be able to track him down.

"I should probably check in with Dr. Isaac and give him an update. Do you have my phone?" asks Carla.

I realize that Gwen has been going through her phone the whole time.

"I updated him," replies Gwen.

"Yeah, but I need to make my video log," says Carla.

Hmm. I suppose that if we break up Carla's routine *too* much, she'll get suspicious.

"Why don't we make one together?" suggests Gwen.

"That would be great!" Carla places her face between our headrests.

Gwen turns on her own phone and starts recording. "This is Gwen, and today I made a new friend," she says into the camera.

Carla pops her head into the frame. "I'm Carla, and I made two new friends today. This is the happiest I've been in a long time."

Gwen aims the camera at me.

I feel the pit of my stomach tighten.

"This is Sloan, and I can't wait to see where life takes me next."

Literally. I have no idea what we're going to do when we get Carla to South Florida, and I'm not sure Gwen does either.

"Wake me when we get there," says Carla before she slumps back into the rear seat.

CHAPTER FORTY
Turnpike

We stop at a turnpike rest stop so I can stretch my legs and get some coffee. Gwen wakes Carla and we all use the bathroom.

This makes it easy for us to keep an eye on Carla in case she makes a break for it. Not that we could legally stop her. We'd have to persuade her to trust us after all the lies.

Carla climbs into the back seat and passes out again while Gwen and I pace around the parking lot.

"How are you holding up?" she asks.

"Good. We can either do a hotel room or you can spot me for a few hours. Probably best if we just keep moving, because one of us will have to keep an eye on Cinderella."

"I can drive for a while," says Gwen.

"Find anything on her phone?" I ask.

"It was wiped earlier today. He probably had her do it. They were using an app called Teleport to talk. It erases the message after it's been read," she explains.

"Any phone calls?"

"No, just the messages. I wouldn't be surprised if she never actually spoke to him. It seems weird, but people can create attachments over text. Some people will even recall conversations as if they were spoken if they heard the other person's voice once or have a vivid imagination about how they would sound."

"I can relate. When I read my friends' text messages, I hear their voices in my head," I admit. "So what's our plan? We can't keep driving forever. We've done a lot of downloading, but when does the deprogramming start?"

"It already did," says Gwen. "Did you see how excited she was to say she made friends? She's been deprived of attention. Isaac put her in a mental cage. Or rather, he instructed her to build one around herself."

"What are we dealing with here, Gwen? This isn't some roadside strangler. He seems too smart and manipulative."

"Maybe. But being manipulative isn't necessarily a mark of intelligence. I mean, have you ever met a child?" she asks rhetorically.

"Fair point. But Isaac has technique."

"That can come from experience. You don't have to be a clinical psychologist to know how to brainwash someone. People have been gaslighting one another for years. It's just a skill," she tells me. "To your point, this Isaac isn't stupid. But he could be anybody. A copy-machine repairman who does this as a hobby. We shouldn't be too in awe of this skill."

I don't want to broach it with her right now. Maybe never. But I get that Gwen is speaking from even deeper experience than she alluded to before.

An observant child watching an alcoholic might gain more insight than she would in a PhD program on substance abuse.

I have a thousand questions for Gwen but try to keep them focused on what's important right now.

"What are you guys talking about?" asks Carla as she gets out of the car.

"Sloan," says Gwen. "She's avoiding an obvious truth."

"And what's that?" asks Carla.

"She's fixated on the approval of male authority figures and people with status," Gwen improvises.

Carla puts her hands on the hood of our rental car. "Dr. Isaac would say that you've let someone else have your remote control."

"Did you know she's working on a PhD?" asks Gwen.

"No. That's cool. What on?" Carla asks me.

"Archaeology," I reply.

"Except she stopped working on it about three years ago. The same time she started working for an older male authority figure. Do you think she stopped because she didn't have the time or because his approval was a surrogate for status?" Gwen inquires, cutting a little deep.

"What do you think?" Carla asks me.

I hate this game. That's what I think. But I play along anyway. "My family had money, then lost it. More than once. I developed self-esteem issues when I realized the kids I was going to private school with were talking behind my back," I admit.

"Then she had an out-of-wedlock child with a young man from one of the wealthier families but never married him. Although they've cohabitated," says Gwen.

I'm feeling anger toward Gwen. But I can't tell if it's justified. Why is she revealing so much about me? Not that it isn't true . . .

"Why wouldn't she marry him?" Gwen asks Carla.

"Same reason she won't finish her PhD?" she replies. "She's afraid that if she completes either one, she'll be unfulfilled and have to find some new way to feel she has worth."

"This isn't very fun," I tell the pair.

Carla puts a hand on my shoulder. "I'm sorry. I feel like I already know you. Why don't you guys do me?"

"You're too trusting," says Gwen. "This has caused you problems in the past. You think the way through this is to trust someone else. But you know that's not the answer either. You're afraid that what happened before will happen again."

I don't know everything that happened to her before, but from the tears welling up in Carla's eyes, Gwen's spot-on, and it wasn't pleasant.

"Fuck me. I know. I know. It's always the same pattern," she replies.

"It's all right, Carla. We'll break the pattern," says Gwen.

Gwen might be a genius at this, though I'm annoyed by her simplistic, if accurate, analysis of me. Still, it seems to have served a purpose.

"I'll owe Dr. Isaac my life if we do," she tells Gwen.

Two steps forward. Three steps back.

"I have a crazy story about trust," Gwen says as we walk back to the car. "I had a high school track coach who encouraged me and helped me win a silver medal at state in cross-country. He saw talent that nobody else did. He'd stay out in the rain and help me practice when I was so angry at the world all I wanted to do was run and scream."

"He sounds like a great guy," says Carla as she climbs back into the car.

"He was to me. But not to two of the other girls on the team. He was molesting them," says Gwen. She turns around to face Carla. "How should I feel about that?"

"Men suck," Carla says simply.

"This is true. But how should I feel about the fact that this person who was so helpful to me was also a monster?"

"People are complex. Dr. Isaac says—"

"Your words, Carla. Use *your* words. How should I feel?"

"You take what helped you and you condemn the rest. We can't be all good. And people who are bad can't be all evil," she says.

"Am I wrong to think positively of him?" Gwen asks.

"No. But you should also recognize the pain he caused. A lot of pain."

"I think you're right." Gwen turns back around.

Carla reaches out and touches Gwen's hand. Gwen places her other hand over Carla's and squeezes.

Gwen's so good at this even I can't tell what's an act and what is true.

"We still have a long way to go," says Gwen.

"You still haven't told me where we're going," says Carla.

"We're going to meet one more person. It's the next step."

I'm beginning to see the method to Gwen's madness. I also have a good idea who this person is.

CHAPTER FORTY-ONE
SISTERHOOD

Carla gently nudges my shoulder. "Wake up, Sloan. We're here."

I wipe my eyes and squint at the sun rising over the ocean.

Gwen shuts the trunk and walks around the car with her leather briefcase. She taps on my window. "Come on, sleepyhead."

I take a sip of lukewarm coffee and regret it immediately.

Carla is already out of the car and holding her arms outstretched, greeting the morning sun. She's full of life and innocence. You can't help but like her. Which makes me worry about what's going to happen next.

I get out of the rental and follow Gwen and Carla as they walk across the beach.

There's a skip in Carla's step. A skip that's not going to last.

Gwen stops at a section of sand just beyond the waterline.

"Is the other person meeting us here? Is it Dr. Isaac?" Carla asks excitedly.

"No, Carla," says Gwen. "This person is a young woman."

"Who is she?" asks Carla.

"Someone who knows Dr. Isaac. About your age. You two are a lot alike."

Carla looks around. "Is she coming here?"

Gwen takes something from her bag. I want to rush out and pull it from her fingers before she shows it to Carla.

It's too soon. It's too cruel.

But I don't.

Carla accepts the photo. She studies the image but seems confused.

"Her name was Nicole," says Gwen. "Tell her, Sloan."

This is a mean game, but I can't think of an alternative.

"Okay. I got called onto the scene because my specialty is crimes that happen in or around the water. Nicole Donnelly had been strangled to death."

I point to where her body lay. "I saw her right there. The rope was still around her neck and her clothes were in a garbage bag floating in the surf."

Carla's face is wrought with anguish. Not because she's made the connection, but because she's a kind and sympathetic soul.

"Is this the game?" she asks.

"No, Carla. It's not a game," replies Gwen.

"I don't understand. Why show this to me?"

"Because Dr. Isaac killed Nicole. It's what he does. He tricks young women into trusting him and then he murders them."

Carla's face contorts. "Y'all are fucking with me."

"No, Carla. We're police officers, like we originally told you. You were next on Isaac's list. It's why he had you in the condo in Miami. Remember when we put your name all over the news? That's why he let you go," explains Gwen.

"He said that was the pharmaceutical companies messing with his research," Carla argues.

"And did you believe that?" I ask.

"I don't know. Sometimes it's just easier to go with it. But Brenda and Diane. All the others. Do they know?"

"Are they even real?" replies Gwen. "Have you actually spoken to any of them other than via text message?"

Carla grows still, and her eyes search around as if she's trying to remember something. "I've spoken to Dr. Isaac."

"How often?" asks Gwen.

"A few times. And I've talked to lots of people who know Dr. Isaac," Carla responds.

"You've talked to accounts," I reply.

"They're real people!" she insists.

"Some of them might be. But their accounts could be copied. This happens in online scams all the time," I explain.

Carla shakes her head. "It can't be."

"I didn't think my track coach could be a monster," says Gwen.

"That was real? That's not some story you made up?" Carla looks searchingly into Gwen's eyes.

"Everything except it being other girls on the team he messed with," Gwen says.

I try not to let my face show the horror I feel at hearing this. As a cop, I've encountered hundreds of stories like this. It doesn't *and shouldn't* get any easier.

"This is all so screwed up." Carla looks at me. "What's your deal?"

"I think we covered it. I'm also told I have a bit of a death wish."

Carla backs away from us. "I don't know who to believe."

"That's easy," says Gwen. "Nobody. Don't take our word for it. We'll go to the police station and talk it over. You can speak to a specialist. Anybody you like. But don't trust *anybody* else. Especially Isaac or anyone you know through him."

"This isn't the game anymore?" she asks again like a helpless child.

"What do you think?" replies Gwen.

Carla wipes at her eyes. "I'm so fucking stupid. I'm so stupid."

Gwen steps up and embraces her. "Join the club." She extends one hand, motioning for me to hug Carla as well.

I can't tell if this is an act for the attention-starved Carla or a sincere moment of comfort, but I give in and join the group hug. But my cynicism fades as I realize exactly how lost and alone Carla feels right now.

CHAPTER FORTY-TWO
TRUST

Gwen and I sit in a conference room at the FDLE and watch on a monitor as Carla explains to two others her emotional and physical journey from her home in Asheville to a condo in Miami where she was on the verge of being killed.

The two people in the room with her are FDLE Special Agent Bridget Harris and Dr. Zoe Serred, a psychologist and expert on cults and the psychological techniques they employ.

Harris is smart and often works with the computer-crimes division on cases that involve online deception and coercion. Serred has worked with various police agencies in South Florida and was brought in at Gwen's insistence.

To get Carla to open up to Serred and Harris, Gwen and I spent about forty-five minutes in the room with her and the others, making casual conversation and getting her to relax.

I made my departure first; Gwen followed ten minutes later. While Gwen and I would have liked to have conducted the formal interview, we need to have others involved to provide some impartiality. Harris and Serred have their own questions that might illuminate more of the technical and manipulative nature of what was done to Carla.

There's also the fact that Gwen and I are exhausted. I haven't had anything other than a few catnaps since yesterday morning. I can tell that it's even harder on Gwen. She keeps drinking cup after cup of coffee, but all it's doing is causing her to take more trips to the restroom.

Through the speaker in the monitor, we're able to follow along with the interview. Harris is the more active one, asking Carla about apps and conversation timelines. Serred spends more time observing Carla and occasionally asking for clarifying details. She seems especially curious about the different people she spoke to, when she talked to them, and through which medium.

It's become apparent that there are three prominent characters in this drama: Dr. Isaac, who according to Carla was a psychologist who dropped out of med school to surf waves in Australia, where he found his spiritual calling helping people find themselves. Brenda, Isaac's wife, is a former model in New Zealand who married Dr. Isaac when he helped her discover that there was more to her than her looks. And Dr. Diane, a senior researcher who helps Isaac on his projects and was his mentor.

There are several other people, mostly women who are also patients, whom Carla interacted with. At one point she says to Serred and Harris, "I thought Sloan might have been Kim. They come across the same way."

Each character serves a different function. Isaac is the spiritual leader with the wisdom. Brenda is proof that happiness can be found and a prototype for Carla to want to emulate.

Just do what she does and you'll marry a handsome rich man and have beautiful children and live in exotic places.

Diane is the voice of reason that intervenes whenever Carla hesitates about something Isaac suggested, like making a recording describing your first sexual encounter or similar intimate details.

Isaac hates this part. But I told him we can't get breakthroughs without revealing ourselves. If you'd be more comfortable, imagine it's a scene in a movie.

The other "students" would point out in side conversations their own hesitations, how liberating it was to give in, and the breakthroughs they made, creating fake peer support for poor Carla.

I'm baffled by all this. Most of what Isaac had Carla do wasn't sexual. It involved mundane things, like doing meditation for five hours or seeing how long you could go without speaking to another person.

Carla even described the other students as competing with one another. She went the longest without speaking, and Isaac told her she did better than anyone he'd worked with before, including his wife, Brenda.

Some of the tasks were just plain odd, like going to a grocery store and counting the number of carrots.

"Why?" I ask Gwen about that.

"Control. That's what Isaac gets off on. Turning Carla into a mindless robot. It's his thrill."

"What about the occult connection? That sounds a little Looney Tunes for someone this manipulative."

"Why? I said it before, I'll say it again: manipulation is a skill. You don't have to be a genius to pull it off. It's like a magic trick. It only looks amazing because you don't know how it works. As far as the occult connection, smart people believe crazy things. Look at who makes up the followers of some of the most extreme belief systems. You'll see doctors, scientists, all kinds.

"Also, Sloan, Isaac knowing how to manipulate vulnerable women doesn't preclude him from having his own irrational beliefs. In fact, some cult groups are actually started by the survivors of other groups. They know the techniques for manipulation because they experienced them firsthand."

"So he chooses some woman at random, strings her along, and then kills her when he gets bored?"

"We'll want to talk to Harris about this, but I imagine this is a wide con. Isaac may be communicating with dozens of women right now, not only Carla."

That's a chilling thought. We may have rescued Carla, but Isaac could be busily luring other women into his controlling trap.

"It seems like a lot of work. Trying to maintain all of those different accounts and identities," I say, exhausted at the very thought.

"So does scuba diving, to me. Or fishing or playing a video game for twelve hours. This is Isaac's thing. The manipulation, the personas, that's the excitement for him. He makes some dumb comment and suddenly Carla's counting the number of Cheerios in a box. It's not a means to an end. It's about the process," she explains.

"And killing them?"

"Final stage. That's the ultimate control. None of the victims showed signs of struggle. Toxicology said there were no substances. I don't know if you realize this yet, Sloan, but they *let* Isaac kill them."

"I don't think they understood that was what he was doing." I point to Carla on the screen. "She doesn't want to die."

"But she desperately wants to trust someone. At what point do you think she'd say no?"

I remember Violet's story and how she trusted "Azrael" even though everything about him screamed danger. Hell, Carla believed she was talking to a clinical professional and his coterie. There were warning signs, sure, but unlike the rest of us, Carla was so conditioned to trust doctors and follow peer pressure, it was too uncomfortable for her to tell him it was too much.

Gwen glances down at a message on her phone. "They want to talk to us before we speak to Carla."

"What are they worried about?"

"'Fragile' is the word Serred used. But I think we already know that."

CHAPTER FORTY-THREE
CONDITION

Carla is taking a nap in Harris's office while another agent watches over her. Our biggest fears are that she decides to leave or contacts Isaac.

She's a free person and we can't stop her from doing either. While we could probably get a judge to put her into temporary medical custody, that runs a huge risk. We could lose Carla's trust and set everything back. Our current plan is to reach out to her family members—the ones she gets along with—and make them aware of her condition.

The FDLE is talking to the North Carolina state police about a safe house or similar arrangement for Carla while we track down the elements of her story. That's the biggest challenge we face right now. Carla told a story that fit what Gwen and I were looking for, but to everyone else, it's only a story at this point.

Part of the reason Gwen and I didn't object to Harris and Serred doing the initial interview is that we don't want to be accused of guiding Carla's testimony. While this wouldn't normally be an issue, with Mazin breathing down my neck and Bennett out to see Gwen fail, we have to proceed with caution.

As we enter, Dr. Serred makes some notes in a binder and beckons for us to be seated.

Harris finishes typing on her computer, then sits back. "Well, that was fascinating."

"Let's cut to the chase," says Gwen. "Do you believe her?"

"One hundred percent," replies Harris. "If anyone has that deep of an understanding about how these kinds of online confidence scams work, they're either pulling one off or a victim. If they're pulling it off, they're not going to talk to us."

"This 'Isaac' is very good," says Serred. "He's created a stable of personalities to manipulate Carla. From father figures to role models, he has this down to a science."

"He's had practice," replies Gwen.

"I didn't go through the other cases, but my understanding is that you believe Carla isn't the only victim of this con," says Serred.

"Um, no. The last one ended up dead on a beach a week ago," Gwen tells her.

"I read the report," says Harris. "Both women seem like they fit the type. The challenge here is establishing that 'Dr. Isaac' is real."

"Obviously he's not real. He's a persona," says Gwen.

"What I mean is that, as Carla was giving us the details, I was looking everything up online. I could find some accounts with the same names, but they belong to real people with no apparent connection to any of this. The specific IDs she mentioned have all been deleted."

"Isaac must have deleted it all when he saw Carla's face in the news," I venture.

"It's what I would do," says Harris. "But it also makes your case that much more difficult. I don't know if anyone is going to believe her story."

"Has everyone lost their mind? She spent hours in here going through everything!" shouts Gwen.

"And we believe her story," replies Serred. "But outside of the people in this room, I don't know how much of it everyone else will accept. It's a wild story."

"It might sound technically hard to pull off, to an outsider," says Harris. "But we interact with fake personas every time we go online and read reviews or comments. Inventing fake people to manipulate us is an entire industry. You can take courses online on how to do this. And there's another problem," she adds.

"Now what?" asks Gwen.

"There's no case here."

"No case? What more do we need?"

"In Carla's situation? A crime," says Harris.

"A crime? Attempted murder isn't a crime anymore? I knew the DAs were getting soft, but this is beyond the pale."

I put my hand on her arm. "Gwen, see it from the outside. Heck, see it from Carla's point of view. She was lied to. She was manipulated. She was even transported across several states under dubious circumstances. But she never gave Dr. Isaac a dime. She never did anything illegal at his coercion. Technically, Isaac never broke the law."

"Absurd." She pulls her arm away to rub her temples. "Just plain absurd."

Harris is about to speak, but I shake my head to stop her.

Gwen is smart. She understands. You just have to let the facts sink in.

She lets out an exhausted sigh. "I know. I know. If being a lying, manipulative bastard were a crime by itself, I could have made a career going after half the people I worked with."

Good old Gwen.

"Without much of a digital footprint, we have to rely on Carla's memories," says Harris.

"I'm not sure if she ever even saw Dr. Isaac," adds Serred.

"She said she spoke to him at least once," I point out.

"Yes. She said he was on a satellite phone and getting over a cold," replies Serred.

"That's a convenient way to mask your identity," I reply.

"It is," she agrees. "And you'd be surprised at how easy it is for anyone to fall for it. This was at the beginning, when Carla was having doubts. He probably made the call to reassure her. She says that Isaac would send her audio files of him speaking but insisted that she delete them after listening."

I nod. "He created a conspiracy theory in which people in the pharmaceutical industry were trying to suppress his research, so it had to be kept secret."

"I played a voice sample for her," says Harris. "She asked me how I got Dr. Isaac's voice. It was a computer-generated voice. She had no idea they could do that. She thought he sounded robotic because it helped the 'brain waves' function."

"Oh dear," says Gwen.

"Carla isn't an idiot, Detective Wylder," says Harris.

"Oh, I know. Trust me, I've fallen for similar lies. It just hits a little close to home."

"My advice for talking to her," says Serred, "is to ask for the details you need, but don't push her. She's going through a tremendous amount of stress and self-doubt."

"Do you think she might try to reach out to Isaac?" I ask.

"Maybe. We've told her that's a bad idea, but she'll want closure and probably wants to give him the opportunity to explain how this is all a misunderstanding," replies Serred.

"That would be bad," I say.

"That could be fatal. If he gets in her head again, he'll have her get as far away from us as possible," adds Gwen.

"Maybe not. He might move on," says Harris.

"Move on? This isn't some grifter trying to max out her credit cards. This is a serial killer who knows she's our only living link to him. Catching him may be a matter of getting what's inside her mind," says Gwen, "and erasing it forever."

CHAPTER FORTY-FOUR
DETAILS

"What's up?" Carla says with a smile as she enters the conference room.

"We're still putting together all the details. We need to sit you down with a sketch artist and give descriptions of the drivers," I reply.

"We also need to know more about this condo," adds Gwen.

"I told Harris it was night and I was half asleep," says Carla.

I can tell she's getting tired of the questions and the emotional roller coaster. If we push her, she might shut down.

"Every detail matters," I reply. "Last year I was involved in a shoot-out in California and I spent weeks getting grilled by everyone, from the local police to federal prosecutors. Some of them were on my side. Some weren't. They were looking for a reason to blame me for what happened."

"How did you manage that?" she asks.

"I told the truth."

Mostly.

I only gave direct answers to direct questions. If an attorney asked me if I saw "Mr. Casado" or "Mr. Galo" directly point their weapon at me before I fired my gun, I'd reply in a way that would be hard to use against me. I live in a world where a cartel hit squad sent to kill me can be spun into a headline like, "Florida Law Enforcement Officer Involved in Deadly Shootout with Mexican Tourists in California Resort."

Now I'm in the awkward position of having to give Carla advice that I would never give to myself: Tell us everything. Don't hold back.

"The condo was surrounded by trees. I never saw anyone else, and there was a gate around the property. Dr. Isaac said I needed to stay away from sunlight so I could reprogram my sleep cycle. I could go onto the back patio at night and use the pool," she explains.

This is interesting. Keeping her inside limited the chance of her talking to somebody else. But why let her use the pool?

"Did you ever get the sense that you were being watched?" asks Gwen.

"I mean, there were cameras all over the house. It was a study. So, yes, I was being watched. You get used to them," she tells us.

"In the bathroom too?" I ask.

"Yes. There was a camera, but it wasn't aimed at the toilet. Thank god."

As far as you know . . .

The cameras enabled Isaac to get his jollies watching his pet day and night. And I suspect the nighttime pool permission was so he could watch her in person.

"What was the furniture like in the condo?" asks Gwen.

"A bed. A couch. A kitchen table and some chairs. That was it. I gave Harris a floor plan."

A floor plan that matches a million condos in South Florida.

Our best bet, besides whatever clues Carla may have that she doesn't realize, is narrowing down locations for Isaac.

This condo sounds like a rental property or something you could book online. Given the prevalence of disposable email addresses and cryptocurrencies, it could be next to impossible to connect him to where Carla stayed.

"You never saw anyone while you were there?" asks Gwen.

"Other than the drivers? No. Not a soul."

"Did you see a sign of anyone? A delivery person? The sound of a lawnmower?" I ask.

"I never saw the delivery person. They always came while I was sleeping," says Carla.

The delivery person? This is something new.

"What did they deliver?" asks Gwen.

"They brought my groceries and took away my trash. But always at night while I was asleep."

Watching her routine on the cameras, they'd know exactly when she was sleeping.

"You never saw this person?" asks Gwen.

"No, I don't think so. I was in the yard one day doing my exercises and I could see a car through a tiny gap in the fence. You know how you can see part of something through a sliver but know what the whole thing looks like? I saw a car drive by and the stop across the street, I think."

"Did you see anyone?" I ask.

"No. I wasn't supposed to be out front, so I went back inside. I was feeling kind of cooped up."

I try to get more details. "Could you describe the car?"

"Yeah. It was like my dad's old work car but dark blue. An Impala. The windows were tinted. Like the maximum amount you can get."

"Do you know the model year?" asks Gwen.

"No. But it looked exactly like Dad's. Except for the tint. He had that in . . . 2012, I think."

I make a note: *Dark blue Chevy Impala, around 2012.*

The first thing Gwen and I are going to do when we're done talking to Carla is see if there's a match between that car and one spotted near the crime scenes or the storage unit.

While Isaac may have used other people to do the driving to and from the victims' cities, it seems more likely that he was the one bringing Carla groceries and taking away her trash.

Why didn't he have Carla fly or drive her own car to the condo? Or do it himself?

Letting her drive would mean giving her an address that someone else could obtain later. Driving her himself might be too risky.

Using two other drivers was also risky, but normally the plan was to only use one. Carla was likely the first victim ever to get a return ride home.

The drivers seem like the most vulnerable part of the scheme, assuming they're not fully in on it. How do you trust them to not talk to the police? A language barrier only works so well. They might be professionals with clean records who transport narcotics. Since they were coming to South Florida, they'd probably be driving clean.

There's also the possibility that they were recruited out of state. Carla thinks the car that took her home had a Texas license plate.

We'll have a team check the highway cameras to see if there's a match, but it feels thin.

The drivers, like the condo, could have been paid with untraceable currency. They'd have no more clue about the source than Carla.

There's also the intriguing possibility that the driver who took Carla home was Isaac.

"When the driver took you home, you said you were talking to Isaac?" I ask.

"Yes," she replies.

"Did you ever see the driver on his phone?"

"No. It was in his pocket the whole time. If he took a call, he pulled over. But I never saw him text," she says.

There goes that theory.

CHAPTER FORTY-FIVE
REQUEST

Monica Kirch, acting district supervisor for the Florida Department of Law Enforcement, holds up the folder Gwen and I prepared for her the night before.

"This is thin," she says.

"It's what we have right now. We have more potential physical evidence, but we want to act on what Carla Burgh said while there's still time," I reply.

"According to Harris, there's not enough here to make a formal complaint because no crime has been committed," Kirch points out.

"That's not true," says Gwen. "This Dr. Isaac claims to be a licensed psychologist and offered his services to her. That's a violation of state law. Plus transporting Ms. Burgh under false pretenses, including over state lines. There are a few other examples. But the point is, we have evidence of crimes."

"Where is she now?" asks Kirch.

"Harris and Serred are keeping tabs on her. Serred wants to make sure she doesn't have a breakdown."

Kirch directs her next question at me. "Why are you coming to me instead of through Mazin? She's your supervisor."

"Mazin hates me with the intensity of a thousand white-hot suns and would rather see me dead than give me an ounce of support," I reply bluntly.

"There's still a chain of command," Kirch reminds me.

"And if I followed that, Carla Burgh's body would be washing up on a beach right now. Thankfully, Wylder and I saw eye to eye on this."

"Why not Miami? How come you're not bringing this to Bennett?" Kirch asks Gwen.

"Is that a serious question? Because I don't think it deserves a serious answer."

Kirch sits speechless for a moment. "You two are quite the pair. It's like some kind of pro-wrestling tag-team match my kids watch."

"We'd like forensic analysis. We'd like some agents assigned to this. We'd like a couple of researchers. But we'll settle for a bulletin and some assistance getting local agencies looking for the car Carla described at the condo," I tell her.

"What did Fort Lauderdale say?" asks Kirch.

"'Keep us posted on any developments.'" I shrug. They didn't want anything complicating a case they were hoping would go away on its own. This is rough. I'm not used to begging for resources. When I worked for Solar, he made things happen. He was a damned miracle worker. When a power broker got our certification pulled, he had us deputized by the US Marshals within minutes. Then the Secret Service. He was always several steps ahead.

And here I am, begging to have some extra police patrols help us find the car belonging to Carla's abductor.

"I don't see why this is so hard," says Gwen, exasperated by the groveling.

"Well, for one, you're not wrong in how much Bennett dislikes you. He's not the only one. To be brutally honest, there are also questions about Carla Burgh's testimony," says Kirch.

"You think the poor girl is lying?" asks Gwen.

"No. But I have heard the word 'coached' thrown around. You two spent a very long car ride with her before she made her statement. It's been suggested that not everything she said was original to her."

I don't have to look at Gwen to know she's seething. I decide to speak up before she goes ballistic. "Care to name names? I'd love to know who is saying that I'm a liar and making an allegation that I'm interfering with a witness. In fact, this might be the time where I bring in outside counsel."

"McPherson, nobody's making that allegation about you," Kirch assures me.

I know that. This is some vendetta with Gwen's colleagues. They want to bring her down, but in doing so, they're pulling me into the vipers' nest with her.

"There were three people in that car. Carla Burgh, Gwen Wylder, and myself. Any allegation against Wylder reflects on me as well," I say. "And we're not making an unreasonable request," I add. "If someone has an objection based upon a belief that we're tampering with the witness, then they need to step forward and make that allegation formally instead of whispering it behind our backs."

Kirch softens her tone. "It's politics."

"It's people's lives!" snaps Gwen. "Do we get the help or not?"

Oh, Gwen. Ever the nuanced negotiator.

"All right. I'll make the calls," says Kirch.

"Thank you," I say for both of us.

"Would you mind if I speak to McPherson?" Kirch asks Gwen.

"Yes, of course." Gwen leaves the room without another word.

"Mazin is not happy with you," Kirch says flatly.

"You noticed?"

"I don't know that I'd say she's your enemy. But she's certainly not a fan." Kirch points to the door. "Wylder, she has enemies. More enemies than fans. I've heard stories about the backstabbing that went on in Miami a while ago, so I don't know who's right and who's wrong.

My suspicion is the whole lot of them have a screw loose. Right now, though, some of that hatred for Wylder seems to be rubbing off on you. I don't know what your career plans are, but at some point you're going to need a favor, and somebody's going to say no because of her."

"I don't know about what happened before. And I won't say that Wylder isn't, well, Wylder. But I've never seen her do anything other than dedicate herself to her work. If being associated with someone like that is bad for my career, then you can have it. I didn't come here for the politics."

"You are definitely Solar's protégé," says Kirch.

"I take that as a compliment."

"It's an incomplete one," Kirch adds. "You may be his protégé, but you don't have his nuance. He'd have seen Bennett being a problem a mile away. He'd have figured out how to make friends instead of acquiring new enemies."

"I don't know if everyone can be turned into friends, and Solar has his enemies," I reply defensively.

"Maybe. But everybody wants something from Solar. He's the one you go to when you can't get it anywhere else. If I said no to you, he'd have been the next call you made."

This is true. "Point taken," I admit.

"Her enemies don't care if you're collateral damage. Be careful with Wylder too. You might only be experiencing her on her best behavior because she wants something from you. When she doesn't get what she wants, that's a side you don't want to see."

CHAPTER FORTY-SIX
LATENT

"I may have a partial print," says Mandy Fonseca from the top of a ladder as she dusts a light fixture.

It took us three days to find the condo, but between a search of rental listings, Google Maps, and a reconstruction of Carla's road trip, we were able to find the location: Sea Castle Cove, south of Miami.

We sent the photos to Carla, currently staying with her brother in North Carolina, and she confirmed that it was the same place.

She seems to be handling things fairly well. Gwen and I both make a point of calling her several times a day to check in on her and make sure she doesn't do anything irrational—like talk to Isaac.

At this point we think she's probably in the clear, but we don't want him knowing how much we know. Finding the condo was only one part of our plan to catch him.

As we predicted, the rental was booked online and paid for with cryptocurrency. The security deposit was held by a third party that, conveniently, doesn't keep records after a rental is completed.

While that trail has run cold, there's the possibility that if we ask around, we might learn that Isaac has done this before and maybe slipped up and used a personal email account or phone number.

We borrowed Fonseca from Fort Lauderdale because she was still attached to the Nicole Donnelly case, and Gwen didn't have too many people in Miami who owed her favors.

Fonseca decided to dust the fixture when we mentioned the layout of cameras that had been installed to watch Carla. She pointed out that this one light looked like it had been recently adjusted to illuminate a dark hallway. Her observation is a reminder that you should always ask experts what they think. In this situation, the quiet woman who has dusted a thousand crime scenes probably has a better idea than I where to look.

"How does he afford to keep doing this?" asks Gwen.

"I've been thinking," I reply. "Isaac never tried to scam Carla out of money, but he easily could have. Maybe that's his main income—running internet scams?"

"We should ask Harris," says Gwen.

"We can add anybody who has done cybercrime to the list—or knows how to do it. Or knows how to Google it, for that matter." I sigh.

At this point in an investigation, you want it to shrink. Unfortunately, our list keeps growing. At the rate we're going, everyone on the planet will be a suspect in a month.

"I'm going to scan these, then check inside the cabinet doors and under the chairs," Fonseca explains as she steps down from the ladder.

It's not uncommon for a criminal who is acutely aware of leaving fingerprints at the scene of a crime to screw up and leave a print in a place they don't realize they touched. There are a hundred places in our homes where we leave fingerprints and don't realize it. That's the advantage of bringing in someone like Fonseca.

While I roam the condo, checking closets and underneath drawers for anything that might have been left behind when Isaac set the place up, Gwen is on all fours, scouring the edge between the carpet and the walls, looking for anything that got wedged in there.

"This is interesting," says Fonseca as she leans over her laptop on the counter.

"What's up?" I walk over to see what she's doing.

"I got a print from the light fixture. It's only a partial, so I got thousands of potential matches, but nothing concrete in the general database," she says.

"I guess that's something."

"Yes, but I also got a potential match from the matchbook you found at that storage unit."

"What's this?" asks Gwen as she bounces to her feet.

"It's not enough to say that both people are the same, but the probability is really high," says Fonseca.

Gwen takes her phone out and starts dialing.

"Where are we on the Impala?" she asks a moment later.

Presumably she's talking to our coordinator at the FDLE, who sent a bulletin to the other law enforcement agencies.

"What? Why didn't anybody tell us?" Gwen yells. She covers the phone and tells me, "A BSO patrol car saw a car matching our description near one of the routes we wanted covered."

"When?" I ask.

"Half an hour ago. Nobody told us because they told Fort Lauderdale instead. FDLE only just saw the memo," Gwen explains with an eye roll.

I grab my keys and my backpack. "You get the address; I'll drive!"

CHAPTER FORTY-SEVEN
Person of Interest

I keep the gas pedal floored as the blue light on my dashboard whirls, warning the other vehicles on I-95 to stay clear. The dark clouds and the rain hitting the windshield don't help.

Gwen is in the passenger seat, getting the latest updates on the location of the vehicle.

We don't know that this dark-blue 2012 Chevy Impala with tinted windows is the one that belongs to our suspect, but it was spotted going down one of the roads we'd marked as a potential route the killer might take on a regular basis.

If you map out where the bodies were found and where we believe they were killed, then draw lines between them, you notice certain roads the killer used more than once and might be part of his routine.

Most of these are high-traffic corridors like I-95, where millions of cars travel every day. But some have less traffic and were worth flagging to other police departments.

"The car was last spotted pulling into the Vista Shopping Plaza," says Gwen. "Are you going to kill the blue light?"

She's even more anxious than I am—which is saying a lot.

"We're ten miles away. I'll turn it off before the exit. I don't want to lose any time getting there."

"I know, I know. Do you mind?" she asks as she pulls her vape pen from her purse.

"Puff away."

Gwen had been a chain-smoker, which comes as no surprise. She switched to a vape pen, which manages to keep the urge under control unless she's really stressed.

Seeing Gwen inhaling from a blue LED device or Jackie play with her VR headset reminds me that I'm living in the future.

Speaking of which, a flying car would come in real handy right now.

"They have two patrol cars watching the exits. I told them not to go into the plaza's parking garage," Gwen updates me.

"Good idea. I want to follow the car and get the plate. We can try to track down the owner later. Where he goes might tell us more."

Gwen answers her phone. "Just now?" She swats my arm. "The car just left. It's heading northbound on 144th Street."

"Tell them to keep a distance," I reply.

"Obviously."

I flip off the blue light and head for the exit. If our suspect is on the move, we don't want him to spot cop lights in his rearview mirror. South Florida is so flat you can see down some roads for a mile or more in either direction and spot emergency vehicles. This means you have to proceed extra carefully when you want to get to a suspect vehicle in a hurry and not be seen.

We pass the shopping plaza and I make a left at the intersection for 144th, speeding through a yellow light.

Gwen doesn't say anything, but the tension shows in her body language. A predator preparing to pounce.

What happens next is another question. We want to pull the car over at some point, but not before we've had a chance to see if he goes to a location that might be informative.

While we can run the license plate once a patrol car or Gwen and I see it, that will give us their official residence at best. If the address on file belongs to a relative, a place of business, or some other entity, that won't tell us much because all we'll know is this person drives the same kind of car Carla saw once.

Also, to compel the driver to come in for questioning or volunteer fingerprints might be a challenge. Even people who have never considered committing a crime can be hesitant to cooperate so freely. If the driver of the vehicle is our guy, then we can expect even less cooperation. There's also the possibility that if we pull him over to talk, the moment we leave he'll drive off and never be seen again.

Ted Bundy was a sloppy serial killer who left behind forensic evidence that could have led to his arrest years prior, but he kept moving and complicated the various investigations into his murders.

There have been incidents where a killer was able to elude authorities simply by moving ten miles away to a different state and jurisdiction that didn't communicate well with nearby law enforcement agencies.

While the FDLE has reach across our state and good relations with our neighbor states and the FBI, the more distance our suspect is able to put between Gwen and me, the better his chances of getting away.

"This damn rain!" Gwen groans as water begins to fall by the bucketload onto our windshield.

The other cars are starting to slow, and a few simpletons turn on their hazard lights, not realizing they're meant for when your car is stopped and not moving in miserable weather. More than a few collisions have happened in weather like this because the person behind the driver with the flashing hazard lights couldn't tell that the other car was braking or making a turn.

I keep us moving and weave between the other cars, doing my best not to cause an accident myself.

Gwen is clutching her phone in one hand and the dashboard in a talon-like grip with the other.

My two biggest concerns are what to do with the suspect if we catch up and how to manage Gwen. Other than our trip with Carla, she hasn't worked in the field in years. I don't think she's going to flip out, but I can't unsee the image of her shoving her Glock into the suspect's mouth as she demands a confession.

In fairness, she's shown more restraint over the past few days. I don't know if that's because of me specifically or whether the presence of other humans in general has made her less feral.

"Ram him if you have to," she says before giving me a nervous smile.

Four cars ahead I see a dark Impala. "There it is."

"Shit," says Gwen as she points to a patrol car one lane behind and to the right of the Impala.

"Tell them to have their guy back off."

Gwen makes the request to the dispatcher on the other end of the line.

The lights on the police car flip on.

"What the hell?" I moan.

"Damn it! He's got another call he has to respond to," says Gwen.

"Let's hope he doesn't spook our—"

Just like that, the Impala jumps forward, weaves through traffic, and starts racing down the breakdown lane.

I push the pedal to the floor and flip the blue light on.

"Hold on!"

CHAPTER FORTY-EIGHT
PURSUIT

Usually in situations like this, you call for a police helicopter and keep a safe distance so you don't escalate the chase and end up killing innocent people when things go out of control.

Usually, you have better weather for a helicopter and you're not pursuing a serial killer.

This is one of those edge cases where your instructors tell you to use your best judgment. Which is a phrase that you learn later actually means, *We're going to blame you no matter what if things go badly.*

I race down the breakdown lane, chasing after the Impala while the other traffic remains still like a herd of cattle.

Gwen takes out her laptop and starts pinching and zooming on a map while she shouts into her phone.

"We need more cars! The suspect is heading north on 144th. What do you mean you can't send any more? What about the helicopter? Grounded? Damn it! What good are you," she cries.

There's an intersection ahead. The Impala shows no sign of braking.

"Don't lose him," says Gwen.

"We're already pushing things," I reply as calmly as possible. "Did you get the license plate?"

"Yes!" She holds up her notepad.

"Call it in. See where he might be headed."

I really don't want to burst through the intersection and T-bone someone, so I slow down.

"Sloan!" yells Gwen.

The light turns green and the Impala accelerates.

Green works for me as well. I gun the engine and fly down the lane, smashing into puddles and vaporizing them. God forbid I have to brake or make a turn with my tires this wet.

"If he keeps going straight, we can probably get BSO to stop him," I point out.

But he doesn't keep going straight. In the middle of the intersection, the Impala swerves to the left, nearly smashing into a utility pole, and races down a side road.

"Damn it!"

At first I think it's Gwen who yelled, then realize it was me. I repeat the Impala's move, but at a slower speed, which allows it to gain critical distance on us.

"Wait! I think he's headed for an on-ramp to 95. We can probably get a car there!" says Gwen.

I'm too busy trying to watch the road through sheets of rain to look at where she's pointing on her iPad. The wipers splash away the water, and I see four cars on this smaller road. None of them is the Impala.

To our left is nothing but the trees of a nature reserve.

"Wait! There's an access road!" says Gwen.

"Where?"

"Right . . . behind us!" she exclaims.

I slam on the brakes, turn the wheel, glide into a slide, and bring my truck around in a 180-degree turn.

The park's access road is a small earthen berm going across a canal into a narrow gap between the trees. I turn onto it and send the truck flying down a gravel path. My scuba tank makes a clanking sound in the back as a strap unbuckles and sets it free.

"Is that going to explode?" asks Gwen as the tank produces a loud bell sound.

"Probably not." I'd rather take that chance then lose the Impala.

"Look out!" yells Gwen.

I slam on the brakes and send the truck into a skid.

The Impala is only few yards away, smashed into a tree with the driver's side door wide open and steam hissing from its ruptured radiator.

I slam the truck into park and leap out of my seat with my gun drawn.

"Stay here!" I order Gwen.

She may have seniority, but she lacks experience in this kind of situation.

Without waiting for a response, I race around the Impala and into the woods.

Twenty yards into the trees, I yell, "Police! Come out with your hands up!"

Silence.

I could start running in a random direction, but my best bet is to wait and listen.

The only sound is the rain hitting the leaves and falling to the floor of the woods. The trees keep going for another twenty yards, and then there's a small hill. If memory serves me correctly, there're a number of trails beyond there, a small parking lot, and then a fence that backs onto a housing development, several apartment complexes, and a strip mall.

I assume that Gwen has already called for backup to search those areas. The bloodhound in me wants to keep going, so I walk carefully to the top of the hill and look around to see if anyone is trying to conceal themselves in the bushes.

Nothing.

In the distance I hear the squalling of police sirens responding to Gwen's call and encircling the park.

With a hundred different ways out of these woods, if the suspect is smart, he'll keep going and slip through our net before it's even in place.

I walk back to where the Impala crashed into the trees. Gwen is behind my truck, gun drawn and talking into her phone.

"See anything?" she asks.

"Nothing."

Gwen flinches first. Then I hear the sound too.

It's a miracle neither of us fires our gun.

We look around for the source.

There's another thump.

It's coming from the Impala.

"Help!" shouts a muffled voice.

I walk to the trunk and silently motion for Gwen to open it from inside the car.

The hatch pops open and a terrified woman with ripped clothes and a battered face looks up at me.

"Please don't hurt me!" she says as she shrinks deep into the trunk and away from me.

CHAPTER FORTY-NINE
RETRIBUTION

Gwen and I are at South Broward Hospital, waiting for one of the female detectives talking to the female victim in her room to come out and give us an update.

The woman said nothing to us other than her plea for help from the trunk. She simply watched everyone around her with a confused look. Her only notable reaction was going nearly catatonic when one of the male deputies approached her.

Her hair was disheveled and her makeup running, but she looked like she was in her early forties and kept an otherwise well-maintained appearance.

We couldn't find a purse, phone, or anything else to help identify her. Right now, it's a waiting game for her to talk.

The car registration belongs to Gladys Fillmore, a ninety-year-old resident of a senior citizens' home in Boca Raton who had no recollection of ever owning a Chevy Impala. We think it's safe to assume the registration was forged.

"This sucks," says Gwen as she fights with a cushion on the waiting-room sofa.

We've been on our phones and computers for the last three hours, keeping updated on the manhunt and trying to get any other details we can.

Other than the car with the fake registration, it hasn't been a productive search. A forensic team will be going over the Impala in the next few hours to lift any prints or other evidence.

The search for the fleeing driver didn't even yield an eyewitness. Apparently, the rain kept everyone indoors. Patrol cars are on the lookout for anybody on foot, but if the suspect has friends or a place to hide nearby, that may not yield anything either.

But you never know. He could be sitting at a bus stop right now, being watched by a police car and only minutes away from being apprehended.

Or he could be on an airplane halfway across the country.

Gwen is quietly shaking her head as she thinks something over.

"What is it?" I ask.

"I think he's gone berserk, Sloan. A second victim in four days? He's never done this before. I think we pushed him over the edge. He may be on a spree. If so, god help us."

It's not uncommon for murder suspects to completely decompensate when their world starts closing in. They make mistakes because they don't care about caution anymore. This is when they'll sometimes start to kill erratically.

Gwen's fear is that we may have pushed him over the edge.

"Everything we need to know is in there!" says Gwen, gesturing to the woman's hospital room.

"Let them do their job. This is delicate work. They know how to deal with people who have gone through trauma," I reply.

"Just give me ten minutes with a sketch artist," she scoffs.

Detective Hayley Laina steps out of the room and sees us in the waiting area.

"Anything?" Gwen asks her before the detective's body has had a chance to make it all the way into the room.

"These things can be slow," she replies.

"Is it possible to be even slower than this? What about the rape kit?" asks Gwen.

Laina shakes her head. "She won't even let a nurse examine her."

"Can we get a judge to compel that?" Gwen asks in desperation.

"Not a chance in hell. You know that. I understand that this is frustrating, but look at it from her perspective."

"Her perspective? Hell, I'd trade the last six years of my life chasing down this son of a bitch for a few hours in a trunk. Sign me up," snaps Gwen.

Laina looks at me to be the reasonable one. Which usually isn't the case when I work with my normal partner, Scott Hughes.

"We need time," she explains. "We can call you if anything changes. Right now, it's just a matter of waiting for her to be comfortable."

"Can you at least give us a clear photo of her so we can ask around about her identity?" I ask.

"I'll see about that when she's communicating," Laina replies.

"Sloan, you manage this. I need to go splash some water on my face and wake up from this nightmare," mutters Gwen as she gets up and leaves the waiting room.

"She's a handful," says Laina after Gwen is out of earshot.

"At times. But definitely someone you want on your side." I feel Gwen's frustration. I'm just better at hiding it. "In your experience, how long does it take for someone to talk?"

"Minutes to days. Some people block out the trauma entirely. It depends upon their mental state before and what they went through," says Laina with a shrug.

Laina's partner, Detective Abigail Richards, shouts from down the hall, "Hey! You're not supposed to be in here!"

I look up and see Gwen walking toward us with her phone in her hand and Detective Richards chasing after her.

Richards reaches out and grabs Gwen's elbow.

Gwen swats it away. "Touch me again and I draw blood," she growls as she spins around to face her.

I launch out of my chair and put myself between them.

"She just shoved a camera in the victim's face and took a photo!" Richards complains.

"You can't do that!" says Laina.

"The fuck I can't. This is our case. She's our witness. You can play your trauma drama all day long, but our suspect is out there. The longer we wait, the farther away he gets. In what condition do you think we'll find the *next* woman he shoves into his trunk? I guarantee she won't be the talking kind."

There's an awkward moment of silence. Nobody wants to speak first.

Technically, Gwen is correct. There's no rule saying we couldn't ask the victim questions or take her photo.

Laina and Richards were following department guidelines, but guidelines is all they are.

"I think you two should leave," says Laina.

"Funny. I think *you two* should leave," Gwen fires back.

This is going nowhere.

"Excuse me," says a voice from down the hall.

"Give us a moment," snaps Richards.

"It's just . . ."

I turn and see our victim standing in the hallway.

"Hey," I say to her.

"I think I'm ready to talk," she says in a weak voice.

Laina glares at us. "Okay, hon. Detective Richards and I will be right there."

"No. I want to talk to *them*." The woman points at Gwen and me.

CHAPTER FIFTY
RESCUERS

"My name is Riley," says the woman seated upright in the hospital bed with her arms wrapped around her knees. Her voice is almost a whisper, but she makes eye contact with Gwen and me as she speaks, then looks back down at the bed. "You're the ones who rescued me?"

"Yes," I tell her.

"How did you end up in the trunk?" asks Gwen, getting right to the point.

"The man put me in there," says Riley. "I was out on my morning walk and . . . just out of nowhere I feel a hand grab me by the neck. He pushed me towards his car. I tried to pull away, but he said he had a gun. He shoved me against his car and told me to get into the trunk.

"I didn't . . . I didn't know what to do. Then I saw the gun and I got in. I should have run. But his grip. He was strong," she explains.

"What did he look like?" I ask.

"He was wearing a hat and sunglasses. I really didn't get a good look . . . I'm so stupid. So, so stupid."

"Was he white or Black?" asks Gwen.

"He seemed tan? Maybe Hispanic? Greek? I don't know. His voice sounded a little different. Like English wasn't his first language. But I couldn't tell you the accent," Riley explains.

"And you've never met this person before?" asks Gwen.

Riley goes silent for a moment. "Like was he someone I knew in disguise? I don't think so. I don't know anybody like that. He had . . . a presence. The other man too," she adds.

"The *other* man?" asks Gwen. "What other man?"

"I didn't see him. But I could hear arguing from inside the trunk."

Gwen and I avoid exchanging looks of surprise. We've been looking for a lone killer and trying to figure out how he could pull this off by himself. Two people working together would make it easier. And it wouldn't be entirely unprecedented. There have been several serial killer pairs and evidence that even some of the most notorious killers may have had accomplices.

"Could this have been someone on the phone he was arguing with?" I ask.

Riley thinks this over. "Maybe. It was hard to hear."

I have a list of questions but decide instead to follow her current story and get more details. "Were you able to make out what they were talking about?"

Riley shakes her head. "No. I mean, I think I heard him say the things he was going to do to me. He seemed angry. Like, very agitated for some reason."

I can think of a few reasons why.

"Do you know if the other man was in the car when they crashed?" I ask.

"I don't think so," says Riley. "And I didn't see him when the man who abducted me made me get out of the trunk."

"Where did he do that?" asks Gwen.

"I don't know. We were like in a garage somewhere. He opened the back and told me to keep my eyes shut. It was weird. He had me sit in the passenger seat and then he got into the back. I couldn't see him. But I could hear the door opening and closing. It was just him. He sat there behind me for a long time. I could feel his breath on my neck, so I kept my eyes shut."

Gwen raises an eyebrow. She's probably wondering the same thing I am. Was the man thinking about strangling her?

"Then he gets out and grabs me by the wrist and tells me to lay down in the back of the car." She pauses. "I was so scared. I laid down and . . ." Her voice trails off.

"It's okay, Riley," Gwen offers.

"It's not like that. I mean, that's what I was afraid of. But that didn't happen. He just forced me into the trunk."

"Were you abducted near your home?" asks Gwen.

"I was house-sitting for a friend," Riley replies.

"What is the address?" I ask.

"My friend's place or where I was abducted?" Riley replies.

"Both would be helpful," says Gwen.

"I don't know what street I was on. I was just walking around. I know the houses, but not the exact street," explains Riley.

"What about your friend's house?"

"You know the Waterway Towers?" she asks.

"I've been by there." It's a large apartment complex in southern Broward near the beach.

Gwen zooms in on the area on her iPad. "Can you show us approximately where you were when you were abducted?"

"I'll try." Riley scrutinizes the map and moves her finger around. "Maybe here?"

She points to a side street near a park and another apartment complex.

"Let's get that out to BSO right away and see if they can look for home security camera footage," says Gwen.

"I think that's where it was. But I'm not so good at directions," Riley replies.

"Is there anyone we should call to tell where you are now?" I ask.

"I broke up with my boyfriend a few months ago, and my friend that I'm house-sitting for is out of town." Tears start to stream down her cheeks. "I could have vanished and nobody would have known."

"That didn't happen," says Gwen. "You're fine now."

"Are you sure? Why me? Why did they pick me? Is it because of the way I look?" she asks.

"We don't know," says Gwen.

"Has he done this to other women?" asks Riley.

"Not like this," says Gwen.

"But you know about him . . . or them? You know they're out there doing this?"

"We don't know much. This is different than what we've encountered," Gwen replies.

"How?" asks Riley.

"It's just different," I reply for Gwen, not wanting to put the images of cult killings in Riley's head.

"Have there been other victims?" she asks.

"We don't know," I respond.

Riley turns to Gwen. "What aren't you telling me?"

"We're still figuring it out," she says.

"I saw a missing woman in the news. Is this connected to that?" asks Riley.

"We're still trying to figure everything I out," I explain. "Any little detail, no matter how insignificant, could make a huge difference."

"I'm sorry," says Riley. "I was so scared. I could barely hear anything when they talked. But I heard them mention another girl. Or it sounded like they were talking about another girl. Getting back at her? He was ranting a lot."

"Which one?" I ask.

"The man who abducted me. I think. It was hard to hear."

Gwen leans in. "I need you to be as specific as possible. What did he say about this other girl?"

"I think he said, 'I'm going to get another one in Orlando'? I don't know!"

"It's okay," I tell her. "He said this to the other man?"

"Yes. I think. Maybe it was on the phone. Maybe he was talking to himself?"

"Sloan, can I speak to you outside?" asks Gwen.

"Can I call my mom?" asks Riley.

"Sure. You can use my phone. Tell her you're safe and we won't let you of our sight," says Gwen.

"Thank god you came along. You're my guardian angels," says Riley.

"That's the first time anyone has ever called me that," Gwen admits with a thin smile.

CHAPTER FIFTY-ONE
BERSERKERS

"We need to tell the Orlando authorities right now," says Gwen the moment the door shuts behind me.

"I'll tell Kirch. We can have the parks alerted too," I reply.

I make the call while Gwen paces and taps away on her iPad.

I explain the situation to Kirch while staring at the vending machine, salivating over the thought of a candy bar.

"She's on it," I tell Gwen after hanging up with Kirch.

"Our killers have to think we're getting close? Right?" asks Gwen looking up from her screen. "And two of them," she continues. "It makes so much sense. Maybe the other man was one of the drivers? Maybe they alternated? Think about that," Gwen suggests.

"It would fit," I tell her.

"Isaac One drives Carla down and then Isaac Two drives her back? It's not as clean as using drivers who don't know anything. But it also means that we should be putting Carla's descriptions of them out there," says Gwen.

"And we need to show those sketches to Riley," she adds. "It would make so much sense if there were two suspects. It also explains how her abductor got through our dragnet. He had his accomplice pick him up."

It certainly makes things tidier.

"Has the car been taken to the lab to be dusted yet?" asks Gwen.

"It should be there now. I'll call and find out. How crazy would it be if the prints don't match and this is some other random abduction?"

The color drains from Gwen's face. "Don't even joke about that. I know this is unlike the others, but don't get lulled into thinking these assholes always follow the same patterns. Hell, they might have abducted her just to trick us."

"Heck of a way to throw us off the scent," I reply.

Gwen makes a face as she stares at her iPad.

"What is it?" I ask.

"Riley may not have been random," she says in a harsh whisper.

Before I can ask what she means, Gwen bolts into Riley's room.

Riley has her arms around her knees again and is rocking back and forth. She barely registers that Gwen has entered the room.

"Riley, you okay?" asks Gwen.

"Yeah. I'm managing. I talked to Mom. Told her everything was just fine. I almost started bawling," she admits.

Gwen sits on the side of her bed. "Think carefully. This man, the one you saw, could he have come into your store? Did you ever see him at work?"

Riley thinks this over before answering. "I haven't worked there in a while. It's really my mom's shop. But it's possible he came through there. It would have been a long time ago. I mean, I stop in. He could have been in the other section and seen me. I guess?"

Gwen casually hands me her iPad to look at.

It's open to an email from a service that matches faces to social media images. The first two results are photos of a bookstore with Riley smiling behind the counter.

Not just any bookstore. An occult bookstore: Sacred Angel. The place we tied to the matchbox in the storage unit. The matchbox bearing the fingerprint Fonseca matched to the one in the condo.

It's too much to be a coincidence. Riley's abductor must have spotted her there initially or else been stalking her for some time before then.

Or maybe she'd been a fixation of his since he first saw her and he decided to act on it when he and his partner realized that Gwen and I were closing in.

Or perhaps Riley knows more than she's aware of. She never saw the second man in the car or on the phone. He could be the one she'd recognize.

"Am I safe?" asks Riley.

"Nobody is coming near you," says Gwen. "Sloan, let's let her rest and talk in the hallway about some logistics."

Riley picks up that this is about her safety. "Just say it in front of me. I get it. I want to know everything."

"Okay. We need to arrange for protective custody for you," says Gwen.

"What does that mean?"

"We'd put you in a house somewhere with people to keep an eye out and make sure they don't come for you," explains Gwen.

"You think they might still be after me?" Riley asks.

"They would be stupid to do that now. But we need to be careful."

"I have family in Montana. I could go there," suggests Riley.

Gwen shakes her head. "These people are very computer savvy. They knew you were house-sitting at your friend's place. They could probably track you to family."

"I know I'd be safe there. I mean, I can go there if I want to, right?" asks Riley.

"You can leave right now," I reply. "But we'd want the police to keep an eye out for you. Whether it's here or there. And to be brutally honest, it's not just for your safety; it's because watching you might be the best way to catch these men. If they're dumb enough to come back."

"I don't want to be anyone's bait. I just want to go home. I want this nightmare to end. I just want to be left alone."

"I understand. Trust me," I reply. "The sooner we catch these men, the sooner it's all over."

"And what if you never catch them?" she asks.

"If this goes on long enough, you'll no longer be of interest to them," I say.

"How long will that take?"

"I don't know. I promise you that things will go back to normal." It's a half lie, but Riley doesn't need to know that.

"None of this makes me feel safe. No offense, but I don't trust the police. Especially when I start to feel like bait," says Riley.

"You're not bait," replies Gwen. "But if you are, there's nobody better to be next to than her." She points to me. "Sloan has stopped more than a few bad men dead in their tracks."

True, but something I don't like to think about.

"You've killed people?" asks Riley.

"I'm not proud of it. But sometimes in the line of duty you have to." Some of us more than others.

Riley stares at me for an uncomfortably long time. "Will you keep me safe?"

"We'll all keep you safe," I assure her.

"I don't trust anyone else." She turns to Gwen. "No offense." She looks back to me. "I can tell by looking at you that I can trust you. You won't let anything bad happen to me."

I can only hope that I'll live up to that.

CHAPTER FIFTY-TWO
MOTEL SICK

"When are they letting you out of jail?" Jackie asks me via FaceTime.

I'm in the outer stairwell of a motel near Naples, Florida, watching the sun set for the fourth time as I say good night to my daughter.

Riley is in the motel room with the television on as she surfs the web on a phone we provided her. FDLE Agent Harris gave her a long lecture about making sure her location services were turned off and not to open any suspicious emails or messages.

If Harris had her way, the only tech Riley would have access to would be a wristwatch and a paperback book.

Carla had to go through the same routine regarding electronic safety. The North Carolina state police have her in protective custody, and even Gwen and I don't know where she is.

FDLE balked at first over me supervising Riley's custody because it's a special skill I'm not trained for. But Riley insisted that it had to be me. And while I may not be qualified at protective custody, unfortunately, I have more experience than most at dealing with bad people when they come after you.

Besides keeping Carla and Riley hidden, the FDLE and local law enforcement agencies have been keeping watch on occult bookstores, shops, and other locations where the men might be trolling for prey—with a particular focus on attractive women who might work in those establishments.

In four days, we haven't had any breaks in the case. Forensics recovered a lot of prints from the Impala. These matched the ones we found in the condo and the storage unit, as well as Riley's own prints, agreeing with her description of what happened, minus the second man.

Forensics also recovered hair. Again, hers and one other person's. There wasn't much else beyond that. The car had been recently cleaned.

Right now, it's a waiting game. That and making sure Riley and Carla are safe.

"I hope I can come home soon," I tell Jackie.

She's growing older so fast and turning into a young woman. I'm afraid I'm going to turn around one day and my little girl will be gone and instead there will be a young woman I love just as much, but who's also different.

I get distracted enough with work. Being gone for this long only makes the guilt worse.

I say bye to Jackie, then call Gwen to check in. She's back in Miami, driving everyone insane by micromanaging every tiny detail until I gave her a project to focus on.

She's now working with narcotics, circulating the sketches of the drivers Carla described and seeing if they match anyone known to work as a drug mule. I don't have a lot of hope for this line of inquiry, but I need to keep Gwen sane and prevent her from driving everyone else batty.

"How is it going?" I ask Gwen.

"Ugh. I know this is busy work, but it's the kind I can't resist. I've been going through all of their cases and photos of unidentified people they knew were involved in narcotics but couldn't implicate. I've sent a few dozen photos to Carla and gotten a few potentials. But don't hold your breath. How is babysitting?" asks Gwen.

"She's on her phone more than Jackie."

"Is that a good idea, given how sophisticated these guys are?"

"I could try to take it away, but she'd throw a tantrum. And just between us mice, we have someone posting to her account with location services turned on in a house in Tampa," I confide.

"A honeypot?" says Gwen.

"Yeah. It was Kirch's idea. Riley was aghast at anyone else posting on her Instagram account but agreed once she saw the logic," I explain.

"Let me guess: Kirch shot down your offer to house-sit at the bait house?"

To catch the Swamp Killer, we ended up having me pretend to be a housewife in an attempt to create a target too attractive for him to ignore.

He didn't. Unfortunately, we weren't prepared for his devious method of incapacitating his victims.

"I never even considered offering. Last time I tried that it almost killed me. Fool me once," I intone.

"How long do you think Kirch will keep this up?"

"She's pretty invested now. We can't keep Riley and Carla seques-tered forever, and we'll have to ease up the patrols on the occult shops and bookstores. But I can see a presence being kept up for a while. Now that Fort Lauderdale is on board with the idea that this is connected, they're not so eager to drop it."

"I'm just glad those slackers finally admitted that Nicole Donnelly wasn't a suicide," says Gwen.

"They came around. Any issues with Bennett?"

"Between Carla and Riley's statements, he's shut the hell up. At least enough that I don't hear him griping."

"And how are you doing, Gwen?"

"I hate to say it, given the fact those assholes are out there and Carla and Riley are in hiding, but it feels good to be useful. I can't lie. And I have you to thank for that."

"Thank me when it's over," I tell her.

"I'll bring the wine."

I end my call with Gwen and head back inside. I want to talk to Riley and do a bit more digging.

Sometimes the most casual observation that doesn't seem important can be useful. While she has no memory of ever meeting her abductor, it could be possible that she's only one degree of separation from him.

I was backup at crime scene once, where a teenage girl got stabbed by another girl she'd never met before. It turned out the victim worked with a young man at a fast-food restaurant, never even spoke to him socially but appeared in a few team photos with him, and that was enough to convince his girlfriend he was having a torrid affair. So she stabbed the other girl.

People are weird.

There's also the possibility that Riley's abductor was someone she spoke to on social media. Given Isaac's reach online, that's not hard to imagine.

Whenever I bring up online chat rooms or dating, she withdraws from the conversation. I know some of my friends her age have had less than encouraging experiences with digital hookups.

As awkward as these topics are, I can't avoid them.

Solar once told me about a high-profile child-abduction case that was never solved. Years later it turned out that the sequence of events described by the mother wasn't quite accurate. When she said she'd left her child alone only for a short period of time, she omitted the fact that she left her child alone in the same place on a regular basis because she was having an affair.

This detail might have made all the difference in the world or none at all. We'll never know.

But that is why we investigators have to keep asking the same questions over and over. Sometimes the answer changes and a solution presents itself.

CHAPTER FIFTY-THREE
DOUBLE DARE

"When can we leave this place?" asks Riley as I enter the room.

"We're still figuring it out," I tell her.

"This is boring. I thought it would be like an action movie where we keep moving from place to place," she complains.

"That's generally a bad idea," I reply. "The other option is the air force base, but that's noisy and even more depressing."

"You guys need better travel planners," she says.

I take the seat by the window so I can watch the parking lot.

"What's the craziest thing you've ever done?" asks Riley as she lies back in the next bed and stares at the ceiling.

We have adjoining rooms, but our habit has been for me to talk to her in her room until she falls asleep. When it's my time to crash, Jane Aranega, one of the other FDLE agents working with me, keeps watch.

I'm never more than ten feet away from Riley, but I do need to sleep and use the bathroom.

I'm even starting to smell like Riley—this after Aranega spent two hours tracking down a bottle of perfume that Riley absolutely, positively had to have.

"Good question. Air, land, or sea? Good crazy or bad crazy?" I ask as I stare up at the ceiling and imagine it's the surface of a swirling ocean.

"Sexy crazy," she clarifies.

"I don't think we're there yet," I reply.

It's a strange question, coming from Riley, whom I've found to be quite guarded. Given what happened to her, I can understand why that would be the case.

She'll ask a question like this, then give some vague answer herself.

She reminds me of some of my friend's friends who will ask you for dirt and gossip and then not offer up anything themselves—treating the conversation like a women's magazine in a checkout line made entirely for their consumption.

"Good crazy," says Riley.

"Having my daughter while I was a teenager," I reply. "Everybody said I was nuts. But for me it was right."

"Why was that?"

"My family, I guess. There wasn't a lot of judgment. There were a lot of us. My mom loves kids. It's not like they were thrilled that I got knocked up. But I never felt an ounce of humiliation. What's your family like?"

"My parents divorced when I was young. Dad had money but moved up north. Mom had her kooky little bookshop. She was a hippie back in the day and into all that. She had a weakness for guys that were into yoga and talked the whole mindfulness talk. I kind of had my fill by the time I was thirteen. Anyway, I moved back and forth between New York and Florida. Never settling into either."

"School?"

"I dropped out of several. It just wasn't for me. I did some modeling and acting. There's some serious bullshit. Anyway. Family. You asked about that. Not my thing. People tell me you'll change when you get older and want kids. Nope. Not yet. I don't mind my friends' kids, but I've never felt the urge to take one home," she says with a sigh.

"The right partner can make the difference," I tell her.

It's a subtle probe on my part, because in all my conversations with Riley I can't tell if she's straight, gay, or something else. I don't care personally, but it might give us some insight into why the abductor fixed on her.

Did he lose a girlfriend to Riley? Did she ignore his advances? Is there something else going on?

How people present themselves can be radically different from how they behave in private. I've never had a witness volunteer to me that his wife and he are members of a swingers' club or that he makes a habit of picking up hookers when she's out of town.

When you find out these details later on, it suddenly makes sense how someone could have made a copy of their house keys when you realize their pants were sitting in a locker at a sex club for an hour or why there's a lot of DNA in the family minivan that doesn't belong to anyone in the family.

If Riley told me that she worked as a dominatrix, it wouldn't shock me in the least. Not that I think she moonlights as something like that, but she's sufficiently guarded with me that anything could be true.

"'Partner,'" Riley responds to my comment. "Where's the love and romance in that? It makes falling in love feel like forming an S corp. Maybe I'll find the right *partner*." She giggles. "Who knows? Maybe the guy who abducted me was my true love. What if he just wanted to take me to some exotic island and shower me with roses and make love to me on the beach in the moonlight? Did you think about that, Sloan? You could have ruined my entire life."

I don't think Riley has completely processed what just happened to her. If she were in a less fragile state, I'd point out how messed up what she said is, but I keep my mouth shut.

She didn't see Nicole on the beach. She didn't see the autopsy photos of the other victims. She's still in a state of denial about everything.

"You're doing that thing where you get silent, Sloan. You don't say what you're thinking, but it's obvious what you're thinking."

"Well, that saves me the trouble of saying it," I reply.

"I'm just kidding. You're the best thing that's happened to me." Riley turns her head and smiles at me.

At times she comes across as a textbook child of divorce trying to get the favor of whatever power figure's in front of her. I can't tell if she likes me or just wants me to think she likes me because she needs me to keep her abductors from harming her.

My phone buzzes. It's Kirch calling. I wasn't expecting that.

"I'll be outside for a second," I tell Riley as I step outside to take the call.

"McPherson," I say into the phone.

"Is everything okay?" asks Kirch.

"Yes. What's going on?"

"We think Carla's safe house may have been compromised," she explains.

"Compromised? What do you mean?"

"Someone emailed us a photo from Google Maps of her location, circled. The subject line said 'She's next.'"

"How could they get that?" I ask. "North Carolina has her locked down like we have Riley."

"We don't know. Carla turned over her phone and didn't have any way to inadvertently let them know where she was. They still found out," says Kirch.

Damn.

"We need—"

A phone rings from inside the room and catches me off guard.

"One second," I say to Kirch and walk back inside.

"Hello?" I reply into the receiver.

Silence.

"Anyone there?"

An electronic voice responds, "We know where she is. We're coming to get her."

"McPherson?" says Kirch.

"Everything okay?" asks Riley, stepping out of the bathroom.

I hang up on Kirch and dial the police dispatcher for our protection detail.

"I need a trace on our motel phone as soon as possible!"

"Sloan?" Riley asks anxiously.

"It's the same area code," replies the dispatcher. "Hold on. A pay phone about a mile away."

Damn it.

"Sloan?" Riley asks again.

"Send a car there now. And get us some backup."

"What's going on?"

"Pack your bag. We're moving first chance we get."

CHAPTER FIFTY-FOUR
SAFE SPACE

Riley has her head down on the conference room table as she tries to nap. I haven't let her out of my sight since the call at the motel.

Aranega was at our door less than two minutes after the call and kept watch while I stayed inside and guarded Riley.

I had to wait for backup before moving her because the call could have been a ploy to get us to leave the motel room and expose ourselves. While we waited, she sat with her arms wrapped around her knees in the bathtub—generally the safest place to be if your motel room gets strafed with bullets.

Once we had backup, we wrapped her in a bulletproof vest and brought her straight to the police station, where we've been all night while the Naples PD and FDLE search the area around the motel and the gas station where the call was made for any sign of our suspects.

"You can stay here as long as you need," says Curt Vincent, the assistant chief of the Naples PD, when he returns to the conference room. "But you're going to want a long-term solution."

He notices Riley at the far end of the table. "Does she want to go in the other room and lie down on the couch?"

"I'm not leaving Sloan's side," says Riley, her voice muffled by the sleeve of her hoodie.

I'm flattered that she feels safe with me, but I think that it's unwarranted. Her abductors found Carla and us. Or at the very least discovered our locations. I have no idea how they pulled that off, but the moment we got to the police station, I confiscated Riley's phone and turned it off.

She didn't put up much protest but assured me she'd never once turned on her location services and had stayed off social media.

Even if she did screw up somehow, that doesn't explain how they found Carla.

We know that Team Isaac has the computer skills to run complex online scams, so it might not be unreasonable to assume they somehow hacked us. If that's the case, we're really screwed. There's no way to know how far they've intruded into our security.

The sound of heavy footsteps comes from down the hall, and a breathless deputy enters the room.

"Captain, I need to speak to you."

The two go into the hallway to talk, getting both Riley's and my attention.

A moment later Vincent reenters the room. "It's probably nothing, but somebody just called in a bomb threat to the station."

"Are you fucking kidding me?" says Riley.

"Like I said, it's probably nothing," says Vincent.

The deputies run down the hall and past our doorway. Vincent chases after them to find out what's going on.

I hear the words "device" and "parking lot."

Riley apparently hears them too. "I don't want to be here, Sloan."

"It's the safest place right now," I assure her.

"Was Oklahoma City the safest place when those fuckers blew that up? I don't want to be here." She stands up and grabs her bag.

"Riley! Where the hell are you going?"

"Anywhere away from here. These people screwed up. Somebody talked. The men who tried to kill me . . . they know I'm here!" She heads for the door.

I get up and follow. I can't force her to stay in protective custody, but maybe I can get her to wait until we find out what's going on in the parking lot. The last thing I need is for her to go running outside and take a bullet to the head.

"Hold up!" I shout at Riley as she hurries for the back exit. "They could be outside waiting for you to come out!"

This stops her in her tracks. "Jesus! What am I supposed to do?"

Our plan to draw her abductors to the honeypot location in Tampa obviously hasn't worked.

First, they found us at the motel. Now here.

If our communications have been compromised, we need to think of something different. Or rather, I need to come up with something different.

Captain Vincent enters through the security doors at the other end of the hallway. "Maintenance found a suspicious device in a trash can near the entrance," he explains. "We have the bomb squad on the way."

"I'm going," says Riley. "I don't want to wait for one of them to dress up as a cop and come in here," she tells us.

"That's not going to happen," replies Vincent.

Her face is flushed with anger. "There've been a lot of firsts today. I don't want to wait and see what's next." She turns to me. "I'm walking out that back door."

"I can have you arrested," says Vincent.

"For what?" Riley practically screams at the man.

"For your own safety."

Sure. We could come up with a reason to hold her, but that would only freak her out worse and complicate our situation.

I have to find a better solution. Maybe not the smartest one, but something that solves our current problem.

"Captain, can I use your car?" I ask.

"My car?" he says, confused.

"Let me get her out of here. It's probably safest here—I agree—but it doesn't feel like it to Riley. If I can keep her moving, maybe that will throw them."

"That's the worst thing you could do," he replies, echoing my own thoughts.

"I know. But there's an FDLE safe house in Tampa. Let me take her there. I just need a car they haven't seen us in," I explain.

"This is a horrible idea. If you were anybody else, I'd say no." He takes his keys from his pocket and hands them to me. "It's the silver Expedition in the back lot."

CHAPTER FIFTY-FIVE
DAMNATION ALLEY

Riley keeps checking the rearview mirror every time a car's headlights are visible behind us. We're halfway across Alligator Alley, the highway that runs east and west across South Florida, and so far I don't think we've picked up a tail.

"Why did you tell him we were going to Tampa?" asks Riley.

"I don't know how they were able to find you and Carla. It could be something as simple as a compromised email system or our phones getting hacked," I explain.

Another possibility that I don't even want to consider is that these people may have resources closer to us than we realized. While they were playing mind games with Carla and the other women, Isaac might have been cultivating the trust of someone in law enforcement. It could be anyone from a detective in the FDLE to some IT person who has access to everything.

We often overlook how much the "little" people know and what they have access to. Edward Snowden was working as a contractor when he stole enough secrets to expose our entire global intelligence operations at the highest level.

Isaac doesn't need huge resources to stay a step ahead of us. He needs the right resources.

"Where are we headed now?" asks Riley.

"I'm still figuring that out."

"I don't want to keep running forever. What if we go to some small town and check in to a motel under another name?"

"And use my credit card or the government's? I thought about that. We don't know how they're tracking us."

Oops. I don't want to scare her with the thought that it could be someone on the inside. So I try for reassuring. "These guys are getting careless. If they keep coming after you, we'll catch them. Every law enforcement agency in Florida is on this."

"But do they catch them before or after they kill me?"

"About that . . . They could be after you because you know something that they're afraid you'll tell us. I know we've asked you this before, but it really might be something simple. Maybe you know the name of your abductor and don't realize it. Hell, maybe you went to high school with him."

Riley lets out a muted scream. "Don't you think I've thought about that? I keep trying, Sloan! I never met him. I have no idea who the hell he is."

"I'm sorry," I reply, trying to calm her down.

God knows how I would be handling things if I were in her shoes. One moment you're out for a morning walk, the next you're shoved into the back of a car afraid you're about to be killed.

"I'm truly sorry this happened to you," I say to Riley.

"What about Key West?" she asks. "I have a friend who has a place there. He's in Europe. We could hide out there."

"Too risky. You have to assume they know everything about you. Everyone you know. Remember how they got you in the first place . . ."

I turn on my blinker and pull into a gas station. After I stop the car, I wait to see if there are any cars following us in the distance. When it seems clear, I get out.

"Come with me," I call to Riley.

"I'd rather wait here," she says.

"No. We're switching cars," I tell her.

"What?" She lowers her voice. "Are we stealing one?"

"Not quite." I toss the keys to the Expedition on the seat and leave the door open.

Riley follows me across the parking lot to an unlocked pickup truck. I get in and find the keys in the ignition. Riley hesitates to join me in the cab.

"Come on," I tell her.

"I have to pee," she says.

"Next station."

"Really bad," she complains.

"No. We can stop on the side of the road. We have to get moving *now*."

"Fine," she complains like a teenager and gets in the truck.

I start the ignition and pull back onto the highway. In the rearview mirror, I see George Solar exiting the store and getting into Captain Vincent's Expedition.

I'd called George back at the police station from a credit-card-size cell phone I keep with me and -don't let anyone else know I have. I've been in enough bad situations to learn that having a backup is a good idea.

"Whose truck is this?" she asks.

"A friend's."

"That's vague."

"I think we need to be a bit more vague, to be honest."

"What's next? Are we gonna hop a train?"

"I'm considering our options."

Solar suggested a few to me in our brief phone call. For my part, I deeply regret not asking for his help sooner. In fairness, I had no idea how quickly things would escalate.

Of course, that could be said for every dumb situation I find myself in.

The only way out of this is to catch Isaac and his partner. Since I'm saddled with protecting Riley, that means I have to let everyone else do the tactical stuff while I see if there's some little detail in her frustrating head that might break the case open and allow us to go on with our lives.

Finding that out will be impossible if we're constantly crisscrossing the state and jumping from motel to motel. We need a place isolated enough to spend a few days not being chased while our tactical people do their work and I do mine with Riley.

"Do you get seasick?" I ask her.

CHAPTER FIFTY-SIX

SUNDECK

I'm belowdecks, watching the waves through a porthole, when I get an update from Gwen on the satellite phone—the only form of communication we trust can't be tracked.

Riley is stretched out on the front deck of the *Azimuth*, a sixty-two-foot cabin cruiser Run had purchased to resell. He and I have taken it for a few trips with Jackie to test out the engines and the electronics. It's not as slick as the other boats on his dock, but it has a lot space for a boat its length.

I figured it would be inconspicuous enough while still giving Riley and me enough room not to be at each other's throats.

To her credit, she's been much more relaxed since we've been out here and has even started to open up to me. It might be the ocean, my personality, or Stockholm syndrome.

"How's the houseguest doing?" asks Gwen.

"Tanning. Topless again," I reply.

She'd wanted to go full commando, but I had to tell her that our goal was to *not* attract attention. And while the days of piracy may be over in these parts, drunken men still roam the waters.

"How's the search going?" I ask.

"Nowhere. When you went off radar, the calls stopped. North Carolina police have Carla at a military base, so she seems pretty safe there. Unless we find her a handsome officer to marry her off to, I don't know how long we can keep that up."

"How about forensics?" I ask.

"We're reaching out to other states, seeing what kinds of records we can look at for fingerprint matches. Security guards. CDL permits. Anything."

"Hopefully something will turn up."

"Hopefully," she echoes. "Has she provided any more enlightenment to why they were hunting her so hard?"

"No. She's a weird one." I lower my voice. "She's self-obsessed yet manages to say very little about herself. Although last night she alluded to something about her childhood. I think it was very . . . unconventional. He parents were flower children. Woodstock and all that. It got me wondering." I put my hand over my mouth and the microphone in case Riley can hear me. "She may have encountered Isaac when she was much younger. Maybe when she and her mother were drifting around. Maybe she can't remember, but he remembers her."

"I'll start looking into her mother's background," says Gwen. "Knew she was kind of a hippie, but maybe it's a matter of asking the right questions."

I'd tell her to go gently, but this version of Gwen is a lot calmer than the one I first met.

"Any new theories on how they tracked our vics?" I ask.

I already talked to Kirch about this, but I want to see if Gwen heard anything different. If Kirch thought it was someone we trusted at the FDLE or some other agency, I don't think she'd tell me until she knew for sure.

"I haven't heard anything. I, for one, never trusted email. I'm old enough to remember a time before we had to use that."

"What was that like?" I ask.

"Sloan, hand to my heart, I can't remember. I'd say we were on the phone more. But I can't imagine being on our phones any more than we are these days. Maybe we just talked. Also, memos were a thing. I used to have a little spike on my desk where I'd stick all the paper memos. Oh, that was satisfying. Anyway, heck if I know. Do you have any other questions to make me feel old?"

"That was it. I'm going to go tell Ms. Hawaiian Tropic that it's time to come in from the sun. We're running low on lotion."

"That'll end a pleasure cruise real fast."

"Not as much as running out of wine. I'm glad I stocked up. She's going through a bottle a day."

"How about you?" asks Gwen.

"I don't touch it. We may be ten miles from shore, but I don't assume for a moment that we're entirely in the clear. This may be a vacation for her, but it's work for me."

"Keep me posted. I'm curious to know what information's locked in that little head."

"Me too."

Hmm. Come to think of it, I might bring out an extra bottle of wine tonight and see what comes out when Riley really feels relaxed.

CHAPTER FIFTY-SEVEN
CONSTELLATIONS

Riley and I are lying on the deck of the *Azimuth*, staring up at the stars as the waves gently rock us. It feels like a summer camp moment where you're hanging out with your new best friend and all is right in the world, but camp will soon be over and you know you'll probably never see them again.

Also, a serial killer and his accomplice are out to kill you. That part too.

"You grew up like this?" asks Riley.

"Out on a boat, under the stars? Basically."

"That must have been fun."

"It was, most of the time. There'd be a lot more of us packed onto a boat like this, and my brothers would be spending half their time trying to push me overboard or playing pranks on me."

"You were always the victim?"

"Well, I only retaliated in self-defense," I reply. "How about you? Any childhood adventures?"

Riley falls quiet for a moment, then speaks. "I think I know you enough to trust you. Right?"

"I guess so. With a secret?" I ask.

"Kind of. I just don't want you to judge me. That's all. You're a very strong person, Sloan. I wish I had your strength."

"It's an act."

"It's a good one." She gets up on an elbow. "Can I tell you something that you *promise* won't end up in some report or deposition?"

"Not if you're about to tell me you robbed a bank," I joke.

"No. It's something that happened to me. And maybe. I don't know. Maybe it's all connected to this and I just didn't want to admit it."

My ears perk up, but I lie perfectly still. "What do you mean?"

"Oh, jeez. I've never told anyone this, Sloan. And you're going to think I'm making it all up." She lies back and looks at the night sky.

"Hey," I say softly, "I have a high threshold for crazy. I find myself surrounded by it all the time. My father is a treasure hunter and my grandfather claims he came face-to-face with a giant prehistoric shark. You'll be in good company."

"That's what I like about you. So, here goes. Understand that I was young, and I'm telling you how I remember it. Things may be distorted, but it's how I remember it. Okay?"

"Okay."

"After my mother broke up with my father, we moved around a lot. I think I told you that. But I didn't tell you exactly where. Mom was always enchanted by charismatic guys who thought they had some insight into the universe. So, some of those places we lived were . . . not normal.

"Like we spent some time on a farm with a bunch of other people in Ohio. Only it was a commune. Everybody lived in dorms. All the kids were in one cabin. At night we could hear our parents . . . well, fucking around. That kind of place," she explains.

"Free love?" I ask.

"Yeah. Basically. But it was gross because some of the people were young. Like there were girls just a little older than me participating."

"That's horrible. That had to be very confusing," I tell her.

"It's like you said. You don't know what normal is. But I think it affected me. I remember being so revolted by it all. I thought that's what adults did normally. It might be why I have trouble with relationships. One trip to a hippie freak-fest farm and, boom, you keep your virginity until your twenties." She puts her hand to her mouth. "Oops. Well, that's embarrassing."

"You never know how these things change you," I reassure her.

"True. But that's not what I wanted to tell you. It's about where we lived later when I was fifteen. That's when it got weird."

"How is that?" I ask.

"Mom met some guy. He had an estate in California up near San Francisco. He was from old money going back to Europe. He invited us to stay there. It wasn't like the farm. This was a nice big house. He'd throw big parties and you'd see famous people. I didn't know any of them. But Mom would tell me that person was a big director or that one was a famous writer. The parties would go late into the night. I'd usually just go to bed. Mom would too.

"One night after I thought everyone had left, the man who owned the house knocked on my door. He told me to get dressed and come downstairs.

"I went down there and there was a group of people gathered around a wooden table with a candle in the middle. I didn't recognize any of them from the party. It was so weird, but it also felt like something they'd done before. I heard somebody say 'another girl' when I sat down, but I didn't know why. I remember the candle because it was the first time I'd ever seen a black candle. I didn't know what it meant back then. Do you know?" she asks.

"I'm not too up on candles," I admit.

"People will tell you that it's to protect you from negative energy. But what it was actually used for was to protect you from negative energy when you were going to summon something evil." She rolls over on the deck and looks at me. "I know what you're thinking. You can't believe any of this. But they did. The host had me sit down across from him and we all held hands. I didn't realize what was going on, but I held hands and the two men on either side of me held my wrists.

"I started to pull away, but the man told me to relax. He had a calming voice. It was kinda hypnotic. He started saying some strange words. Like something out of a movie. He mentioned a visitor. Or welcoming someone. That's when I started freaking out. I've always been a little psychic, I guess. I don't talk about it. But I get these intuitions.

"Anyway, I pretend not to be scared, so the guys holding my hands ease up. Then I feel something cold, like a breeze, and I jump up. I push my chair back and run back upstairs to my mom's room. She's had a bit to drink, so I have to shake her. By the time she gets up, everyone's gone. I couldn't really explain it to her. She thinks to this day that the man tried to molest me.

"But that's not what happened. When I pushed my chair back. When I ran. It was because I could feel somebody's hands starting to strangle me."

CHAPTER FIFTY-EIGHT
RECALL

Riley looks up at me from her cup of yogurt as we sit in the galley the next morning. "Can you just forget I told you that story last night? You're probably thinking I'm the biggest weirdo in the world."

"Not at all," I assure her.

Honestly, I have no idea what to think. Riley passed out shortly after, and I didn't get a chance to ask for details.

I wanted to call Gwen and tell her first thing, but I forgot to charge the satellite phone. I also need to get more information from Riley, then tell her I'll have to break confidence about what happened to her as a teenager.

"What do you think those people were doing?" I ask.

"At the party around the table? I thought they were going to kill me," she replies. "I was fifteen and maybe not the most aware, but I felt clear on that."

"And you said it seemed like they'd done this before."

"They seemed comfortable with the routine. Like everyone knew what they needed to know. And when someone mentioned 'another girl,' I definitely got the feeling I wasn't their first."

"Do you remember the man's name? The one who owned the house?"

"It was a long time ago. Marvin? Martine, maybe?" Riley replies as she looks to the side.

"What about where the house was located?"

"California. Somewhere north. I didn't drive back then, so I wouldn't remember how to get there."

"But your mother might. I'll have my colleague talk to her. She might have more details."

"I doubt it. She's bad with that stuff, and she doesn't believe me about all the rituals I saw. Also, in retrospect, I doubt that guy actually lived there. I think he lied to my mom about being rich. I think everything was off. Like they all moved around a lot."

"Could one of them have been your abductor?" I ask.

"I've been asking myself that. I put that story out of my mind for so long. But now, it kind of makes sense. Doesn't it?"

I don't want to get too excited over this. She was drunk last night, and stories have a habit of fitting the audience. Also, stress can make you ascribe relationships between things that aren't connected. Riley may have walked in on a magic show and only now connected it to how Nicole Donnelly was killed. Or everything she said is exactly how it happened. Whatever the situation, I need to tell Gwen.

Given all of Riley's weird travels, it wouldn't seem all that odd if she'd encountered Isaac somewhere in the past.

I notice a flashing light on the satellite phone.

"Excuse me, Riley."

I leave the table and head up to the upper bridge to take the call.

"McPherson," I reply once I'm on the next level.

"It's Scott," says my once and hopefully future work partner.

"What's going on?" I hadn't been expecting a call from him.

"You know when people tell you 'I don't want you to worry, but I have to tell you something'?" he asks.

Just hearing him say those words makes my pulse start racing. "I'm already worried, Scott. What's going on?"

"It's complicated. First, everyone is safe—"

"What do you mean everyone?"

"Jackie and Run. That's who I'm talking about. They're safe. Trust me," he says calmly.

My heart begins to pound through my chest. I want to start yelling a million questions and scream at him for not answering all of them.

"Tell me what's going on," I manage.

"Someone called Jackie's school this morning and made a threat."

I want to interrupt him but I restrain myself.

"They said if you don't turn over Riley, they're going to start shooting children. They evacuated . . ."

He keeps talking, but I feel like I'm going to be sick. I look out at the ocean and hate myself. Here I thought I was being clever . . . and I'm as far as I could be from the most important thing in my life.

"The kids were sent home," Scott continues. "And Jackie and Run are with Solar and about a dozen other cops that he trusts personally."

"Can I talk to them?" I ask.

"Yes. But I need to tell you something else. FDLE brought me back from training to help find out if they'd been hacked. I started double-checking all their logs and details about this case and I noticed something unusual."

"We were hacked?"

"I can't say. There was a phishing email that was sent to different agencies, and we think it might have been an intrusion attempt, but we don't know yet. But . . . about the calls that were made to your motel in Naples and to Carla Burgh's safe house . . ."

"Yes? Just tell me."

"The preliminary trace put them both to a pay phone near your motel. But I went and pulled the logs and found out the caller was using software to hide the true origin. We had to pull different logs to get that number, but we were able to unmask it." Scott slows down and takes a breath. "It came from a government phone."

"Damn it. Someone on the inside? Do we know who?"

"Yes. The calls came from Gwen Wylder's phone."

I can feel the blood rushing in my ears.

"It's also the number that called Jackie's school."

Oh fuck.

"And where is Gwen?" I ask evenly while screaming inside.

"We don't know. Miami is searching for her, and FDLE's issuing a bulletin."

"Why?" I ask, trying to make sense of it all.

"Only she knows, I guess. I talked to someone at Miami . . . Bennett? He says they'd long worried she might snap. The signs have been there. Apparently, they tried to get rid of her a while ago for planting evidence but couldn't prove it. I don't know the details."

I think of the evidence Gwen found, like the matchbook with the fingerprint, and her keen intuitions about the many cases.

Was she trying to find Isaac by any means necessary or protecting him?

Was she really searching for clues in the Miami condo or scouring them before Fonseca or I found them?

"Are you *sure* Jackie and Run are safe?"

"Absolutely. You should probably come back to port, though. We can have the coast guard meet you."

"I will, but I need to squeeze every detail I can out of Riley. Then we need to find Gwen."

CHAPTER FIFTY-NINE
FRAGMENTS

Riley is sitting at the bow of the boat with her legs over the edge. I try to slow my breathing and regain my composure before I approach her. If she sees how frantic I am, it'll make her nervous.

Once I'm able to fake being calm, I take a seat next to her on the other side of the anchor rope.

"Everything okay?" she asks.

"It's all under control, yeah. I have some questions before we head back."

"Head back?"

"We can't stay out here forever. We need to get some fuel and supplies, and we might be trying something different," I say, with no idea what that might be.

"Did they catch them?" she asks.

"No. But we might be close. I have a random question for you."

"If it's about the night at the weird party, I can't remember anything else. Maybe if I saw a hypnotist . . . Would that help?"

"Possibly. Actually, this is about something else. Detective Wylder, the woman who helped rescue you when you were in the trunk. Do you recall meeting her before?"

Riley thinks for a moment. "No. I think we would have recognized one another. Why?"

"Just curious. She knew about your mom's shop. Did you maybe see her in there or talk to her?"

"It's possible. I'm bad with faces. Maybe. I never spent a ton of time there. The people who go there are kind of kooky, to be honest. Why don't you ask her?"

"I will when I get a chance."

I get up and head back into the boat to get everything ready for the trip back to port.

Riley pokes her head into the galley. "Need a hand?"

"No. I'm just locking the cabinets."

And trying to think.

"Let me know," she says.

"I'm going to take a quick shower," I say as I head into the master cabin.

I get undressed and climb into the shower.

Everything is hitting me all at once. I don't know how to process it all.

I should be racing back to Run and Jackie, but that won't help me catch Isaac or figure out what happened to Gwen.

It's nuts.

It's crazy.

It's just too damned much.

Nothing makes sense. It feels like every revelation takes me in a new direction . . . the wrong direction.

My hand freezes before I turn on the water.

Somewhere in the back of my head, things start to click into place. Comments made. Convenient observations. Details that came out of nowhere.

Anxiety gets the better of me and I step out of the head and put my clothes back on.

"Riley?" I call out.

"Up here," she says from the bridge.

I walk up the steps and find her sitting in the captain's chair, staring at the horizon.

"I have another question," I tell her.

"Shoot."

"Why my daughter's school?" I ask.

"What?" She looks at me blankly.

"Why threaten my daughter?"

"I don't understand."

"If it had just been the calls to our motel room and to Carla, I would have fallen for it. But that . . . that just hit too close to home."

"Sloan, what are you talking about?"

Riley's convincing. She's so damned convincing. She was the victim when she needed to be. She was the ditzy, self-obsessed woman when the scrutiny should have been directed at her. She was like water. But she tried to be too much.

"You asked to use Gwen's phone back at the hospital. That's how you got her number. She's so technically illiterate that you could have swapped her SIM card for the one in the phone you've been hiding," I explain.

"Um, I have no idea what you're saying. This is getting scary. Shouldn't we be heading back now?"

"It's crazy how obvious it is now. When we chased the Impala, you weren't in the trunk. You climbed in after you crashed and had your accomplice lock you in. Either way, you didn't want to take your chances running. You climbed in there to play victim."

Riley stares at me in stunned silence.

"That didn't make sense. But then I realized . . . from your point of view, you didn't know how close we were to catching you. If we found you in the trunk, then you could be the victim and slip away. But you didn't. You had to see what would happen next. You didn't want to stay in police custody because you didn't need the extra scrutiny. With me alone, it would be easier to do what you wanted to do next. And what is that?"

Tears start to stream down Riley's face. "You're scaring me so much right now, Sloan. I don't know what's going on."

"I don't even know if you're you. Sometimes you reminded me of Carla. Just in passing. Were you obsessed with women like her and Nicole and tried to emulate them? Is it their youth? Is it control? What was it like watching me fall for it? That had to be a thrill . . . Then what? Were you going to slip inside my bed one night and try to strangle me in my sleep? Is it sexual for you?"

Riley wipes away at her tears. "I'm so fucking confused right now. If this is a test, please stop it."

"You're never going to break. That's what's fascinating to me. You're like a clever animal that only knows one trick."

"Will you *please* tell me what's going on," she pleads.

"I'll tell you what's going on. You're so committed to this act I probably don't even have to handcuff you. But I will because you're going to try to do everything you can to get away when you realize how you fucked up—and how I'm going to nail you with that."

Riley wraps her arms around her knees and starts to rock. "This is so insane."

I take the handcuffs from my pocket.

"What are you doing?" Riley shrieks as I grab her wrist.

CHAPTER SIXTY
UNWANTED

Riley Devereux is sitting in a conference room, wiping tears away with the sleeve of her hoodie as Grant Frowst and Erin Sabin, two FDLE agents, talk to her.

Kirch sent them in because I didn't know either one and she wanted as impartial an interview with Riley as possible.

Given the cloud of suspicion around Gwen, whose innocence Scott Hughes is trying to establish at this very moment, and my heated interactions with Riley, it's the smart move. Frustrating for me, but the right call.

Kirch, Dr. Serred, and I are watching Riley on a video screen. I can't tell what either is thinking. They're both making notes and following along as Frowst and Sabin interview her.

Riley's responses are short, spoken through tears, and peppered with frequent queries about why I would do this to her.

I catch Kirch watching me from the corner of her eye from time to time, assessing my response.

Serred is focused on Riley and taking copious notes.

Frowst suggests they take a break, and Sabin escorts Riley to the bathroom. They took her handcuffs off when they came in to talk to her.

Riley had no prior history of violence, and my claim against her is circumstantial at best.

I'd hoped she would break somewhere on the way back to the dock. Instead, she just sat quietly with her wrist cuffed to the rail and glared at me.

I thought my lie about knowing how she messed up would cause her to adapt her story. I wanted her to admit to some made-up detail, then twist it to misdirect me. I fully expected her to tell me that Gwen put her up to this or that she'd been misled by Isaac.

She admitted nothing and didn't change a single detail. If anything, the parts of her story that were fuzzy before—Was it one man in the car? When was she in the trunk? What happened in the back seat?—all have concrete answers now.

Riley has established a consistent timeline from when she was abducted to when we found her in the trunk.

The one clue I was hoping to find was the phone she'd surely used to talk to her accomplice. I never found it on her or the boat. And it wasn't on her person when she was searched at the police station.

She probably ditched it when she realized we were too far out at sea for cellular service to work. And in the end, thanks to me, she didn't need it. I'd showed her how to use the satellite phone to talk to her mom and only realized in retrospect that the battery kept dying because Riley was using it at night.

When I checked the call logs, the same number appeared five times. If you dial it, you reach a standard voice mail service.

I had two questions for Frowst and Sabin to ask Riley:

First: Whose number is this?

"I thought that was my mom's cell phone. I didn't have my phone so I couldn't remember for sure."

Follow-up question: Did she answer?

"No. She never picked it up when I called that number. But I left really long messages letting her know I was okay."

Your usual sociopath confronted with a question like this might say they never called the number or accuse me of lying.

Riley is smarter than that. While a refusal response might be tempting, it wouldn't satisfy the investigators. It's the kind of thing a liar would say.

Riley is an expert at social manipulation. She might be the best.

I don't think this just because of how she had me fooled but because she's been doing this for years, and thanks to social media and a mobile phone in everyone's hand, she could experiment on hundreds or thousands of people.

If a serial killer keeps letting his victims get away, he won't be in the business very long. There's no room to practice or make mistakes.

Riley, on the other hand, could learn how to push and pry and find vulnerabilities by repeating the process over and over again. She could get better through repetition with little risk of getting caught.

Since finding her in the trunk, we haven't done a lot of digging into her history, other than what she's told us. FDLE agents and BSO detectives spoke to her mother, but nobody has done a deep dive into her finances or asked her mother for more background.

I suspect she overheard me talking to Gwen and this is why she faked the call from Gwen's phone to the school. Riley didn't want anyone on the outside digging too deeply.

A missing piece of this puzzle is how someone as adept at online fraud as "Isaac," aka Riley, could end up being a forty-four-year-old woman who has to live off her parents' money and couch-surf.

I suspect she doesn't. Not all professional fraudsters live like millionaires, but someone as smart as Riley probably wouldn't have to beg for a friend's spare room.

She mentioned a place in Montana and one in Key West as potential hiding spots that belonged to "family" or "friends." It's likely she owns properties in each location under a false name.

We wouldn't have dug too deeply if we had decided to use one of those locations—especially because Riley wasn't a suspect. She probably felt comfortable suggesting them because of that. She also might have wanted to use them because it would give her a home-field advantage in case she needed something to "happen" to me.

My next question for Frowst and Sabin to ask Riley was a simple one that she should have had an answer for.

She wasn't expecting to get stopped and had to improvise by climbing into the trunk. She was quiet for so long in the hospital because she was trying to come up with a story that would misdirect us. The one detail she gave that no one pushed back on was where she'd been staying when she was abducted.

She named the Waterway Towers (house-sitting for a friend), and we immediately processed that as where she'd been living and moved on.

It was a clever nonanswer.

There are four hundred units in that complex. It's the size of a small town.

Riley never told us what building or apartment. She only said the Waterway Towers.

Her real home—or where she was actually staying—would have told us more than she wanted us to know about her.

I asked Frowst and Sabin to have her give us the apartment number of the unit where she was staying.

Riley replied that the Waterway Towers were confusing and she knew it by sight.

When Sabin offered to drive her there to find the apartment, she said she would try, then started crying and asking why I would do this to her.

I turn to Dr. Serred after Riley walks off the screen to use the bathroom. "Well?"

She rotates her chair to face Kirch and me. "I see two possibilities. Either she's the most convincing pathological liar I've ever encountered. Or you are."

CHAPTER SIXTY-ONE
SOCIAL

Kirch speaks up. "While one might call McPherson's behavior irrational at times, I don't think sociopath is a word that describes her."

She should see how some people described me on social media. There was even an article in an anti–police brutality blog after the Catalina incident with the headline: "With a Kill Count This High, Who's the Real Sociopath?"

"I agree," says Serred. "I was just trying to point out that, in the abstract, if you only heard Ms. Devereux's and Ms. McPherson's testimony, you'd either draw no conclusion or possibly lean towards Devereux's."

"No offense, McPherson," Serred says to me. "But she's very compelling. She's emotional and seems very distraught by all that has happened."

"You have to—" I start to protest.

"I said *seems*. I'm a professional. I know how to spot the tells. Most people don't. Sabin and Frowst are exceptionally good at interrogation, and they haven't managed to get her to trip up or backtrack yet. Devereux isn't just a competent liar; she's very thorough and sees traps before they're even set. The only question that threw her was yours"—Serred nods to me—"about where she was staying."

"Should we follow up on the offer to drive her there?" asks Kirch.

"You could. But I suspect she'll say the stress of everything has made her forget the precise number and that she only knows the friend by their first name. Or if she really wants to disarm us, she'll say she was having a tryst with a married man and doesn't want to involve him in all of this. There will *always* be an excuse. She avoids complicating things because she knows that could trip her up—although I suspect she's capable of keeping track of even a complex narrative.

"I don't know if you observed this, McPherson, but when they asked her about what happened after you found her in the trunk, she had very precise details about what food she ate, what people specifically said to her, and other kinds of information directly relating to her."

I nod.

"She has an exceptional autobiographical memory. That's closely correlated with high-order narcissism and some degree of sociopathy," she explains.

"How does she keep her story straight if she's also playing 'Isaac' and other people online?" asks Kirch.

"The same way a fantasy author keeps track of all the characters in an epic novel. They have their own backstories and journeys. Devereux could probably tell us what Isaac was doing June 22, 2002, and give us the same answer a year later." Serred shrugs.

"Could it be multiple personality disorder?" asks Kirch.

"I don't believe that's a real thing. There's no evidence that someone can have different unconnected personalities that they're unaware of. Other than in rare instances, like physical damage to the brain separating different regions. But supposed MPD sufferers aren't typically this high functioning," says Serred.

"Maybe she's not unaware of them?"

"Then what's the difference between MPD and someone *pretending* to have different personas, or anyone who has moods and changes in temperament? None. It makes for exciting fiction and narcissistic patients craving more attention. Mental health professionals with little regard for empirical testing will continue to be attracted to the idea. But it's pseudoscience.

"Riley Devereux is on top of every persona she's constructed as well as innumerable details about the people she's been deceiving," explains Serred.

"Why get on a boat with a cop?" asks Kirch. "That would be the last place I'd want to be if I was trying to get away from the authorities."

"I can think of three reasons. First, it's a contained environment with just one person. You often use two or more people to interrogate someone so you can wear them down. One gets a rest while the other asks questions. With only one interrogator, Devereux could think through her answers and keep planning ahead. She's so used to playing her manipulation games she could probably outlast McPherson in an interrogation. No offense."

I shake my head. "None taken. I'd ask her for details and she'd go sunbathe. When I was pressing her for more information about her friends, she'd do something distracting like go topless or ask me to teach her to fish."

"She was controlling you," replies Serred. "She probably had your entire routine down."

It's painful to have someone explain this to me, but it's true. Riley was controlling things even more than I suspected.

I'm a light sleeper but never caught her using the satellite phone. She'd make a show of stomping to the bow of the boat when I had to make a call, but she could have positioned herself to listen in, timing it so I wouldn't realize she was close by.

Our entire time at sea, *I* was the one under surveillance.

"You said there were three reasons she wanted to be with Sloan on the boat. What are the other two?" asks Kirch.

"Being protected by just one agent would make it easier for her to escape if she felt like she was about to be revealed. If she's the killer we suspect she is, that also would make it easier for her to have killed McPherson if she had to. The boat would provide extra cover, and time. If she killed McPherson and dumped her body, she could have created a scenario where we thought there was an accident and they both drowned. But that's just speculation. You two would have a better idea of how she could have pulled it off in actuality.

"The third reason she chose to be around McPherson is that I think you presented an incredible prize to her. A worthy challenge. Manipulating you, getting you on her side. She lives for that.

"Her exhibitionism may have been an attempt to get you to lower your own inhibitions. If she could break down those barriers, she could start to peel away the others," says Serred. "On the surface it might look sexual, but I don't think it was. Getting someone to overcome their nudity taboo is common in forming trust bonds. The first thing they do in the military is make you get naked with others. Locker rooms, fraternity hazing . . ."

"Asking Carla Burgh to take nude photos," I add.

"Exactly."

"For the record, I did not sunbathe in any state of undress or do anything like that around her," I tell the room.

"Of course not," replies Serred. "If Devereux could have really read you, she'd have realized that the wall between your professional and personal life is so well defined that it extends all the way into your family life and makes it difficult for you to get your mind off work."

Um, thanks for that?

"How do we break her?" asks Kirch. "We can't keep her forever."

"She'll answer your questions as long as she knows they won't pin her down. She doesn't want to be a suspect and will try to act like someone who believes they're being wrongfully accused for as long as she can. But she knows that *we* know at a certain point an innocent person protests and asks for a lawyer. That's when you lose your chance to catch her in a lie, because a good attorney would have her shut up," says Serred.

"How do we catch her in a lie?" I ask. "She has an answer for everything."

"You'd need something physical. Something that definitively ties her to a crime or to a reasonable question she can't answer. You have to catch her on her back foot. Make her lie on the spot in a way that we can catch her."

Kirch motions to the interrogation room on the monitor. "I don't know how much longer she's going to cooperate."

"We can't let her run," I say.

"Well," Serred tells us, "maybe we can give her a reason to stick around while we build a case."

CHAPTER SIXTY-TWO
Dark Brew

Gwen is sitting in the back booth at the Blue Moon Diner drinking a cup of coffee as I enter. Her head's down as she reads a newspaper. She's the only person in the place reading something physical. The few other people in the diner are on their phones or tapping away on computers.

"I see you found the source of my secret," I say as I slide into the seat across from her.

"He's in the back making me another pot." Gwen looks up and greets me with a weak smile. Her eyes are tired. More than usual. She seems run-down.

When I first met her, she was like a mousetrap ready to snap and break your fingers at any moment; now she's a rusted spring with no deadly tension left.

"I'd ask how you're doing, but that's a stupid question," I say, not sure where to begin.

"How's the little bitch?"

"Ms. Devereux? Still cooperating, in her way. Although they took her to a safe house to break for the day."

"She kind of set that trap up for herself," says Gwen. "As long as she's the next potential victim, we have an excuse to stay on her ass morning, noon, and night. But she'll figure something out. Maybe she'll try to swat her accomplice like he tried with me this morning."

"*What?*"

To "swat" someone is slang for calling the police on them at their home by claiming there's an active gunman there. This will typically prompt an armed response, often including police in tactical gear with flash-bangs and semiautomatic weapons.

People have been killed by these malicious pranks.

"Apparently, this morning, around the time it was being circulated that I was the mad bomber and mastermind for all of this, someone called 911 and said they'd been shot by me and were hiding in my closet," Gwen tells me. "Your partner? Hughes? He called me after he spoke to you. He decided to dig a little deeper and see if the spoofed call had indeed been spoofed. Too little too late. The police were already surrounding my home and battering down my door."

"Oh, Gwen. I'm sorry. That must have been horrible!"

"I'm sure it was." She holds up her mugful of Lao's coffee. "But I was sitting here. Thanks to you. Nobody was home. Although it must've scared the hell out of my neighbors."

I can only shake my head.

"Point is, if Hughes hadn't kept pushing, I'd be in handcuffs right now, fake 911 call or not. And that's what hurts, Sloan." Gwen's voice falters. "I'm mean, I have my faults. But I'm mostly harmless. The people that came after me? Those were my colleagues. The captain who called in the SWAT team? I've known him for twenty years. That little conniving bitch Riley? I expect this from *her*. She's like a poisonous snake in a hole. You poke your hand in there and you're going to get bit. But these people were supposed to be my friends. These are the folks who are supposed to look out for me."

I nod and tell her, "I know. It's so disheartening."

"Look," Gwen says. "What it *is* is Riley Devereux doing what she does best. But it shouldn't be that easy to twist cops around like that.

God knows, I haven't made it easy for everyone else. But this? This is just beyond the pale."

"The record has been set straight. We'll sort things out," I assure her.

"Will we? Let me ask you a direct question. When they told you that I'd called Jackie's school and made a threat, what did you think? Be honest."

This is hard. This is really hard. "I was scared for Jackie. At the time I was focused on Riley. And when Scott tells me something, I take it as the gospel. Thankfully he second-guessed himself after I talked to him."

"But did you think it was possible I could do that?" asks Gwen.

"Yes, Gwen. I could see you doing that. Or my dad, if he was drunk. Run, if he had some kind of brain damage. You know as well as I do that we can't be good cops if we walk around with preconceived notions of who's capable of good and who's capable of evil."

She stares down at the table. "What does that say about me?"

"I don't know. But I'll tell you what else. I didn't want to believe it. The assholes you worked with? Yeah, they did. They wanted to put you in a box, and that was a perfect way to wrap it. 'Gwen really flipped out this time. The End.'"

"Me? I didn't want to think my friend did this. In fact, it was my worst fear come true. But that's why I thought it could be true. Because it was motivated by fear."

"I appreciate you being honest. I'd probably believe it too. Hell, I half wondered if maybe I *had* made those calls after mixing wine and meds. Self-doubt is a hell of a thing." Gwen shakes her head.

"We can doubt ourselves all we want later. Right now, we gotta nail Devereux and find her accomplice."

"We can be pretty sure he looks nothing like either of the men she described," says Gwen. "That's for starters."

"Maybe. But she was always very vague. I've learned from Serred that that's part of her brand. Riley thinks well ahead and always avoids being trapped by having said he was Black or he was white, for example.

She doesn't make it easy to catch her in a lie. But somewhere in her fuzzy details we might have something to go on."

"Like whatever she told you on the boat?" asks Gwen.

"Maybe. But I have no idea how much of that was designed to intentionally mislead us. I suspect she hoped we'd waste effort chasing down mysterious satanic cults in other states. I think the really telling details are what she told us shortly after we found her. The vague description of her abductor. Where she was found and where she was staying."

"You think she may actually live near there?" asks Gwen.

"She didn't know what we knew. She didn't know how we found the Impala. For all she understood, we could have tailed her from her home all the way to South Broward. Something that I didn't recall until after I spoke to Kirch and Serred today was exactly what Riley said when we asked her where she lived."

"She said she was house-sitting at a friend's apartment in Waterway Towers," replies Gwen.

"No. That's how I remembered it at first. But then I thought about it. What she *actually* asked was if we knew the Waterway Towers. We assumed she meant that's where she was staying. She was testing us. We never brought it up again or challenged her on it. That's when she knew we weren't going to follow up on that and had no idea where she actually lived."

Gwen stirs her coffee. "The Towers are visible all around that area. You could use it as a landmark."

"If we'd asked, 'Isn't your house ten blocks away?' she could have said, 'Well, the Towers are visible from there.'"

"I don't think I would have even registered that as an evasion," Gwen admits.

"What if we started looking at property records around that area? We might find something suspicious," I suggest.

Gwen nods. "This is Florida. Of course we'd find something suspicious. We'd need to have a better idea what we're looking for." She pauses, holds up a hand. "Wait. You've got me thinking. Another detail that she tried to keep fuzzy was when we asked her about her mother's store, the Sacred Angel. Riley tried to make it clear that she rarely worked there."

"You think she did?" I ask.

"Maybe not work there. But it would be a good place to spot potential marks for social-engineering scams. You ever heard of *The Psychic Mafia*?"

"No . . . ?" I reply, intrigued.

"It was the name of a book that described how psychics would share notes on the clients they were ripping off. They'd give each other details like the names of lost loved ones and pay each other commissions," Gwen explains.

"That sounds like something out of a movie."

"It happened. The author got shot in an attempted assassination after the book came out and had to move and change his name," says Gwen.

"Okay . . . if Riley were using Sacred Angel to find financial marks, then that means her mother is probably in on it at some level."

"Getting money for referrals, maybe," Gwen adds. "I'd be surprised if she knew what her daughter was really up to. But I don't see her cooperating with us in any case."

"Also, the moment we call her mother in for serious questioning is when Riley will lawyer up."

"What about her accomplice?" asks Gwen. "Could it be her mother?"

"I doubt it. Remember, she needed to be vague about her abductor. If she thought we suspected she was working with another woman, then she wouldn't have told us it was a man who abducted her. Having spent time with her, I suspect her partner's a bit of a lackey. Someone for her to order around. Maybe a man infatuated with her. She'd crave that and use it to manipulate him," I explain.

"Is he the one doing the killing?" asks Gwen.

"I don't think so. I think he's the one dumping the bodies for her. But he might not even be around when she kills. I think it's something special for her. I wonder if there was some truth to Riley's stories about the cults and occult groups that she and her mother spent time with," I ask out loud.

"Who knows. Maybe she's got an S&M dungeon in her garage," Gwen replies.

I slap my hand on the table, nearly knocking Gwen's coffee into her lap.

"I think that's it!"

"The S&M thing? I was joking."

"No. Her house. I think I know why she didn't want us to know where she lived!"

CHAPTER SIXTY-THREE
BEACH PARTY

Kirch, Waterman, and Suarez arrive at the same time on the beach near where Nicole Donnelly's body was found. I called their offices from the diner and told them to meet us as soon as possible. Kirch was hesitant, but I insisted she come.

The sun is starting to set behind us and my anxiety's burning at the thought of Riley deciding she's had enough, leaving the hotel where she's staying, skipping town entirely, and never coming back.

"McPherson, Wylder," says Suarez as they reach us. "How's your suspect?"

"Cooperative. In her own way," I reply.

"I'm not questioning your judgment," Suarez begins in what I'm sure is going to be an indirect questioning of my judgment. "But if she did all this, why is she still around? You brought her in for questioning, but she could lawyer up or leave at any time."

"For the same reason you don't skip town every time you crash your police car," I reply.

This gets a "heh," from Waterman. Which would be a standing ovation from anyone else.

I get serious. "Seriously, you have too much at stake here to skip town. Same with Devereux. She doesn't want to leave unless she has to. And if she can talk her way out of this, then she gets to keep what she has."

"What's that?" asks Waterman.

"Killing is her hobby. Fraud is her business. She uses the same methods she used to trick Carla Burgh and Nicole Donnelly to rip people off."

"And does what with it?" asks Suarez.

"That's the interesting part. She answered a lot of questions and volunteered even more, but she always avoided certain topics . . . or let us come to our own conclusions. I know I did. I assumed she was a forty-something with arrested adolescence sponging off her aging mom, but that's what she wanted me to believe. Which should have been a clue. She's a narcissist with a fragile ego, but she was totally comfortable with us thinking she was a happy-go-lucky failure who had to live on her friends' couches.

"Why would she do that? Because it hid the one truth she didn't want us to pay attention to, because *that* would reveal something even more damning," I explain.

"Come on, McPherson. Get to the point," says Suarez.

"You have something more important to do?" asks Gwen.

Kirch hasn't said a thing. She's only been listening. I can't tell if she's following this or drafting my termination letter in her head.

"I'm getting there. I'm also getting to why we found Nicole on this beach. Riley had a pattern. She'd meet vulnerable young women online. See how much control she could exert over them. And from time to time, invite them to Florida for one reason or another and then kill them.

"She was smart enough to hide all connections to her. And she was able to do this for years.

"She also had an accomplice who'd do the dirty work of getting rid of the bodies. God knows what kind of relationship they had. Whatever the dynamic, he knew Riley's pattern. By the time Nicole Donnelly arrived, he was already thinking about how to get rid of the body.

"And that's the giveaway. She used him to solve the body problem because he was good at it. But the solution was *too* good this time."

"He dropped her at sea? We already went over this," says Suarez.

"He dropped her out there a little while before she was found. We were confused because of the saltwater in her lungs. But my shark experiment showed that she wasn't drifting in the ocean for long," I remind them.

Waterman shakes her head. "The ME's adamant that she was in the ocean for at least twenty hours."

"No. That's not what her body says," I tell her.

"So you're saying Kaperman's wrong?" asks Suarez. "This will be interesting."

"No. What I'm saying is, the report only observed that she'd been in saltwater for twenty hours."

"Nice try, but we actually checked to see if she could have been drowned in an aquarium or a saltwater pool with a chlorine generator. We're not idiots, McPherson. There are tests for that," says Suarez.

"I know. I discounted that at first too. Then I remembered the house we lived in when I was a child. My dad bought it because of the pool. It wasn't a saltwater pool like people have today, where a generator produces the chlorine. It was a true ocean water pool with the same salinity as the sea. He bought the house so we could test scuba equipment. Those kinds of pools are rare and hard to maintain. Gwen?"

Gwen takes her iPad from her purse and shows Waterman and Suarez the screen. "This is where Nicole Donnelly was found. This building two miles away is the Waterway Towers, a place Riley claimed to have been staying when we first 'rescued' her. There are only two residential homes with that specialized kind of pool anywhere near the Towers."

I pick up where Gwen left off while she flicks to a new image. "This secluded house with the high fence and palm trees blocking the view has one such pool. It belongs to a company called Accurate Advisors LLC. Their board of directors lists three people. Two are deceased. The third is Gladys Fillmore. That's the same woman on the registration for the Impala we found Riley in. Fillmore lives in a nursing home in Boca Raton," I explain.

"I called the home and they said the woman has dementia," adds Gwen.

"Well, that's not helpful," says Suarez.

"Tell him, Gwen."

"Then I asked if the place had any employees who hadn't shown up for work in the last few days. They mentioned a handyman named James Damask had been out sick all week. I asked for a description. They said he was a very tall, muscular man in his late fifties," says Gwen.

"The Michael Myers guy from the storage unit in your report," says Suarez. "Holy shit."

"Where is he?" asks Kirch.

"Palm Beach Sheriff's Office is looking for him; they're also going to try to get fingerprints from his workplace," says Gwen.

"I'll get everyone I can at the FDLE on this right now," offers Kirch.

"Before we put his photo out there, I'd like to take another crack at Riley," I tell them.

"You mean talk to her? She hates you right now."

"I know. That's what I'm counting on. I think we can back her into doing something if we take away the one thing she wants more than anything," I explain.

"And what is that?" asks Suarez.

"Control."

CHAPTER SIXTY-FOUR
Suite

Riley is sitting on the queen-size bed of the bridal suite in the Atlantic Hotel, flipping through channels as I enter the room.

She looks up, glares at me, then goes back to watching television.

How long did it take her to calculate what the appropriate expression would be for someone who felt betrayed and wrongfully accused?

"Before you go, I'm curious about one thing," I say to her.

The word "you" in "before you go" catches her off guard.

"Go where?" she asks petulantly.

"Wherever the hell you want." I point to the door. "Your guards are gone. This protection detail's over."

"What about the men who're after me?" she asks, sitting upright with the appropriate amount of shock.

"There are no men after you. You know it, I know it, and I finally was able to convince everyone else, once I realized that you could use a robocaller to make the threatening calls. I was sitting next to you in the motel when that call came in. It was clever. It made me think you were really being chased by someone who wanted you dead. I feel stupid. Especially because I realize, the moment you saw the police lights flash behind the Impala, you probably thought you'd been caught.

"When Gwen and I found you in the trunk you tried a Hail Mary to throw us off your scent. You were assuming we had more on you than we did.

"It worked. The abduction story, the details. You had us convinced that other people were involved, or at the very least you had an accomplice." I put up a hand. "I know, I know. You're thinking, 'Do I have to sit through another monologue where she comes close but doesn't get it?'

"You don't. The door is open. You're free to go. I wish I could say I had the forensic evidence to prove that you killed Nicole Donnelly and the others. Or that Carla Burgh could positively identify your voice as 'Dr. Diane's.' But I can't."

Riley's giving me nothing. Not even moving.

"It's funny how you mentioned Carla and I didn't even notice it," I continue. "I just assumed you'd overheard me talking about her. But I couldn't figure out when. Of course, now I know it's because you already knew who she was. But I can't prove it. In fact, you don't even have to worry about coming up with an explanation for any of it. Nobody's asking for one. We all know you'll have a story that fits or you'll play it off like you don't remember." I shrug.

Riley remains silent. She's working to figure out what trick I'm trying to pull.

"What's my game? you're wondering. How is Sloan trying to trap me? I'm not. There's the door. You may leave," I offer.

"Sloan—" she begins, but I cut her off.

"The broken record 'but men are trying to kill me' thing is just tedious at this point. You're like a zombie that keeps doing the thing you were doing before you died. Oh, and now the tears. You want to elicit sympathy, but all I feel is revulsion. I don't think you know what tears are for, to be honest. You're like some kind of robot on the Pirates of the Caribbean ride, doing the same thing over and over. Now it's just tired and mechanical."

"I want to talk to somebody else," she says.

"Go. I keep telling you. The world is yours. Talk to anyone you want."

"I want to talk to someone at the FDLE."

"They don't care. They don't believe you. But we can't prove you did it. So it's over for now. Emphasis on 'for now.' That's because it's a long game. Somewhere we'll find a little clue that ties you into all of this. Maybe it'll be a fingerprint on a body. I'm hoping the hair we pulled out of the saltwater pool drain at your house in Fort Lauderdale is Nicole's. That would be fun because then we'd get to have a real deposition and I could start going through all of your financial records and those of your mother."

Her breathing slowed when I mentioned Nicole's hair in the drain. I don't know what they've actually found, but it sounds plausible.

"I keep saying 'go.' But here you are. You think it makes you look innocent. But it doesn't. That's because in your model of how people work, you imagine that an innocent and betrayed person would sit here and look confused and hurt.

"What they'd actually do is call a friend or their parent and ask for help. But you're not doing that. And it's because of your weakness. It's your kryptonite.

"I know you're dying to know what that is but can't think of a way to ask me. So I'll do you the favor and tell you. It's your one and only tell. The one thing that gives you away.

"You have to make the person directly in front of you *like* you. You think that if you just keep this up, I'll feel guilty and start to doubt myself.

"No. I see you. So I'm going to do you a favor. Since you won't go, I will. I'll make it easier for you to call your mom or whoever and slink away."

I turn around and leave the suite.

CHAPTER SIXTY-FIVE
SURVEILLANCE

I watch the camera feed streaming from the surveillance van as Riley's Uber drops her off at her mother's house in Pompano Beach.

Scott Hughes is tapping away on his laptop next to me at our command center at the FDLE office. Kirch and several others are gathered around, also watching and curious to see what Riley will do next.

"I'd pack my bags and leave," says Harris.

"She's got a lot of loose ends in South Florida. Money in real estate, bank accounts in her name. She spent years building that. She's afraid if she leaves, she'll look guilty to us," I explain.

"That's a mistake," says Kirch.

"The next time we call her in for questioning, she might go for a big lawyer and a PR firm," says Serred. "When executives are afraid they're going down, they often try a scorched-earth strategy." She addresses me directly. "She might go directly after you, McPherson. She could claim that you intimidated her on the boat. Or worse."

"Let's hope we get what we need before that happens," I tell her. "Any update, Scott?"

"Nothing at the moment. She just got to her mother's home."

"Too bad we couldn't bug the house," says Harris.

"I'm sure she assumes she's under surveillance right now, and I don't think she's going to tell her mother much. Maybe she'll explain why she came here instead of one of the properties she owns. But I think that's it," I reply.

"It was an interesting gambit you played back in the hotel," says Serred.

"Interesting. But did she fall for it?" asks Kirch.

"I don't know that it matters," says Serred. "It forces Devereux to make a choice of believing McPherson or not. Either way, it compels her to make a choice. If she thinks Sloan was lying and that we actually suspect she has an accomplice, then she's going to be panicking about what to do about James Damask. If she thinks Sloan was telling the truth, then she'll be somewhat relaxed and take different next steps, but ones that are equally predictable."

"We just picked up a cell phone call from the house," says Scott.

"What's the originating number?" asks Kirch.

"One we haven't seen before. Probably a burner phone she kept there. We have a connection. Hold on." Scott studies his screen. "The call was placed to a phone that's in Hollywood, Florida. I have the cell tower location."

"Tell us when you have the other number," says Kirch.

"Looks like a burner too," he says.

"Do we have a location?"

"Just the towers. The call ended," says Scott.

Kirch takes control. "See if we can get a more precise location. Harris, start looking at records. I'll send some unmarked cars to the area."

"I'll see if I can track the other number if it makes another call," Scott offers.

"McPherson, Dr. Serred, is Devereux calling Damask to arrange a meet?"

"I don't think she'd chance meeting him in person right now," I reply.

"I agree. She's paranoid by nature and probably convinced she's being watched," adds Serred.

"All right. So then what?" asks Kirch.

"I think she might be telling Damask that he needs to go on the run. He's the biggest loose end she has," says Serred.

"Maybe . . ." I think it over.

"McPherson?" asks Kirch.

"Oh. Damn! Call the dispatcher for Hollywood right now!" I yell.

CHAPTER SIXTY-SIX
BLOCK PARTY

The four Hollywood, Florida, SWAT team response vehicles are parked half a block down the street. Officers in street clothes just finished moving people from the houses on either side of the one at 893 Pine Tree Avenue a minute ago.

As far as we know, the occupant of the house has no idea that police have surrounded the property.

If we hadn't called the dispatcher in time, the SWAT team would probably be bursting through the door right now and tossing in flash grenades to stun the man they believe to be holding a family hostage at gunpoint.

I was surprised that Riley would pull this trick twice, but she had good reason to think it could work again.

After she used her burner phone to call someone—presumably Damask—she or someone working with her made a call with a computer that couldn't be traced.

This one was to the 911 operator, and it used a realistic but computer-generated voice whispering that an armed man was in the house. To ensure a well-armed response, the caller confessed this may have been about the "drugs and guns."

My current theory is that she called Damask with a late heads-up that the police were coming. That way Damask would be armed and ready, guaranteeing a shootout that would leave him dead.

It might be a stretch, but the facts are pretty simple: Riley is a killer. She likes to control things. And right now, Damask is a risk.

She's probably watching local television right now, waiting for a breaking-news interruption to announce that there's been a standoff in Hollywood, or better yet, a suspected gunman has been killed.

Her worst-case scenario is Damask getting taken alive.

Even if he doesn't want to tell us about the murders, he'll have to help explain how patients with dementia at the nursing home facility where he works are leasing cars and forming LLCs and S corps.

A woman with a Kevlar vest visible over her blazer walks up to Kirch and me by our car behind the perimeter. "I'm Hollis. I'm the hostage negotiator. Are you the FDLE people?"

She looks like a middle-school librarian. Maybe that's the point.

"I'm Kirch, this is McPherson. This situation is a bit complicated."

"They usually are," says Hollis. "Someone gave me a phone number for a line in the house. Was that you?"

"Yes," I reply. "We think that's the number for the phone he's using."

"What else do I need to know?"

"We don't believe there's anybody else in the house. The 911 caller was trying to create a situation where the man inside got killed," explains Kirch.

"Is he armed?" asks Hollis.

"Very likely. And dangerous. But he's also an important witness."

"Do we know who made the call?"

"We have a good idea," says Kirch. "It's a woman he knows. They're accomplices in multiple crimes."

"Are they lovers?" asks Hollis.

Kirch turns to me for an answer.

"I doubt it. She's the one in the power position in the relationship. He'd do anything for her. Except, I hope, die," I add.

"Okay. This is helpful. Any other details?"

"Yes. She likely told him the police were coming to get him, though he might not understand that she's the one who swatted him. Either way, he's probably ready for a shootout."

"All right. Let me get a phone and call him."

CHAPTER SIXTY-SEVEN
Alpha

James Damask is sitting across from me in the interrogation room with his hands secured to an eye bolt on the table. Although he's unarmed and can't lift his hands, there are two other FDLE agents in the room with me because Damask is so physically imposing.

When the gang members said he was built like Michael Myers, they weren't kidding. Even though he's in his fifties, he could be in the WWE and winning.

That's the first thing you notice about James Damask.

The second is how exceedingly polite the man is. He answers every question with a "ma'am" and even reflexively attempts to stand when a woman enters the room.

He knew exactly who I was when I sat down and hasn't pretended to be ignorant about why he's here. While he won't answer questions about Riley or what he has done, he hasn't lied to us.

He's fiercely loyal to her, and even playing the audio of the 911 call didn't convince him that his loyalties are misplaced.

Grant Frowst and Erin Sabin spent two hours talking to him, and he gave up very little. I insisted to Kirch that she let me give it a try, and now I can feel her eyes burning into me through the camera in the corner of the room.

"You love her, don't you?" I say to Damask. "I understand that. I spent a long time with her, and I like her—despite what she's done."

Damask doesn't respond.

"And even though she tried to have a SWAT team come kill you, that doesn't deter you. I admire that. We forgive the ones we love. It's what love is about. It's about protecting them. I have a daughter. I'd do anything to protect her. I'd even kill.

"You don't have to answer me, James. But I know you understand what I'm talking about. Unfortunately, Nicole Donnelly and the other women didn't have anyone protecting them, did they?"

Damask stares at his hands. Riley has probably coached him a hundred times what to do in this kind of situation. She has controlled and manipulated this man like a German shepherd. It only took her a few weeks to get Carla Burgh to trust her enough to put herself in mortal danger. What has years of being around Riley done to Damask?

I have to play upon his insecurities. What is he afraid of more than anything?

"When I was on the boat with her and she talked on the phone, I couldn't help but overhear. She told me you were her boyfriend, so I didn't think anything of it. The cute little nicknames. It was adorable. It was also hard not to hear her when she was talking sexy with you on the phone and all the things she whispered she wanted to do when this was over."

Damask's cheeks are turning red, and his hands are starting to clench into fists.

I lower my voice the way I do when I want Run to do something for me. "It was hot, the way she talked about you."

Damask's jaw tightens, and he avoids eye contact as he processes everything I said.

All of it was a complete fabrication. I never heard Riley say anything like that to anyone.

But Damask doesn't know that.

He stayed loyal to her because he was the only man in her universe. Maybe they weren't having sex, but she'd know how to maintain his interest through exhibitionism and manipulation.

I reach my hands out and put them over his large fists and squeeze them.

"I get it, James. If I talked to my boyfriend the way she talked to you . . . he'd do anything for me. Anything. Even kill."

He looks up at me. There are tears in his eyes as he finally speaks.

"I wasn't the one who killed those girls . . ."

❦

"Damask flipped on Riley," I tell Gwen over the phone two hours later.

"Really?"

"Really. They're still talking to him. But he's not holding back. I could tell that it had been wearing on his soul. I don't think this is what he originally signed up for. But little by little he became her minion."

"How did you do it?"

"I stole a page out of Riley's playbook. It almost felt bad, but then I thought about when I first saw Nicole on the beach. That made it easier. I made him believe that Riley had been seeing another guy on the side."

"The only thing worse than a jilted love is a jilted unrequited love," observes Gwen. "Have you told Solar?"

"Yes. I just spoke to him and Scott."

"I bet they're proud. God knows I am."

"Solar complimented me on my interrogation tactic. Scott asked if I had any special tricks. I told him I actually did have one special trick, but it wouldn't have worked if he'd been the one to talk to Damask."

"What was it?" asks Gwen.

"I was wearing Riley's perfume."

CHAPTER SIXTY-EIGHT
EXIT PARTY

Gwen is leaning back against the counter in the break room for the Miami Police Department Homicide Unit, rapping her fingernails under the edge of the Formica-covered top. I can tell she wants to reach for her vape pen but won't in case someone walks in and sees her.

I've realized that her vaping and other little nervous habits are usually on display only when I'm around. Otherwise, she manages to keep a steely exterior that would make an armored tank envious.

She's expecting her colleagues to arrive so they can get the formality of her retirement party over with and she can head for the door and leave all the internal drama behind.

Gwen had wanted to leave for a long time, but she wanted to go out on a high note—to close a case that would settle once and for all the question of whether she was a good cop. The work she put into catching Riley was enough to prove her worth. The other cases I helped her solve took care of the loose ends that had made her feel trapped in her job.

"For heaven's sake, how long does it take to walk down a hall and hand me a plaque? Of course, this is Bennett we're talking about. He could have lost it in his own ass—" She's interrupted by someone entering the break room.

Emile Rouje, a member of Miami PD human resources, steps inside. "Oh, there you are. They're ready for you, Detective Wylder."

"I've been ready for the last twenty minutes," she growls.

Emile, unflappable, replies, "Sorry. There was a mix-up. Just follow me."

We let him lead us down the hallway toward the elevators.

"I'll bet you five bucks they're going to give me the plaque out on the sidewalk and the cake in a to-go box so they can get me out of here as quickly as possible," Gwen says as we enter the elevator.

"You have your f-you speech ready?" I ask in jest.

"I've been working on it for twenty years, hon."

I'm not sure if she's kidding.

The elevator opens and Emile takes us through a set of double doors and down a corridor.

"Where are we going?" asks Gwen.

"Back exit," I reply.

"What?"

"I'm kidding. Just hold on," I tell her.

"Let me tell them you're ready," Emile says, then slips through a door.

"Sloan?" asks a nervous Gwen.

"You don't get to slip off into the night," I reply.

"I'm pretty sure that's what everyone here wants."

"Not everyone."

The sound of an amplified voice booms from behind the door. "We don't do enough to thank the tireless men and women of law enforcement . . ."

"Is that the governor?" asks Gwen.

"Yep."

"I didn't vote for him."

"Don't tell him that," I reply.

Emile steps back out and holds open the door. "That's your cue. Just wait at the edge of the curtain until he calls you," he tells Gwen.

The governor continues his speech. "I can think of nobody more tireless than the woman we're here to honor today. For over two decades, Gwen Wylder has worked to protect the people of Florida . . ."

Beyond the door, the packed auditorium is visible through a gap in the curtain. It's filled with law enforcement officers, local officials, and South Florida media, all there to celebrate Gwen's storied career.

It didn't seem right to me for Gwen to fade away quietly. Closing the case was a nice coda, but it deserved an exclamation point.

With minimal urging from me, Solar got on the phone, nonstop, telling people they'd better get their asses in here or send someone in their place, lest they face his wrath.

They came. Partly out of loyalty to Solar but also out of respect for the fact that, as cranky, difficult, rude, stubborn, and all the other things Gwen was, she cared, goddamn it. Her ego could be her enemy, but she was always the victim's ally.

Other than when I eventually watch Jackie graduate, I can't imagine a more special moment than seeing the look in Gwen's eyes as she stands on the edge of the stage, gazing out at the people there to congratulate her for a job well done.

I'd like to think the almost maniacal smile on her face is from all the love in the room, but I know it's really because she can see the sour looks and barely concealed jealously of Bennett and her other nemeses sitting in the front row.

God bless you, Gwen. Never change.

My phone buzzes and I take it out to check the message.

It's from Solar: Sh!t just hit the fan. I'll explain 9 AM tomorrow at the old UIU HQ. TLDR: The band is back together.

ABOUT THE AUTHOR

Andrew Mayne is the *Wall Street Journal* bestselling author of *The Naturalist*, *Looking Glass*, *Murder Theory*, *Dark Pattern*, and *Angel Killer*, as well as an Edgar Award nominee for *Black Fall* in his Jessica Blackwood series. *Sea Castle* is the fourth book in his Underwater Investigation Unit series, following *Sea Storm*, *Black Coral*, and *The Girl Beneath the Sea*. The star of Discovery Channel's Shark Week special *Andrew Mayne: Ghost Diver* and A&E's *Don't Trust Andrew Mayne*, he currently works on creative applications for artificial intelligence as the science communicator for OpenAI.